Behind the Wall

Ira Hughes

Behind The Wall

This book is a work of fiction: A product of the author's imagination.

Printed in the United States of America

To my
Grandchildren: Brandie, Noah, Casie and Adam.
You each have your own special talents. You make me proud.

State Hospital: The first time I heard those words I was six years old. Rose McGee, a ten-year-old, weaver of tall tales and niece to my mother's best friend, was visiting from somewhere in Mississippi and told me more than I ever wanted to know about a state hospital and the loonies who resided there. She quieted my wailing a bit when she assured me state hospitals weren't the same as the hospital where I was to have my tonsils removed in just two days.

Later, I asked my mother if she knew that loonies with collars around their necks were kept chained to walls in dark rooms in state hospitals. "Sweetie," my mother said. "No one would put collars on those poor unfortunate souls. And don't say loonies, dear. The correct word is lunatics. Common folk would say loonies."

Years later a few people tried to convince everyone I was one of the loonies, or lunatics.

I've heard it said life's a journey and everything happens for a reason and it may all be planned out for us even before we are born. All that may be true. But one thing I know is an absolute truth: I'm not at all the same young woman who first came to Gatewood State Hospital. But to tell you the whole story of what happened to me behind the wall at Gatewood, I need to go back to the day when I arrived there. I was twenty-three.

Chapter One

GATEWOOD STATE HOSPITAL: I stared at the rectangular sign, shivered and rubbed sweaty palms on the skirt of my pink linen dress. Suddenly, I was six years old, and a little girl named Rose McGee was telling me all about what happens inside a state hospital. I tried to shake the memory, reminding myself I wasn't six years old. I was a twenty-three-year old who had come here to get well. Everything was going to be all right. I had to get that thought to stick in my brain.

Dr. Cole sent me to this hospital. So it had to be a good place. Remembering Dr. Cole's soothing words lessened the fear just a little: *'They are having tremendous luck with the new drug. I'm confident it will work for you. Go to Gatewood, Jordan. Let them help you.'*

Thomas drove onto a winding paved drive. A wall about four-foot high, made of several sizes of stones, climbed a small hill before disappearing down a valley. I stared at the well-kept lawns; a few benches sat vacant in the lush green grass.

"They tell me," Thomas said, "that this wall was built by the patients here in the early part of this century.

At the end of the drive sat a large, two-story brick building. A sign read "Administration Building".

Dr. Cole had said, *'It's only ninety days. The time will pass before you know it.'*

"The grounds are absolutely lovely, Jordan," Julia said, looking into the back seat at me. "I think you are going to be happy here."

Happy! I wanted to scream at my elegantly dressed sister. How could coming to a state hospital possibly have anything to do with happy? Had it only been a year since my life had changed so drastically? There had been Mama dying suddenly, of a heart attack, and a few months later the accident. I had been driving home from my office when from out of nowhere came the other car. That was all I remembered until three days later when I awoke in the hospital.

Julia said she wasn't happy with the care at the hospital and transferred me to a private clinic: Run by a friend of hers, a Dr. Cole.

I could still hear *Dr.* Cole's words, *'You have suffered brain damage, Jordan. I'm so sorry, but it's most likely you will be an epileptic for the rest of your life, but maybe with medication the seizure can be controlled.'* After I'd spent a few hazy weeks in Dr. Cole's private clinic, he said none of the medications he had were effective. But there was one hope for me: A special hospital where a drug study was being conducted. Dr. Cole said he thought I would be an ideal candidate.

"It's for your own good, Jordan," Julia said. "Here you will get treatment and be with your own kind." *Your own kind:* That had slipped out without Julia meaning for it to. "I mean," She quickly added, "there will be others in the hospital with the same condition you have."

I didn't remember any of the seizures. The terrible headaches I'd had after the accident were gone, but most of the time I was still unable to think clearly. Sometimes it was as if a thick, gray fog floated across my mind, especially after taken the daily medications prescribed by Dr. Cole.

Yesterday, accompanied by Julia, I'd returned home. The first time since the accident I'd been anywhere outside the hospital and Dr. Cole's private clinic. I'd been unable to stop crying when I'd stepped into the foyer. I'd crumbled onto the floor, beneath the portrait of my great-great-grandmother.

"The accident has left you emotionally handicapped," Julia said. She had put me to bed saying she'd pack what would be needed at the special hospital.

My father owner of a publishing company, which published college textbooks, died when I was a teenager. I inherited most of the company, with conditions: In my father's will, he left me the major portion, which I was to receive on my twenty-fifth birthday, keep it as long as I lived; then it was to go to the stock holders. I was also to get a huge trust fund. Until then I was to draw from a special account as I needed. Upon finishing college I had gone to work at the company. I was listed as head of the company. I wasn't sure it was something I wanted for my life, but felt I needed to give it a try. I was apprehensive about being the head of a company, but was assured that people who had been with the company for years would be there to help me. I started off as president, but I was little more than a nameplate. My skimpy knowledge about how the company was run came from the few weeks during the summers I'd spent there helping around my father's office. Mrs. Copple, the vice president, ran the whole show, and I was glad to let her.

Thoughts of the future scared me. What if this new drug couldn't help the seizures? How could I return to sit at my lovely desk behind my nameplate? How could I hope to run a company in more than name only? How could I take my place in society? Coming to the state hospital had been my only choice. I'd had to chance it; Dr. Cole had said so.

Thomas pulled the car into a parking space, got out, and came around to open the door for Julia. Julia climbed out. "Come along, Jordan," she said, opening the back door, offering her hand. I didn't want to get out of the car. I just wanted Thomas to drive me home. But I took Julia's hand and climbed out.

The door of the building opened. A white-haired man, in a gray suit, walked towards us. He was closely followed by two men in blue uniforms: A yellow patch on the sleeve of each of the men's uniforms read "Security" in white lettering. The security men walked to a car parked nearby.

"I'm Dr. Grayson, the superintendent here at Gatewood," the white-haired man said, extending his hand to Julia. "Please come inside. We've been waiting for you. And how is the patient today?" he asked, not looking at me.

"She's very confused: Has trouble thinking clearly." Julia said, falling into step beside the doctor. Actually my thinking was clearer. The night before I'd not taken the medication Julia had given me. I'd meant to, but had accidently dropped the pills into the glass of water. I'd poured the water along with the pills down the sink. I'd not told Julia, afraid she would think me more unstable than she already did. That was the last of Dr. Cole's medication. He said I would be put on the drug study medication when I got to Gatewood.

Thomas took my arm and we fell into step, following along behind. "We have great hopes you will be able to help her here," Julia said, smiling at the doctor.

"That's what we're all about," the doctor said, holding open the door to the administration building. "There are some papers that will need to be signed, and we will need a more detailed history than what Dr. Cole sent." The doctor led us inside and down a long hallway to a large office, talking all the while about great, new programs at the hospital. "Please have a seat," he said, motioning to four chairs in front of a large, highly polished desk.

As Julia, Thomas and I took seats; the doctor went behind the desk, lifted the receiver off a phone on the desk and dialed. "The new admittance, Jordan Walker, has arrived," he said. "Send a couple of attendants to take her to the Wallace building. We'll place her on A2." He replaced the receiver, sat down, and smiled at Julia and Thomas, still not looking at me.

"We are very excited about the drug study," Dr. Grayson said. "For certain types of seizures this drug is working wonders. Two of our patients, who have suffered seizures for years, are now seizure free."

"Wonderful," Julia said.

My heart leaped. Perhaps there was a normal life awaiting me, after I got beyond this place.

The doctor flipped open a folder, pursing his lips as he silently read. No one made a sound. My heart thundered inside my chest. Could the others hear? Finally the doctor looked up, rubbed a hand through his hair and smiled at Julia. "So your sister is twenty-three?"

"Yes." Julia said.

The doctor read about my accident. He was interrupted by a sharp rapping on the door. The doctor swiveled his chair a half turn. "Come in," he called. Two middle-aged women, dressed in crisp, white uniforms with matching shoes and hosiery, entered the room, accompanied by one of the security guards who had been outside. For the first time the doctor looked at me. "Go with these ladies," he said. "They will take you to your new home. I'm sure what we have to offer in our institution will be very beneficial to you. If luck is with us, your seizures will be under control in no time. And the other problems will be addressed."

The word *"institution"* filled me with a cold fear. In the back of my mind I could see little Rose McGee waving a finger in front of my face telling me about dark rooms, collars and loonies. And why had he said *other problems?* My heart began pounding harder than ever. I felt I was choking. I wanted to bolt from the room, run down the long hallway and out the door. Frantically, I turned to Julia. "I don't think I can stay here!" I cried, grabbing onto her arm. "Please, Julia, take me home!"

"Nonsense," Julia said sharply, prying my fingers from her arm. "Now, you listen to me, Jordan!" she said, gripping my shoulders firmly. "You will have to stay here! Dr. Cole has gone to a great deal of trouble to get you in here; you're lucky he was able to get you placed. Patients are waiting for months to be admitted. This is the only place for you, the only hope to get your epilepsy under control! So don't be immature, go with these ladies. You don't want to get off on the wrong foot by causing any trouble. So go! These ladies are waiting."

“What other problems, Julia!?”

“Just a formality. Part of your work-up,” Julia said. “Now you need to go on and get started on your treatment.”

"Gatewood is a fine hospital," the doctor said, smiling at me. “All our patients at Gatewood are well cared for. We have the finest staff around. You’ll see."

Calm, got to be calm, I thought, trying to breathe deeply, trying to blink back tears stinging my eyes. *It will be ok. Just ninety days.* The ladies in the starched white uniforms took hold of my arms, helping me out of the chair. I forced my wobbly legs to move, telling my brain to just go on, get the ninety days over with. As I was led out the door, I looked back once; Julia was smiling across the desk at the white haired doctor.

I was put into the back seat of a blue car with one of the ladies, and the other got into the front with the security office. "Oh, it's not going to be so bad here," the attendant sitting next to me said, for the first time looking directly at me.

"We'll treat you right so long as you don't cause any trouble," the other one said, looking into the back seat.

I scrunched into the seat, clasped my sweaty palms together and held them in my lap, and tried to keep my hands from trembling as the car snaked up a winding road. I was vaguely aware of the voices of the attendants and the security officer talking to each other. Soon, the security officer pulled the car into a parking space before a large green lawn. Through the lawn was a wide cement walkway. At the end of the walkway, situated between two giant oak trees, was a gray two-story building; a sign engraved above the entrance read "Wallace Building 1905".

"This is your new home," the attendant said, getting out of the car and holding the door for me. "This building has four wards. You’ll be on A2."

I tried to swallow the lump in my throat and climbed out of the car and stared at the gray building. *It will be ok, it will be ok,* I tried to convince myself. *Only ninety days. Only ninety days.*

“Come along. Come along, now,” the attendant said.

Inside, I followed behind one attendant and guard as they walked down a hallway. The other attendant walked beside me. The attendants' clothes made swishing sounds as nylon rubbed against satin. We went through a kitchen and dining room, into another hallway. At the end of the hallway, to the left was a gray door marked **"A2".** The attendant fumbled, trying to get her key into the lock. To the right was an identical door with a window in the top half. Above the door was a small sign **"A1".** I looked through the window; several females with short hair, dressed in drab dresses, walked aimlessly around in a long, gray hallway.

My knees trembled as the attendant opened the door marked **A2.** She took my arm and we stepped through the doorway. Her keys jingled as she turned, closed and locked the door behind us, leaving the other attendant and the guard on the other side. Down another long, gray hallway, more people, some dressed in drab gray garments like I'd seen on the people in the next ward, most were in brighter clothing.

"You sure are lucky you are getting to live on A2," the attendant said. I noticed her nametag read: Mrs. P. Bailey, Psychiatric Attendant 5. On the left shoulder of her uniform was a patch of gold and blue and the words in a circle: Psychiatric Attendant 5. Halfway down the hallway we stopped at an open door to a small office. Two attendants, dressed exactly like attendant Bailey, sat at a desk. Behind the desk was a large rack filled with metal files in individual slots. The attendants looked up and stared at us.

"This is your new patient. What's your name?" Attendant Bailey asked, turning to me.

"Jordan Walker," I said slightly above a whisper.

"Well, Jordan Walker, I'll leave you to Miss Hakes and Mrs. Winningham. They will tell you what you are expected to do." She gave me a tiny smile, then turned and walked back down the hallway; jingled her keys in the lock on the door then swung it open. I stared at the open door. It seems everything was moving in slow motion as the attendant walked through the door, closing it behind her. I wanted to run after her, tell her it was all a mistake; that I didn't belong here. But I just stood there beside the office door and listened to the faint sound of jingling keys as the door was locked from the other side.

Biting my trembling lips, I stared at the two women inside the office. "I'm not giving the bath," the one with the nametag of Winningham said. "I gave the last one. I'll start the paper work."

"All right," the other whined, puckering her lips into a pout.

By now, several patients had gathered around, looking me up and down. One tall, dark haired woman with bright, dark eyes smiled at me. "I'm Lee Ann Dodson. Now, honey, you look scared but don't you be afraid. Everything is going to be all right," she said.

I wished I felt as certain as the woman sounded.

Miss Hakes came out of the office, "Come along. We're gonna have to give you your admittance bath," she said.

"I...I bathed this morning," I stammered.

"Makes no difference," the attendant said. "Every new patient gets a bath. Come on."

I followed to a room across the hall and watched as the attendant opened a gray door and went inside. "Get on in here," the attendant said, turning the faucet on a large, white bathtub in the center of the room. A stream of water began flowing into the tub. I stepped inside and looked about the room. There was no screen for privacy, and the door was open. Patients were walking along the hallway, looking in. I reached for the door and started to push it shut. "No! Can't have the door shut!" the attendant said sharply. "We have to hear in case anyone needs help."

"I will need privacy." I managed to say.

The attendant stared at me for a few seconds. "Privacy ain't something we have here at Gatewood. You'll learn one naked body is all the same here. Don't worry, just take off the clothes and let me do my job. I have to mark down any scars or marks you have on your body. We have to record all this on your admittance form. Now, hurry up. I don't have all day." The attendant took a small notepad and pen from the pocket of her uniform and again looked at me. "Shed the clothes," she said impatiently, tapping the pen against the pad. "Come on. Quit stalling."

I didn't want to take off my clothes in front of the attendant, much less the patients who were still looking in at the door. But the attendant was beginning to tap harder with the pen. So, slowly, I began unbuttoning my dress. When all my clothes were on the floor, I crossed my arms over my naked breasts and tried to pacify my spinning brain with the thought of *ninety days. Just ninety days.*

A small, gray haired woman entered the bathroom. She suddenly reached down and patted the air. "Stay, Koko," she said.

"What are you doing in here, Mossie?" The attendant said, looking disapprovingly at the little woman. Now go on. Get on out of here!"

"I want a bath," Mossie said, grinning up at the attendant. "I want my dog to have a bath, too. See, Miss Hakes, Koko is sooo dirty." Mossie, still grinning, reached down and picked up the imaginary dog.

"I've told you a hundred times, Mossie, there ain't no Koko! There ain't no dogs allowed at Gatewood, real or only in your head. And you get your bath on the afternoon shift. Now, get on out of here! Or I'm gonna have to call security and send you to C3! I don't have time to fool with you today. Go on. Get out! Now!"

The smile left Mossie's face, and her lower lip trembled as she stroked the imaginary dog. She slowly backed out the door, glaring at the attendant. "I'm a telling Dr. Kelso! He'll fix you. He knows my Koko is real!"

"Dern fool," the attendant muttered under her breath. "Ok. Ok," she said, turning back to me. "You don't have any unusual marks. Go on. Get in the tub, so I can wash your hair. Gotta check you for lice. That's the rules."

I climbed into the tub of warm water. By now, more patients were in the bathroom. The attendant chased them out, waved her notepad and pen, and yelled, "Come in here again and all you are in for it!"

The attendant dipped water from the tub into a small bucket and ignoring my protests my hair had been washed that morning poured the water over my head; then lathered shampoo into my hair. I closed my eyes tightly and tried to pretend I was far away, safe at home, and Mama was still alive.

Soon the bath was over. I stepped out of the tub and the attendant handed me a large towel. She tossed a drab gray dress, along with a dingy bra and panties onto a straight-backed chair. "Put these on," she said and turned to let the water out of the tub.

I stared at the clothes, not wanting to touch them. *My suitcases were in the trunk of Julia's car. Would she and Thomas have remembered to drop them off at the clothing room? That was what the instructions from the hospital had said to do.* "I'll just put my own clothes back on," I said, reaching for my pink dress.

"Not today, you won't," the attendant said. "Your things have to go to the clothing room to be marked; might take two or three days. You'll have to wear what you can get. Just put on that ward supply, and hurry up about it."

Please, just let me put my own clothes back on."

The attendant sucked in her breath. "I told you, your things have to go to the clothing room!"

"But these look dirty," I said.

"They are not dirty," the attendant said. "Nothing at Gatewood is dirty. These clothes have been through very hot, soapy water at the laundry. The reason they look so dingy is because they probably got in with some of the dark clothes. Just put them on!"

Trembling, not wanting to even touch the clothes, I forced myself to pull them on and asked for a comb. The attendant unlocked a small cabinet on the wall, took out a comb and handed it to me.

I stared at the comb: Hairs of many colors clogged the teeth. "Do you have a comb that hasn't been used?"

The attendant stared at me. "Ward supply," she said. "If you don't have your own, you use what you can get."

Where were my combs and brushes? Had Julia packed them? I placed the comb on the chair and began to run my fingers through my hair.

The attendant rolled her eyes and shrugged her shoulders. "Come on. Hurry up now," she said. "It's almost time for lunch."

I quickly put on my shoes and followed the attendant out of the bathroom, wondering why she wasn't sending my shoes to that clothing room, but didn't say anything for fear she would see the oversight and strip them off my feet.

"Come on, I'll show you where you'll sleep," the attendant said, looking over her shoulder as she hurried down the hallway. "Hurry along, now."

I almost had to run to catch up, thinking at least I'd have some privacy when I got to my room. I almost went into shock when I saw where they expected me to sleep.

To the right just off a large room, which the attendant said was the dayroom, was an open doorway and the attendant went through it, calling over her shoulder, "Hurry along."

I followed into a large room filled with identical, single, brown, iron beds, covered with identical white bedspreads. There were four rows of beds. One row lined the north wall, another south, and two rows were in the center, head to head, barely leaving room for the straight-back chair between each bed. Windows began about four feet up the wall, allowing someone to see out, while preventing anyone outside from seeing in. Curtains, made from fabric with small, yellow flowers on a white background, were pulled back at the windows.

"This is where you'll sleep," the attendant said, pointing to a bed against the north wall. "Now that you are here, all the beds are filled.

I fought back tears. How in the world would I be able to share a bedroom with all these others? Never in my entire life had I shared a room. *Ninety days*. I tried to find comfort in that thought.

"Come on, I'll show you the dayroom," the attendant said.

I followed into the large room. Along each wall were rows of cushioned chairs of red plastic. In the center of the room were two, long tables, surrounded by straight-back chairs. In one corner was a piano. The room had two large picture windows through which I could see the sun shining brightly beyond. A desk was positioned near the door leading into the hallway. A black phone hung on the wall behind the desk.

A small, dark haired attendant was seated behind the desk, writing in a notebook. Several patients were in the dayroom and some began to crowd around me, looking me up and down. I stared at the faces surrounding me; some looked as normal as myself; others were obviously retarded. The tall, bright-eyed woman, who had been in the hallway, grinned at me from across the room. I nervously smiled back.

The attendant at the desk looked up. She got up and came across the room. "I'm Mrs. Holt. I hope your stay here at Gatewood will be most pleasant and you find the help you need."

"It is almost time for lunch." Mrs. Holt said. "Lee Ann, show Jordan the lavatory," the attendant called to the bright-eyed woman across the room.

Lee Ann quickly came across the room to my side. "Follow me, honey," Lee Ann said, walking towards the hallway. Not knowing what else to do, I followed. Lee Ann went into a lavatory. The room had an open doorway. Five sinks lined one wall; each had a small mirror above. And along the other side of the room were five stalls with commodes; the stalls were open, exposing anyone using the toilets. "You can wash up here," Lee Ann said, "while I go and make sure all the others are in line."

I gripped the sides of a sink and stared in the mirror at the frightened-faced, young woman staring back at me. I hardly recognizing myself: my eyes were sunk into the too-white face. My dark hair, still wet, was pressed close to my head. My eyes, which Mama had so often called beautiful, midnight blue, looked sad and glistened with tears. I thought I was going to be sick.

Mrs. Holt and Lee Ann appeared in the doorway. "Lee Ann, take the new patient up to the dining room," Mrs. Holt said, "Hurry up now, or you won't have time to eat before they bring the cart down for A1." The attendant left the lavatory and seconds later, I heard her say, "Everyone go. Get on up to the dining room, hurry along now."

The thought of food made me feel even sicker. Maybe I'd just go into the dormitory and lie down. And I said to Lee Ann, "I'm not feeling well and think I'll just stay here and rest on my bed."

"Honey," Lee Ann said. "Nobody gets on the beds during the day. And nobody on A2 ever misses a meal. If you're ever too sick to go to the dining room, you can be sure you're half-dead and then they will send you off to the hospital ward. And believe me, honey; no one who has any sense at all wants to go to the hospital ward. You just come along to the dining room and do as you're told and you'll be all right. Hurry up now; all the others are already gone."

"Lee Ann, get that new patient up to the dining room," the attendant who wore the name tag of Winningham yelled, coming out of the office and locking the door.

"Come on," Lee Ann said.

I followed Lee Ann, who was following the fast walking Mrs. Winningham. Soon, we were in a line at a steam table. I thought I couldn't possibly eat anything, but followed Lee Ann through the line and got a tray anyway, remembering what she'd said about no one ever missing a meal. On the tray was a plate with mashed potatoes, a dab of cottage cheese, meatloaf, something green and a cookie. I sat down next to Lee Ann and looked about the room. Most of the patients had already gone through the line and were eating. The attendants carried trays to some of the others who either weren't able to carry their own trays, or as Lee Ann said, "Don't have sense enough."

"How come you came to Gatewood?" Lee Ann asked, digging into a mass of mashed potatoes.

"My doctor advised it. He thinks the new drug will help my seizures."

"The drug study," Lee Ann said thoughtfully. "They say the new drug is helping some of the patients here. They asked me if I wanted it. I refused."

"Why?"

"I don't want untested junk going into me: Won't allow myself to be a guinea pig."

"Why are you here?" I asked.

Lee Ann looked directly into my eyes. "I'm here," she said slowly, because I'm an epileptic. Because they say I'm mentally ill---and, of course, a disgrace to my family." She looked past me, shrugged her shoulders and said almost in a whisper, "Why would anyone blame them?"

"When will you be leaving?" I asked.

"Leave!" Lee Ann said. "Why?"

I didn't know what to say. I looked down at my plate and forced myself to take a bite of mushy looking meatloaf. Off to the right, was a dining room in which several men and women in white uniforms were eating.

"How come the only people eating in that room are wearing uniforms?" I asked.

Lee Ann laughed. "Oh, the staff have their own dining room. They don't ever eat near us patients. See the stack of dishes in the cupboard just off the side of this room." I saw a glass-door cupboard containing what looked like fine china. I dropped my eyes to the dishes before me; they were a plain, old looking, thick, white material.

"They don't eat out of the same dishes as we do," Lee Ann said. "Watch that cook take the special dishes out of the cupboard." A woman, carrying a tray, walked to the cupboard and began putting dishes on it. She then went to the serving counter and filled the dishes, and then took them to the room where the uniformed people were.

"I know a patient who tried to eat out of the staff's dishes." Lee Ann said. "She got herself sent to C3 for two whole weeks."

"What is this C3?" I asked, remembering the patient with the invisible dog who had been threatened with C3.

"That's the lock-up." Lee Ann said. "Honey, you don't ever want to get sent there.

"I won't be here very long." I said, trying to keep my voice steady.

"Really," Lee Ann said, staring at me.

Looking over my shoulder, I could see beyond the kitchen, to a dining area like the one we were eating in. "Are there wards beyond that dining room down there?" I asked.

"Yes. The hospital wards are down there: A3 and A4. A3 is a women's ward and A4 is for men. Anybody sick or hurt, or about to die gets sent there." Lee Ann said. "You don't wanna go there."

I was more than certain, I didn't.

When we got back inside the ward, most of the patients headed for the lavatory. I needed to use the toilet, but don't want to with it being open. I waited until most of the others had left. "Why don't they put doors on these stalls?" I asked Lee Ann.

"Honey," Lee Ann said. "They told me one time the stalls are open because if a patient has a seizure the attendants can get to them. The lack of privacy will be hard for you at first, but you'll get used to it."

I didn't think I ever could.

Chapter Two

"Lee Ann," Mrs. Holt said. "You won't be going to work until later this afternoon. I need you to take Jordan to see Dr. Kelso."

Dr. Kelso? I'd heard that name before. Yes, of course, the patient with the invisible dog had threatened the attendant who had given me my admittance bath with Dr. Kelso.

"Dr. Kelso is the psychiatrist here at Gatewood," Mrs. Holt said. "You have an appointment at 1:30. You'll ride the shuttle bus."

"Why am I seeing a psychiatrist?"

"Routine," the attendant said. "Part of your workup."

The shuttle bus was green, about the size of a school bus. "The bus makes rounds of the hospital every hour. We ride it to get to our appointments and jobs," Lee Ann said, as we boarded the bus. I followed Lee Ann and slid into a seat next to her. We went past several building shaped like the Wallace Building, and eight cottages. The bus went into a valley which had the stone wall all along the road. In the valley, in neatly mowed lawns, were several buildings.

"Over there's the school," Lee said pointing to a large, brick building. "Sometimes they show movies in there on a Saturday night. And that building next to it is the clothing room. The garage, where you'll find the security guards when they aren't out on a run, is that long building. The laundry is the block building next to that smokestack. And the maintenance building is the one near that bunch of cedar trees. There are children in Gatewood: boys and girls. The girls are on Blake cottage. The little boys are over on Hunter. Now, a few young ones, who are badly disabled and in crib beds don't live on the cottages. The little girls, I think there are two, live across the hall from us on A1. And the boys, who are in cribs, I am told, live on the Stringer building."

Good Lord! I thought. Children here. How sad.

The road stretched several hundred yards through the valley, crossed a highway; and then went up a long hill onto another campus, much like the campus which contained the Wallace building.

"This is the east campus," Lee Ann said. "All the male patients live on this side of the valley. When this place was built, a Dr. Coffin was the superintendent. He made it a rule that all female patients were to be housed on the west campus, and all males were to live on the east campus and that's the way it's been ever since."

"Why is that?" I asked, not really caring. I'd be leaving in ninety days. What did it matter where these others lived?

"Oh, there was the fear that epileptics would get together and produce little epileptics, and it was Dr. Coffin's aim to see that never happened. It was a great offense against the rules of this place for a female and a male to be found together. And still a rule today. Girl, the stories I could tell you," Lee Ann said laughing.

"How long have you been here?" I asked.

"About thirty years."

Had she said thirty years? "You have lived here for thirty years!" I said, looking at Lee Ann in disbelief.

"Thirty years," Lee Ann said, looking out the window.

"Don't you ask to leave? I asked.

"No. I'll never do that." Lee Ann said, turning back to me. "To some patients, Gatewood might seem like a place where the devil lives, but to me it is where I see my Sir Lancelot. He comes to me, you know, when the moon is full. He comes to me and we dance by the light of a lovers' moon." Lee Ann's face had a soft glow about it.

I thought I might have witnessed an entirely different person inside the body of this person called Lee Ann. I remembered she had said she was mentally ill. I stared out the window, longing to leave this place called Gatewood and to be back home again, safe with the only worries I'd have would be of what to choose to wear, or which contract to sign, or what function to attend.

The driver stopped the bus near a long, gray building. "This is the Parr Building," Lee Ann said. "Come on. Dr. Kelso is in there."

I followed Lee Ann out of the bus, past the attendant standing by the door. I had wondered what the attendant was doing on the bus. She had stood up all the way, just standing there by the door, talking to the bus driver, and from time to time scanning the patients. "Why is that attendant on the bus?" I asked Lee Ann.

"Honey, attendants are everywhere. They have to be. One of the rules of this place. All patients must be watched at all times. The same rules made by Old Dr. Coffin over fifty years ago. That damn fool has been dead for years, was dead when I came here. But the idiots who run this place still follow along with anything he planned, just as if he was still here."

I followed Lee Ann up the walk to the building. She pushed open the door and we walked inside.

A middle-aged lady with silver hair and a nametag that read "Miss Page" sat at a desk at one end of a long room. I stood beside Lee Ann at the desk. "I have Jordan Walker here to see Dr. Kelso. Mrs. Holt sent us."

"Dr. Kelso had to leave, had an emergency at home. Sorry, you came over for nothing. The appointment will be rescheduled," Miss Page said. "You two may wait here until the bus makes another round."

"Fine and dandy with me" Lee Ann said, turning and making her way to chairs along one wall. I followed and sat beside her.

"Let me tell you a little something about Dr. Kelso," Lee Ann said, "Just let him think you accept everything he says, just nod in agreement, like you believe he couldn't possibly be wrong about anything. If you do that, he'll write up a good report on you. He believes every action us patients have has something to do with sex. It's all based on research from some old doctor named Freud"

"My God!" I said, wondering what I was in for.

"Oh, Dr. Kelso is harmless enough," Lee Ann said, giving my arm a reassuring pat. He just has stupid ideas, but don't you dare disagree with him. He gets upset if you do."

We sat in the waiting room and waited for the bus to return. Lee Ann crossed her arms and sat with closed eyes. I didn't know if she was asleep or if she just didn't want to be disturbed, but I knew one thing absolutely: I wasn't going to try to find out.

After a while the bus returned and I followed Lee Ann outside and we got on. The same attendant was on the bus and reminded an older male patient he was to sit on the right side of the bus with the rest of the male patients when he tried to sit next to a cute, red haired patient named Susan. "Don't try that again, Bobby", the attendant said, not sounding too angry with Bobby.

When we got back to the ward, Mrs. Holt told Lee Ann she wasn't to go to work. “Mrs. Sloan went home sick so the shop is closed for the rest of the day.”

"I don't give a damn," Lee Ann snapped.

"We'll have none of your attitude," Mrs. Holt said.

Lee Ann said no more, but smirked at Mrs. Holt when the attendant turned her back.

A large, red headed woman sitting in a corner yelled, "Lee Ann made a face at you, Mrs. Holt. She's making faces behind your back."

"Shut up, Gladys!" Lee Ann snarled.

"Both of you stop it!" Mrs. Holt said. "I don't want to hear another word out of either of you." Gladys dropped her head, and Lee Ann stomped off down the hall.

As the afternoon wore on, I studied the patients on the ward, wondering how they got to be there. Mrs. Holt had said some of the patients had jobs about the hospital and in a few days I would be assigned some type of job. I learned in a hurry that Gladys was the tattletale of the ward. She seemed to just sit watching and waiting for another patient to make a mistake so she could yell, “Attendant. Attendant, so and so is eating a crayon, or so and so is picking that sore on her arm.” I learned there were thirty-five patients on the ward, not thirty-four as I’d thought when I’d seen the thirty-four beds in the dormitory. Lee Ann had a private room, down the hallway from the clothing room near the back of the building.

Gladys informed me of this. Gladys said, “Oh, yes. Lee Ann has that room cause she’s too mean to sleep in the same room with the rest of us. They put her in that little room so they can keep watch on her. She’s mean. That Lee Ann is. You'd better watch out for her."

Good, God, was I in physical danger here?

And then I learned of the hideous side room. Gladys had been telling a young patient of about nineteen that she was going to go to the side room if she didn't straighten up her act. Finally I asked Gladys about the side room. "Come on, I'll show you," Gladys said, waving me to follow as she went into the hallway. I followed, and about halfway down the hallway, Gladys stopped before a door with a small window in it. "Shh," she whispered. "If they catch us hanging around the side room or talking to the one in there, they just might take them out and stick us in there."

I looked in at the small window; a face stared back at me.

"That's Matilda in there," whispered Gladys.

"Her name's Tillie," came a singsong voice from within.

I looked into the blue eyes of Matilda. "Why are you in there, Matilda?" I asked.

"Her name's Tillieee. Her name's Tillieee. Mom calls her Tillieee," the woman shrilled, biting her hand.

"She's a dummy," Gladys whispered. "Bout all she knows is the names of us patients and attendants on this ward. And she gets mad when anybody calls her Matilda. Says her name is Tillie. Mrs. Holt said that was cause her mother always called her Tillie when she was a little kid. It's all there in her record book. They have record books on everybody. They'll fix one on you, too. She's not been here but a few months. Spends a lot of time in the side room. She hits a lot."

Suddenly the attendant who had given me my admittance bath came charging out of the office and stood glaring at us. "You patients get away from that side room, unless you would like to trade places with Matilda!"

From inside the side room came, "Her name is Tillieee!"

"We're sorry! We're getting away from the side room, Miss Hakes! We're getting away right now!" Gladys said, and then hastily made her way towards the dayroom. I stood as if frozen, staring at the attendant.

"Well! What are you still standing there for?" the attendant demanded.

I felt my knees knocking, but manage to quickly turn and go as fast as I could without running to the dayroom. As well as feeling fear, my feelings had been hurt by the way the attendant had talked to me. I didn't know if it was her tone of voice or the words which had cut me so deeply, maybe it was both. When I got into the dayroom Lee Ann was sitting by the window and I went to her. She looked up as I approached. "Well, how's it going?" She asked.

"Why do some of the attendants talk so hateful?"

"Cause some of them are hateful," Lee Ann replied. "They have to be in control of every situation, and some think they have to talk tough to do that. Been like that since I've been here. I don't expect it to change any. Most treat us decent, but I think even they think of us as beneath them. You know, I think it was the separate dishes that first told me the employees in this place see us as inferior pieces of humanity. Think about it."

I didn't want to think about it. I wanted to go home. I sank into a chair next to Lee Ann, thinking, dear God what have I gotten myself into?

"I'm not going to put up with them talking so hateful to me? Isn't there someone I can report them to?"

"Ha!" Lee Ann laughed. "Listen, girl," she said, leaning forward and talking low, "You don't ever tell on an attendant. There are rules here at Gatewood, lots of rules and one of the biggest one is a patient's word is never to be taken."

"Surely you don't mean that," I gasped, unable to believe just because I was suddenly a patient in a state hospital I would be considered to always be a liar.

"Well, you just wait and find out for yourself," Lee Ann said. "Some of the patients lie, so they just say none of us ever tell the truth. It's easier for them that way," she said, nodding her head up and down.

Was it possible I had lost my right to be heard? I thought, with deep despair that perhaps I had no rights left at all. I try to chase the terrifying thought away with: *Ninety days. Ninety days.*

"I heard them yelling at you for being near the side room. You don't want to do anything to get in there," Lee Ann said, shaking her head. "That's almost as bad as getting sent to C3."

C3? What was it with this C3? Not sure I was going to be better off knowing, I asked anyway. "I've only been here a few hours, but C3 seems to be a popular subject. Didn't you say it was some kind of lockup?"

"C3," Lee Ann said, looking out the window, rubbing a finger across her lips. "Everyone fears C3, even me. That's the lock-up for women. It was included in the plans when this place was first built. You get sent there, you might be gone for a month or two. The lockup for the men is on the other side of the valley; it's called the Hadley building."

Lee Ann's words sent cold chills through me. *Was she making all this up? Why was there a need for a lockup in a hospital?* "Well," I said, "I don't think I will have to worry about going there anyway. What could I do to get sent there?"

Lee Ann looked at me out of the corners of her eyes. "You never know. You just never know," she said, then changed the subject. "It's getting about time for the afternoon shift. Most of the attendants on afternoons are pretty decent people."

Soon two attendants, a Miss Jones and Mrs. Casper, came on the ward. All the patients seemed happy to see them. The two women introduced themselves, telling me they were the afternoon shift.

Thinking perhaps things had lightened a bit, I said to Mrs. Casper, "I don't think I'll go to supper, I'm not hungry. If it is just the same to you, I'll just go lie on my bed."

The smile left Mrs. Casper's lips. Raising a thinly plucked eyebrow, she snapped, "There will be no lying on the beds until bedtime! That's one of the rules around here; I'm sure the day shift already told you. And no one stays back from supper; that, too, is one of the rules." Mrs. Casper quickly turned away from me and went to the desk and sat. I just stared after her, stunned. I looked at Lee Ann

"Girl, you have a lot to learn," she said, then rested her head against the back of her chair and closed her eyes.

I didn't know what to do, so I just sank down into my chair and closed my eyes too.

By suppertime, all the patients who had been out on jobs had returned. The woman with her invisible dog was telling the dog to stay under a chair while everyone went to supper. Matilda was out of the side room, dressed and sitting, with her legs pulled up under her, in a chair across the room. She was grinning at no one in particular.

I followed in the line to supper, got my tray and sat at a table with Lee Ann and Gladys. But I didn't eat anything. "Suit yourself," Mrs. Casper said. "You are allowed to miss three meals before we have to force feed you."

"You don't want them to ever do that to you" Lee Ann said, shaking her head. "I've had it done to me. It'll gag your guts out."

Gladys, who had been taking it all in said, "Are you gonna be a troublemaker? Bet you're gonna end up in that side room before you're here a whole day."

I just turned away, feeling as if my heart was going to break as I fought to keep back the tears.

After supper, the patients who were on the afternoon shift's bath list were given their baths. And everyone else changed into pajamas and bathrobes. "Ward supply," the attendant said, tossing me gray pajamas, along with a gray bathrobe. I took the bundle, thinking the favorite color at the state hospital had to be gray.

After I'd changed into the night clothes, I settled in one of the red plastic chairs beside Lee Ann. The television was blaring, but I hardly noticed. If I closed my eyes maybe I could imagine myself away from this place.

About eight o'clock, Mrs. Casper wheeled a cart into the dayroom. A large tray containing little cups of medicine and water glasses were on top of the cart. The attendant began calling off names. With each name she called, someone went to the cart. When it seemed all the medication had been passed out, I, wondering why my name hadn't been called, went to the cart.

Perhaps the attendant had my special medicine still in the office, surely the doctors would have wanted me put on it right away, and the sooner it had a chance to work on my seizures, the quicker I'd be out of here, maybe even before the ninety days were up. "Don't I get any medication?" I asked. "I'm on the drug study."

"Not yet, you are not," Mrs. Casper said. "You won't get any medication until all the workups have been done. This is routine. However, you are allowed to have aspirin."

A headache that, all afternoon, had been threatening to move from dull to pounding, now, began throbbing at my temples. "Please, may I have the aspirin?" I asked. "My head is hurting."

Mrs. Casper reached into the cart, taking out a bottle of aspirin. She shook two pills into my hand, then handed me a glass of water.

"Thanks," I said, downing the aspirins and water. I then went and sat beside Lee Ann.

Mrs. Casper picked up a notepad and yelled, "Who has not had a B.M. today?" Two patients raised their hands.

"What is she talking about?" I whispered to Lee Ann.

"The shit list," Lee Ann said. "If you don't have a bowel movement at least every three days you have to take that god-awful dose of Milk of Magnesia, topped off with even worse Cascara. And if that doesn't work," Lee Ann said, her eyes getting brighter, "well, honey, they bring on the enemas. Four days without a B.M. gets you one of them hot, sudsy enemas."

Oh, God, I thought, can this be real?

"I always tell them I had a B.M., whether I did or not," Lee Ann continued. "Everybody's name is on the shit list. You're on there, too."

After all the medicine had been given, Miss Jones began trimming toenails. "I can do that myself," I said, when she stopped, with clippers in hand, beside my chair.

"No patient is allowed to have sharp objects," Miss Jones said.

I was thankful when at last we were allowed to go to bed. Lee Ann said goodnight and went down the hallway and out of sight. I went with the rest of the patients to the dormitory. I lay in the small bed, wondering how I was ever going to be able to sleep in a room with thirty-three other people. How was I to survive this place called Gatewood? I turned my face towards the wall; thankful I at least had a bed that allowed me not to be looking directly into someone else's face. Hot tears trickled down my face. *Ninety days.* If only I could stand it ninety days, then it would all be over, and if the new medications worked, I could get on with my life. I listened to the sounds in the dormitory: soft breathing and snoring, someone clearing their throat. Gladys had warned there would be no talking after lights were out, 'You'd better not talk when the attendant turns off the lights. You'd better be quiet. You gotta go by the rules. You'd better mind the attendants.'

It seemed everyone else was asleep. I lay there, remembering my life before the accident. I had never in my life--before Mama and Daddy died-- had to depend entirely on myself for anything. I'd never wanted for anything materially, and I had an abundance of unconditional love from both parents.

My father had often said his little angel would never want for anything. *Oh, Daddy, if only you could see me now.* Julia, fifteen years my senior, was my mother's child from a first marriage. I'd never felt close to my sister. When I'd been about four, Julia went off to college and wasn't home much after that. She married Thomas and they lived in a big house in Cincinnati. I'd heard a cousin remark at a family reunion that Julia was the society queen of Cincinnati. Then after Mama's death Julia wanted to help me manage my financial affairs. She told me, 'You have to have someone with knowledge to handle your inheritance, Jordan; else you'll mismanage your fortune.'

I had declined the offer. I'd stayed on in the big old house I'd grown up in, despite Julia's nagging for me to sell and move to a place more suited for a young woman all alone. I'd felt the house was my protector: a huge, warm thing that at night lovingly put giant arms of wonderful memories around me. I never told that to Julia or to anyone. I had a few close friends, and Mandy who'd been the housekeeper since I could remember still came two days a week. Then after the accident, Julia had become my guardian (temporarily court ordered) she and Dr. Cole told me. Letting Julia be my guardian, gaining total control of all my finances, I'd felt uneasy from the beginning, but didn't know just why or what else I could do. Certainly, I wasn't capable.

Suddenly, a vision of Paul floated across my mind. We'd been engaged to be married. But that was before the tragedy with his brother. I could still feel the pain I'd felt that day when he walked out of my life. Mama had said life must go on and to get out there and meet someone new. Reluctantly I'd started to date again. But none of the young men I met even half-measured up to Paul.

I heard voices coming from the dayroom and turned over to face the door. Two attendants came into the dormitory. Their voices turned to whispers as they walked between the rows of beds. It must be the change of shifts. Soon the attendants were by my bed. I pretended to be asleep as they began discussing me.

"Cody, this is the new patient," Miss Jones whispered. "She had a quiet evening and the day shift reported she didn't have much to say. Lee Ann has sort of taken her under her wing." They moved on, their voices fading as they went out of the dormitory. So Cody was a night shift attendant. *So many names to try to remember.*

I turned towards the wall and exhausted both mentally and physically, drifted into sleep.

Sometime later, I abruptly sat upright in bed, wide-awake, and my heart was thumping wildly. What had awakened me? Perhaps it was the newness of the situation; maybe it was something else.

In the dim shadows, it seemed everyone else in the dormitory was sleeping. I let my eyes travel the length of the room, over the rows of various sized, white humps in bed after bed. I was so afraid. Of what? I wasn't sure, maybe the hospital, maybe the patients, the likes I'd never even dreamed of. I eased back my sheet and blanket and pulled myself onto my knees, steadying myself against the windowsill. The window was raised, letting in a soft breeze through a sturdy, locked screen. Moonlight glistened pale silver on the world outside and leaves on the many trees fluttered lightly. To my left I saw, a great distance away and partly blocked by evergreens, a structure somewhat like a tiny gazebo. There appears to be two shadows in the structure dancing back and forth in the moonlight. What had Lee Ann said about a Sir Lancelot and of dancing when the moon was full? Surely I was dreaming, and the gazebo and the people like shadows were only a figment of that dream. I sank back on the bed, pulled the covers tightly around me and soon drifted into a restless sleep.

Chapter Three

Just before daybreak, an attendant came into the dormitory and flicked on the lights, telling everyone to, "Hit the floor." And I began my second day in that place called Gatewood.

Sometime during the night someone had placed neatly rolled bundles of clothes on the foot of each bed. Some of the patients began dressing as others headed for the lavatory. I picked up the bundle; it contained a dress and underwear much like the same dull gray clothing I'd worn the day before. "That's a bath bundle," Gladys said.

"Why do they call it that? Is everyone going to take a bath before breakfast?"

"Nope. They ain't," Gladys said. "They call it a bath bundle, just because they do. That's all I know."

"Why don't the patients get their own clothes?"

"Nobody gets in the clothing room but the attendants. We get to wear our own clothes, if we got any. If we don't have any, we gotta wear ward supply. You have your own stuff? Don't you?" Gladys asked, grinning.

"Of course I do. They sent my clothes to a clothing room."

"The clothing room for the whole hospital is down in the valley. Miss Vera works there. Everybody's clothes goes there first to be marked. When the clothes are marked with the patient's name, the clothes goes to the ward or cottage where that patient is living. We have a clothing room on this ward. You might have seen it, next to the shower room. Everybody's got their own clothing bin," Gladys continued," but the attendants picks out our clothes. They save our very best clothes to put away for our burying bundle. Everybody's got one; you'll have one, too, just as quick as your clothes comes out of Miss Vera's clothing room. They'll pick out your best and make up your burying bundle and put it on the top shelf of your bin."

Was Gladys making all that up? Why would anyone in a hospital need burial clothes? A chill rippled down my spine. Were some of these patients destined to live out their entire lives in this place, their whole lives planned from the time they arrived in the hospital until they died? My fingers shook as I pulled off my pajamas and slowly began pulling on dingy underwear.

Soon everyone was dressed and assembled in the dayroom. The attendant: Miss Cody wheeled the medicine cart into the room and started giving the morning medicine.

At breakfast, I sat at a table with Lee Ann and Gladys and force myself to take a few bites of soggy looking eggs. "Eighty-eight days from today, I'll be going home," I said, needing to hear the words my time in the hospital was becoming shorter.

Lee Ann raised her left eyebrow and stared at me. "Where did you get the idea you could just up and leave in eighty-eight more days?"

A sick feeling played in the pit of my stomach as I stared at Lee Ann. Did she know something I didn't know? "Because," I finally answered, trying to make my voice sound strong. "My doctor on the outside told me I was only coming here for a workup and drug study and I'd only be here for ninety days."

"Well, good luck to you then," Lee Ann said, getting up and taking her tray to the dumping table.

I couldn't stop the panic rising in my throat, and needing to feel some kind of assurance, I asked the attendant to come to my table. "You know, don't you, that I was only sent here for ninety days!?"

"Hey, don't ask me. I only work here. That's something you'll have to take up with the doctors."

My heart was racing. They couldn't keep me here any longer than what Dr. Cole had promised, could they? *Of course not.* I was letting my mind run away with itself. I just needed to calm down.

Later as I brushed my teeth over the sink in the lavatory--the attendant had a large stash of toothbrushes, and I was thankful for that.

The attendant said, "Jordan, You will see Dr. Kelso at nine o'clock."

"I don't know why I have to see a psychiatrist," I said. "I'm not mentally ill; I have a brain condition that causes seizures."

"Every patient in this hospital must see the psychiatrist," the attendant said. "One of the rules. Your session was canceled yesterday, so you have to go back. Just go on, get on the bus and go, and don't be questioning everything. Since you know where Dr. Kelso is, you can ride the bus on your own."

As I rode through the campus, I noticed how beautiful the grounds were: Grass and scrubs were trimmed just so. And flowers, in soft, spring colors, adorned rock-bordered beds. When the bus stopped at one of the cottages, a middle-aged woman got on the bus and slid into the seat beside me. "Hi," she said, "You're new, aren't you?" Without giving me time to answer, the woman continued. "My name is Rosa. I've been at this hospital for fifteen years. It used to be called, **"The Village"**. They changed the name to State Hospital a few years back. My husband sent me here," Rosa volunteered. "He's a doctor, ashamed, you know, of my seizures. He loved me before the seizures started---told me so anyway. He used to visit sometimes, before the divorce. We had two children."

I stared at the woman. She didn't seem to be too sad about her situation, just matter of fact. Fifteen years? How had she stood it? "When are you going to get out of here?" I asked.

"Oh, I'm never leaving the Village," Rosa said. "There's no place for me on the outside. This is where I belong, with my own kind."

Oh, my God, I thought. Could life outside ever be so bad I'd rather be in here? And that phrase "*With my own kind"*. Julia had used it. I felt like the bottom was going to fall out of my stomach. I tried to chase the feeling away and began talking to Rosa.

"What's way over there behind those tall evergreens?" I asked, pointing towards a line of green, remembering what I thought I'd seen last night?"

"Well, I've been told that years ago there was a lookout tower over there and to the side was a gazebo where they once held dances for some of the patients. That was before I came here. They told me in years gone by when one of the patients would try to run away, that from the tower the security guards could see all over the grounds. I heard that many years ago a storm blew down the tower and they just didn't put it back. I've never actually seen the gazebo, for all I know it has long ago rotted away. Anyway, they say it's haunted."

"Haunted? Who said?"

"Well, I heard it from the attendants and patients too. And even from some of the security guards. And see that yellow brick building, right over there," Rosa said, pointing to a building we were passing. They tell me that place is really haunted. They told me it used to be a morgue, back in the day when this place was first built. They say it has a basement and ghosts roam the place. Now, I think they store stuff there."

I shivered. Perhaps I'd only thought I'd seen two shadowy people dancing in a gazebo. Of course it wasn't real, it couldn't be real, I thought, turning back to Rosa, realizing the woman was speaking again.

"I live on Rose Cottage," Rosa said. "You should try to get transferred there. It's the best in all the hospital."

"I 'm only going to be here for eighty-eight more days."

"Really," Rosa said, gazing at me through lowered eyelashes, "I was only going to be here for about six months when I came. Now I'm a fifteen-year veteran."

I wanted to scream at the top of my lungs: Eighty-eight more days is it! Why did everyone seem to doubt I was sent here for only ninety days?

I got off the bus at the building where Dr. Kelso had his office. I was still not happy about having to see a psychiatrist, but don't think I had any choice except to go on inside. Soon, I was inside the doctor's office and seated in a chair across the desk from him: a little man with graying hair and wearing brown rimmed glasses. "Well, how are we today?" Dr. Kelso asked.

I managed a smile, remembering what Rosa had said when I'd gotten off the bus. '*The Dr. likes happy patients.*'

"The information I have on you is from your sister, Julia," Dr. Kelso said, leafing through a folder on his desk. "It says you suffered a brain injury due to an automobile accident, causing your seizures," Dr. Kelso continued.

"Yes," I said, thinking maybe the interview wouldn't be so bad after all.

"When was the last time you had a seizure?" the doctor asked.

"A few days ago I guess."

"Does any one thing seem to trigger them?"

"No. I don't remember anything about them. They tell me I had a seizure."

"You don't have an aura?"

"No. I've never had a warning at all."

"Some epileptics see lights, hear bells, or sometimes just a feeling before the onset of a seizure," the doctor said, removing his glasses and began chewing on the earpiece.

"I've read about that. But I've never experienced any of those things."

"How about a boyfriend? Do you have many male friends?"

I was startled by his abrupt change in subject, but manage to answer. "I have some male friends from school, but no one special, not anymore." I said, remembering Paul, wondering what my having a boyfriend had to do with my seizures. Then I remembered what Lee Ann had said about Dr. Kelso thinking everything had something to do with sex. Surely that couldn't be true.

"I see here in the report that Paul, to whom you were once engaged, is away in the Peace Corps," Dr. Kelso said.

"Yes." I said, not really wanting to talk about Paul.

"How does he feel about you being an epileptic?"

"I.... I.....I really don't know. You see, I haven't been able to contact him. I wrote him, but I haven't gotten an answer. Anyway, he went away to be alone. He was gone before the accident.

Dr. Kelso stared at me, put his glasses back on then said, "Don't you think that is strange? Don't you wonder why he wouldn't at least answer your letter?

I didn't want to talk about Paul. All I wanted to do was get my seizures under control and get out of that place. "My relationship with Paul has nothing to do with my having seizures," I said sharply, causing the doctor to draw back in surprise.

"Now, just calm down," Dr. Kelso said. "Your sister said you are high strung."

But that's not true!" I almost yelled.

"She also said you are in denial. Would you like to tell me about your childhood, some of the things that happened then?" Dr. Kelso asked, peering at me over his glasses.

"My childhood was good."

"Sometimes we don't want to talk about things that make us uncomfortable. Want to tell me about drowning your kitten?"

"What! That's an absolute lie! Why would you say such a thing!?"

"Well we have your history, from your sister."

I couldn't believe Julia had told a deliberate lie. And I couldn't imagine why she would do such a terrible, hateful thing.

"You, you must have misunderstood!" I said, gripping the chair arms, my knuckles turning white.

"Now, now, Jordan," Dr. Kelso soothed. "We must not get ourselves upset. We could give you medication to help you with your mental outbursts, but we don't like to do that because it could interfere with the drug study medication. Perhaps we had better end this session.

What's he saying. I didn't need mind altering drugs. "I'm ok. I'm ok." I stammered. "I just don't understand why Julia would say such things about me."

"I tell you what; I'll set up an appointment for you each Thursday at 2 P.M. How does that sound? We'll work through all your issues."

"I'll be leaving in eighty-eight days."

The doctor stared at me. "Why do you say that?"

"Dr. Cole told me before I came here," I said, feeling my heart beginning to beat fast. *Surely Dr. Cole shared that with the doctors here.*

"Hum," Dr. Kelso said. "I'll have to look into that. And I will set up the appointment for next Thursday."

I stared helplessly at the doctor. I wanting to scream at him that I didn't think I would ever have another appointment with him, and that I would be leaving in eighty-eight days, I didn't care what he thought. Eighty-eight days was it and I most definitely didn't need appointments with a psychiatrist. But I just nodded and with shaking knees left his office.

As I waited for the bus, I thought about what the doctor had said Julia had reported. Surely Dr. Kelso had misunderstood Julia. But I couldn't help wondering what else was in the report lying on his desk?

As I rode the bus back to the ward, I began to feel a dark dread, of what I didn't know. Maybe it was being in that place. *Stop. Stop it!* You will be out in eighty-eight more days. Dr. Cole promised. And he signed me in here so he can sign me out. So no matter what Dr. Kelso had in his report, I'd be leaving in eighty-eight more days. Just one day at a time would get me through it. With those thoughts, I felt a bit better as I walked up the walk to A2. I knocked on the outside door.

Mrs. Holt opened the door. "Well, Jordan how was your session with Dr. Kelso?"

"Fine," I said, wondering if she was just asking or really cared.

I looked around for Lee Ann. "She's gone to her job in the beauty shop," Gladys said. “Lee Ann works different times. Sometimes she has a schedule, and sometimes the beauty shop lady calls the ward when she is needed. Lee Ann was a beauty shop lady before she got here, had her own shop over there in Louisville, thinks she's the best hair fixer in the United States of America. But I know there's better than her. I go to the beauty shop every Friday, but I don't let Lee Ann curl my hair. I let Miss Sloan do mine. They'll let you go too, if you want to. Just ask Mrs. Holt and she'll set you up with the beauty shop, but don't you let Lee Ann curl your hair. You get Miss Sloan."

"Come along, Jordan," Mrs. Holt said, "it's time to get your bath. I went along to the bathroom, peeled off my clothes as instructed, climbed into the tub, and had my hair washed. Without a word I put on the bundle of gray clothing, and picked out the multicolored hair from the ward supply brush Mrs. Holt offered, and ran it through my wet hair. "I really need my own things," I finally said, choking back tears.

"In a day or two you should receive your things from the clothing room," Mrs. Holt said.

After lunch, a group of people came on the ward. Lee Ann, back from her job, said they were from the recreation department and they came two afternoons a week. "They're here to play games and sing and make us happy," Lee Ann smirked. "Come on over by the piano and let them hear you sing your heart out."

"I don't want to," I said. "I think I'll just sit here and watch."

"Better not," Lee Ann said, raising her eyebrows at me. "You'll get bad marks on you in the incident report."

I'll what?"

"I'm telling you, they will write you up in the incident report. See that brown notebook over there on the attendants' desk. That's called the report and they write down anything about you they think is bad. And refusing to take part in this ward recreation is considered bad, and they'll sure write you up. That's called nonparticipation; they have a chart for that."

"How can it be held against you if you refuse to play their games or sing?"

"Well, it can and it will." Lee Ann said, and then walked across the floor to the piano.

I stood up and walked to the window, wanting to shut out the sounds of singing. As I looked out across the lawn, a large black cloud was rolling across the horizon, and a deep fear filled my heart. I'd seen that cloud before. On the morning before my mother died, I'd noticed an identical cloud. I'd been in the garden behind our house. My mother had been there with me, and the sun had been shining warm upon us. I'd told my mother to look at the odd, black cloud. Mama had looked at me strangely and said, 'Jordan dear, there's no black cloud. Honey, there isn't a cloud in the sky. Aren't you feeling well?' I'd watched the cloud dissipate, feeling sick and fearful, but didn't know what to make of it, and thought perhaps my mind was playing tricks on me. I'd smiled at my mother and jokingly said maybe I needed glasses.

As I'd driven to work, the feeling of fear stayed with me. Later that day a call came in; my mother had suddenly died from a heart attack. The second time I saw the cloud, I was in the clinic, just before Dr. Cole came to tell me I would be going to Gatewood. Then, too, the sky had been clear and the sun shining brightly. But the sinister, black cloud had come rolling in from the eastern horizon. I'd yelled at the nurse to look at the black cloud. The nurse had looked out the window and then looked puzzled at me. 'Miss Walker, there's no black cloud out there. There isn't even a white cloud out there; the sky is as clear as can be. Now, you go on and get back to bed, it could be those seizures are going to come on you.'

Standing in the A2 dayroom of Gatewood State Hospital, I felt my knees begin shaking as I watched the cloud as it grew bigger and then retreated. Soon all I saw was bright afternoon sunlight. I stared at my hands: my knuckles were white where I'd been gripping the windowsill. I hadn't called out to anyone when I saw the cloud this time. I didn't think I would tell anyone about the cloud, ever again. Perhaps the cloud was an omen, of some impending doom?

I sat in a chair in the corner of the room. I shivered, although I knew the room was warm. Someone from the recreation group was playing the piano and a group of patients were gathered around singing "You Are My Sunshine."

Mrs. Holt came over to me. With her was a woman dressed in white, with a nurse's cap perched on her head. Her nametag read M. Margo RN. "This is Nurse Margo," Mrs. Holt said.

The nurse was a large woman, not fat, but big-boned and tall. She said she was happy to meet me and that I was on a good ward. I said I was glad to meet her as well. The nurse told everyone to have a great day, then left.

Mrs. Holt said, "Come on and join the group."

"I'm not singing today," I said.

"I wish you would." Mrs. Holt said. But she left me alone, and went and sat at the desk.

After the party people left, the afternoon dragged on. Some of the patients slept in their chairs. I dozed off, awakened to someone announcing, "Suppertime."

After supper, an attendant approached me, "Go take your bath."

"I had a bath on the day shift."

"It don't matter how many baths you had on the day shift. You're on the afternoon's list now. So get on in the bathroom and get the bath!"

I sighed and got up and followed along behind the attendant as she headed towards the bathroom. I was learning fast to just do as I was told.

My own pink satin pajamas lay on the chair next to the bathtub. I rushed over and picked them up, caressing their softness as I hugged them to my chest. *When had my things arrived, maybe while I was sleeping in the dayroom chair this afternoon?* "Could I please have my blue skirt and white blouse to wear tomorrow?" I asked, looking at the attendant bending over the tub as she tested the water for temperature.

The attendant stood upright, turned her dark head and stared at me for a moment. I noticed for the first time her nametag read: MISS S. ABNER.

"We don't pick out your bath bundle, we lay out the nightclothes. The night shift will make up your bath bundle."

"If you will show me where my things are, I can pick out something," I said, wondering about the burial bundle Gladys had talked about. *Was my new green dress, from Bloomingdale's, on the top shelf of a clothing bin?*

The attendant sighed heavily. "We can't allow patients into the clothing room; if we did we'd have a terrible mess."

Thinking how stupid some of the rules they had were, I undressed, then stepped into the bathtub. Later, I dressed in my pajamas, and then went towards the day room. As I passed the side room, I couldn't resist going up to the small window and looking inside. I could make out the small figure of a nude woman, crouched in the far corner or the room. -- Matilda had gotten herself put into the side room again. I'd seen her sitting quietly in a chair just before I'd gone to take my bath. Matilda looked up, slowly rose to her feet, and came to the window. "Hi," I said impulsively.

For a moment, Matilda stared at me. Suddenly she broke into a smile, showing a missing front tooth. "Her name is Tillie," she giggled.

I smiled back. "I know. Glad to meet you, Tillie."

Matilda looked at me with childlike wonder in her eyes. "Her name is Tillie. Mom calls her Tillie."

Just then Miss Abner came rushing out of the bathroom. "You! Get away from that side room door!" she yelled. "The rules around here are no one talks to anyone inside the side room! And that means you, too, Miss Walker! Unless you want to trade places with Matilda!"

I was stunned and just stared at the angry Miss Abner.

"Her name is Tillie," came the voice from inside the side room.

"Do you want to trade places with Matilda?!" the attendant said, her voice even louder now, her eyes squinting into slits.

Again the voice from inside the side room said, "Her name is Tillieee. The pretty lady says her name is Tillieee!"

For a few seconds longer, I eyed the angry attendant, then quickly turned and rapidly walked towards the day room, wondering why the attendant got so hateful, just because I dared to speak to the poor creature in the side room.

Some of the patients were watching "I Love Lucy". Others were already asleep in their chairs. I just wanted to go to bed, pull the covers over my head and try to let sleep wipe everything away. Miss Abner was still back there somewhere towards the bathroom, and I sincerely hoped she stayed there. I sat down at a table beside Lee Ann.

“I see you have on your own pajamas,” Lee Ann said. “Your things must be in our clothing room. We aren’t allowed in there. My black sequined dress is hanging in there in my bin. I haven’t had it on in years, but I like to know it’s there. A bit of who I was in my younger day,” she said softly. “I used to wear that dress when Joe and I went dancing.” Lee Ann sighed deeply then continued. “I loved Joe so much, but that all ended when I started having the seizures." Lee Ann closed her eyes. I didn't know if she was reliving a memory or trying to shut one down. But I felt very sad.

Lee Ann opened her eyes and looked at me, shrugged her shoulders as if she was letting the memory go. She took my hand, turning it over in her own, intensely studying my fingernails. "Honey," she said. "Your fingernails need attention. You know, I was a manicurist as well as a fine beautician when I lived in Louisville. They won't let me do nails here on the ward, but if you'll have them make you an appointment, I can do them at the beauty shop."

"Why can't you do nails on the ward?" I asked.

"Oh, just one of rules around here," Lee Ann replied.

"I never heard of a place with so many rules."

"You'll get used to it," Lee Ann said.

"Thank God, I only have eighty-eight more days to go."

Lee Ann shook her head. "Honey, I wish you wouldn't count so much on leaving so soon."

There it was again, someone doubting I'd be leaving! I didn't think I could stand it a moment more, if I wasn't assured I'd be leaving in eighty-eight more days. Total panic seized my body. My heart began pounding so hard I thought it might come out of my body. My throat was tightening up, like steel bands cutting off my air. I knew I was losing control, but I couldn't stop the panic attack. Someone had to help me! Someone had to! My eyes locked in on Miss Abner who had just sat down at the desk. "Help me! Help me!" I screamed and ran to the desk, latching onto the startled attendant's arms. "You have to tell me I'm going home in eighty-eight more days!! Tell me! You have to tell me!!!"

"Stop!! Let go! Casper! Get in here, Casper!!" Miss Abner yelled, struggling to get to her feet, frantically trying to shake free of my grip. I only griped her arms tighter, digging in with all my might. I could hear my own voice, screaming, "I'm getting out of here in eighty-eight more days!! You look it up! You'll see! It says

I’ll be getting out of here! I'm going home in eighty-eight more days!!!" The terrified face of the attendant was now a blur.

"Get her on the floor!" Miss Casper yelled, running into the dayroom, tackling me. In an instant I was on the floor. Soon both attendants and Gladys were sitting on me. I can hardly breathe as I struggle in vain to break free.

"Call security!!" Miss Abner screamed. "We'll hold her! Just get over to the phone and call security!!! Do it now!!! Hurry!! And call Margo! Tell her an emergency and to bring the Thorazine!"

Miss Casper released her grip on my legs, ran to the phone and dialed. "Get security down to A2 immediately!!!" She bellowed into the receiver. I heard her yelling into the phone again, “Nurse Margo! Emergency on A2! Hurry! Violent patient! Bring Thorazine!”

I made a last desperate attempt to kick myself free. Then the attendant was back sitting on my legs. I found I was unable to move a muscle. The only thing I could do was lie there and sob: wrenching sobs that seems like they would tear my insides out. Soon two security guards and the supervisor Mrs. Sales rushed onto the ward.

"We gotta get her in the side room," someone panted, near my left shoulder. “She's a wild one!"

Oh, God no! Not that little dark, smelly room!! They were pulling me to my feet. I frantically tried to break free, and was able to twist one arm free and dug into anything my fingers could find. Immediately, large fingers grabbed my hand, pinning it behind my back.

"Just get her down to the side room!!!!" someone yelled. Iron like hands bound my feet and arms, as I was half carried, half dragged into the hallway.

"Get Matilda out of the side room!" Miss Abner yelled. The supervisor ran to the side room, fumbled with her keys, finally opening the door. "Get out of there, Matilda!!!"

Matilda wailed, "Her name is Tillieee!" as she ran naked towards the dayroom.

"Get her out of those clothes!!!" Miss Abner shouted. Hands began ripping off my pajamas.

I screamed, kicked, and bit at the people tearing my garment from my body. A sharp pain shot through the back of my neck as someone grabbed my hair, dragging me farther down the hallway, into the doorway of the side room. Wrenching my arm free from Miss Abner's grip, I desperately grabbed onto the doorframe. Strong hands pried my fingers loose.

"Let me tell you this, missy," the supervisor panted, gripping my wrist even tighter, as she and the others dragged me farther into the room. "From this day forward, you will have a standing order for Thorazine! If you attack us, ever again, you can be sure you'll find yourself in this side room with a shot of Thorazine in your hind end!"

Soon Nurse Margo ran onto the ward, needle in hand. Powerful hands held my legs and arms to the floor, others pressed into my back, shoulders and head, pinning my left cheek against a gritty floor. I no longer had any energy to fight, and just lay there sobbing as sticky tears streamed down my hot face. Soon I felt the sting of a needle being pushed into my right hip. Slowly, I went limp, as much from exhaustion as from the medication flowing into my blood stream. Sweat drenched and naked, I lay still, whimpering.

"I think she's given up," a faraway voice said. "On the count of three make a run for the door. One! Two! Three!" Suddenly the weight lifted from my body. I was fading into blackness when I heard the door slam shut, it seemed so far away. A long, dark tunnel beckoned, and the attendants in their starched, white uniforms were drifting farther and farther away. *Was that an angry black cloud waiting at the end of the tunnel? Would it be safer to stay in the tunnel or try to go past the cloud?* The last thing I heard before total blackness was the jingle of keys.

Chapter Four

I awoke sore and stiff. I had no idea what time it was, but the room was dark. As my eyes became accustomed to the shadows, I saw that a thin, plastic mattress had been placed in the room with me.

Suddenly a loud screeching voice pierced the silence, "Attendant! Attendant! Just give her a pillowcase with her name on it, attendant, honey!"

I crawled over to the door, stood up and looked out the small window. A little woman with a walker was creeping down the hall, pushing the walker ahead of her. *Maylene*. I had noticed the woman last evening sitting at a table in the day room coloring in a coloring book. Lee Ann had volunteered: 'Maylene was once an intelligent woman with a family. She suffered a brain tumor which left her without much sense at all. She's mostly like a child.'

From the office to my left, someone said, "There's that damn Maylene, wanting her pillowcase."

Maylene inched on down the hallway, towards the office, saying all the while, "Attendant! Attendant, honey! Just give her a pillowcase with her name on it!"

A white pillowcase was draped over the top bar of her walker. An attendant I didn't recognize came out of the office. "Maylene," she said, "you get yourself right back in that bed! Do it now!"

Maylene made no attempt to go and calmly said, picking up the pillowcase, holding it out towards the attendant, "See here, attendant, honey, she needs a pillowcase with her name on it. This one don't have her name."

The attendant grabbed the pillowcase. "It don't have any name on it, Maylene! Now you just go on back to bed!"

Maylene ignored the attendant's demand. "I say, attendant, honey, she has to have her name on her pillowcase."

"Do you want to go to the side room?" the attendant asked. And I found myself hoping I would soon find myself on the other side of the door. The room smelled of urine and I felt my skin had absorbed the terrible smell. A sudden wave of guilt came over me as I realized I'd just wished this horrible room on another person.

Maylene seemed to have no fear of the threat of going into the side room and continued to demand, her voice starting to screech again, "Give her the pillowcase, attendant, honey!" That would be the answer to your problem!"

Suddenly, another attendant rushed out of the office, raced down the hall, disappearing into a room next to the bathroom. Soon, she emerged holding a pillowcase. *Miss Cody*. I realized the night shift was on duty. "Here, take your pillowcase and go on back to bed!" Miss Cody said, tossing the pillowcase onto Maylene's walker.

Maylene picked up the pillowcase, calmly unfolded it, and seeing the large black printing stamped on it, smiled and said, "Thank you, attendant, honey." She placed the pillowcase over the top rail of her walker, smiled again at the attendant, then turned her walker around and slowly inched towards the dorm. The printing on the pillowcase had been, "**Gatewood State Hospital**".

"You are spoiling that Maylene," the attendant I hadn't seen before said.

"Oh, what does it hurt if the poor thing gets a pillowcase that has Gatewood State Hospital on it?" Miss Cody said. "It makes her happy and shuts her up. I did what I thought was best for all of us. Did you want to hear her screeching all night?"

"No," the other attendant said. "But she believes her name is printed on the pillowcase."

"So what?!" Miss Cody snapped.

"Oh, well, who gives a damn anyway?" the other attendant said.

I felt the need to get to the bathroom and called out to the attendants, "Please, I need to go to the bathroom."

"Well. It has come to life," one of the attendants said.

Miss Cody came to the door, peering in the window. "You will have to wait until the supervisor makes her rounds before we can let you out."

"But I have to go now! Please just unlock the door and let me out!"

"The rule is," Miss Cody said, "that no disturbed patient is allowed out of the side room without three attendants being present. The supervisor will be down here in about forty-five minutes and we will let you out then."

I could not believe what I was hearing. "Please, please just let me out to use the toilet! I'm not disturbed anymore. I won't cause any trouble."

"Sorry," Miss Cody said. "You'll just have to wait."

I watched in helpless disbelief as Miss Cody returned to the office. There was no way I could wait forty-five minutes. I suddenly realized why the room smelled of urine. And to my dismay I heard the other attendant yell, "You had better not piss in that side room, missy, if you know what's good for you!"

"Why are you so hateful for tonight?" I heard Miss Cody ask. "Did you have a fight with Ben?"

"No," the other attendant said. "I just want these patients to mind us."

I couldn't hold my urine any longer and, with tears running down my face, I squatted in the far corner of the room, thinking I had been sent to the depths of hell.

I crept to the sticky plastic mattress.

After a while footsteps echoed down the hallway. A short time later voices, and finally keys jingled in the lock. "You can go to the bathroom now," Miss Cody said.

I crawled off the mattress, stood up and walked past the three women, shielding my exposed breasts, wishing I had a bathrobe to cover my nakedness. As I sat on the commode I heard the attendant who was working with Miss Cody say, "She went ahead and pissed on the floor!"

A moment later, the attendant appeared in the lavatory doorway, a mop in her hand, her face red with anger. And for the first time I noticed her nametag, it read Mrs. G. Sullivan.

"You piss on the floor! You will mop it up. Don't ever get the idea we're your slaves!"

I stared at the angry attendant, wondering how in the world I was going to survive another eighty-eight days in this place. "I...I...I couldn't wait any longer," I finally managed to stammer. "The only thing I could do was go in the floor."

"I don't want to hear any excuses!" the attendant said. "You're new here and think you can pull the wool over our eyes. Well, let me tell you something, missy, I've been working here at this state hospital for twenty years, and I've seen lots of patients with plenty of tricks up their sleeves and there ain't one of them been able to pull anything over on this old girl! Now, grab this mop and get that floor cleaned up!"

I didn't say anything. I just got up off the commode and took the mop from Mrs. Sullivan, wishing I dared to slap it up the side of her head. The thought surprised me, I‘d never in my life struck another human being.---*Maybe Miss Abner last night. No. I don't think I struck her. Maybe I did when I was trying to get loose. Don't know. Can't remember it all.*

"Go on in the side room and start mopping," Miss Cody said. "I'll get a mop bucket. I headed for the side room, closely followed by Mrs. Sullivan and the supervisor, a middle aged woman with jet-black hair.

I began swinging the mop through the urine, as Miss Cody rolled a mop bucket into the room.

"You mop that piss up, and get it up good!" Mrs. Sullivan snapped, standing in the doorway. "No sense you patients making messes like this. You stink up the whole ward! "

"Oh, lighten up, Sullivan," Miss Cody said.

"You baby these patients!" Mrs. Sullivan snapped.

I finished mopping and handed the mop to Miss Cody. "May I please take a bath?"

"I'm sorry," Miss Cody said, "but we can't give you a bath tonight."

"See!" Mrs. Sullivan said. "You give them an inch and they'll take a mile."

"Sorry," Miss Cody said.

"Do I have to stay in here all night?" I asked, unable to keep my voice from trembling.

"You sure do!" Mrs. Sullivan said. “And you'd better not cause any more trouble.”

"Don't cause any more problems," the supervisor said. "Stand over there against the wall while we get the bucket out of here. You don't want to get into any more trouble than you already are."

I stood against the far wall as Miss Cody and the supervisor pulled the mop bucket through the door. Mrs. Sullivan quickly slammed the door shut; then turned her key in the lock.

I stood by the security-screened window at the back of the room, trying to suck in what little fresh air that came through.

Made of thick mesh wire, the screen securely fitted into a metal frame that had a lock. No chance in the world of anyone escaping. Everything looked so peaceful out there in the moonlight. Not wanting to return to the sticky mattress, I stood at the window for a long time, trying to sort out my situation. And I, Jordan Katelin Walker, didn't know what I was going to do with the life fate had recently handed me.

Exhausted, feeling my body was covered in gritty dirt; I finally went to the sticky mattress, and soon drifted into sleep. I dreamed of fresh air, and flowers, and of Mama and Daddy. I was a little girl again, safe and happy.

I awoke to the sound of the ward's activities getting under way. Getting of the mattress, I tried to rub the stiffness from my legs and arms. I had never in my life been involved in a fight before last night. Fighting had always been beneath me. Even when I'd been a child and a playmate hit me, I'd never fought back. Mama had always said, 'Jordan, dear, well-bred people are never violent, in speech or in action.' What would Mama have thought if she had seen me last night, acting like a wild animal? Well, I thought, going to the window in the door, Mama never saw Gatewood, never even dreamed of such a place.

Patients were going into the bathroom, and Miss Cody pushed a medicine cart down the hall. Matilda came to the side room door, peered through the window and smiled. "Her name is Tillie," she said.

Mrs. Sullivan came out of the office, "Matilda, you get away from there! Now!"

"Noooo! Noooo!" Matilda cried, biting her hand and stomping her foot. "Her name is Tillieee! Mom calls her Tillieee!"

"I don't care what Mom calls her," Mrs. Sullivan yelled. "If she doesn't get away from that side room, she'll be in it!"

Matilda ran towards the dayroom, yelling, "Her name is Tillieee! Mom calls her Tillieee!"

Miss Cody pushed the medicine cart into the office. Soon she was at the side room, followed by Mrs. Sullivan and the supervisor. I backed away from the door as Miss Cody unlocked and opened it. "You can go to the bathroom now," she said.

"When can I get out of this room?" I asked.

"That's not for me to decide," Miss Cody said. "The afternoon shift put you in; they will have to release you."

"You mean I will have to stay in here all day!?" I asked, thinking I was going to be sick.

"Maybe even longer," Mrs. Sullivan smirked.

"But, how can you do that? This isn't a prison. Is it?"

"Now, don't you go getting smart with me," Mrs. Sullivan said. "Or you just might be in there for a week or two."

I didn't say anymore. But I hoped Mrs. Sullivan was just trying to scare me, but another part of me almost wished I had the guts to slap her face. Mama would not be proud.

After I went to the bathroom, they locked me back in the side room. I watched from my tiny window as the other patients got in line for breakfast.

As the patients passed the side room on their way to the dining room, Lee Ann whispered, "Sorry, girl, you have to be in that stinking room. I know it's bad. I've been there many times, myself."

"Lee Ann, are you loitering near the side room!" Mrs. Sullivan yelled as she came from the dormitory.

"Got to go," Lee Ann whispered, quickly heading towards the dining room. Gladys didn't even look towards the side room as she went by, and I felt anger at her for helping to hold me down the night before.

"Sullivan, you go on to the dining room with the others," Miss Cody said. "I'll stay on the ward with Jordan."

Why did someone need to stay with me? After all, I certainly wouldn't be likely to go anywhere. Could they possibly think I needed a guard? Maybe this was a prison, disguised as a state hospital. Miss Cody went into the office as the others disappeared towards the dining room.

I went to the security window at the end of the room. Leaves, fresh and green danced in the early morning sunlight. I longed to be out there, to run free through the dew damp grass, to feel its cleanliness on my skin. As tears slid down my face, I realized I had cried more in the last two days than I had in my entire life, except for the times just after my parents died. I wanted to scream to the outside world--It did exist somewhere out there beyond these desperate walls, didn't it? I wanted to scream for help, for someone to come and rescue me from this place.

I heard the patients returning from the dining room. And a little while later the jingle of keys. Miss Cody, Mrs. Sullivan and Mrs. Holt stood in the doorway. The day shift had come on duty. "If you have to go to the bathroom you can go now," Miss Cody said, "while we are checking with the oncoming shift."

"I don't have to go," I mumbled, wishing they would just go on and leave me alone.

"She wants to wait and piss on the floor," Mrs. Sullivan said. And at that moment, I felt a raging hate for the woman.

Lee Ann appeared at the door, handing a tray to Mrs. Holt. "Here's your breakfast," Mrs. Holt said, bending down and sliding the tray across the floor. I stared at the tray. *How could they just put the tray on the floor? Surely they didn't expect me to eat off the floor.*

"I'm not going to eat that!" I said.

"Suit yourself," Mrs. Sullivan said. "Miss three meals and you get forced fed." The attendant grabbed the door, slammed and locked it.

I sat there on the gritty floor, thinking that Mrs. Sullivan was the most hateful person in the entire world.

Chapter Five

An appointment got me out of the side room. About ten o'clock, keys jingled in the lock. The door opened and Mrs. Holt stood there, holding a gray bathrobe. "Come on, Jordan. You have to take a bath so you can go to EEG. That's an electroencephalograph, an instrument that measures and records brain waves."

"I know," I said. I'd had two of the tests since the accident: One in the general hospital in Harper City, and another in Dr. Cole's clinic. The technician attached wires to my head with glue, which took days to wash out. I didn't think I was going to mind the glue this time. Getting out of the stinking side room was worth almost anything. The only thing I dreaded was the horrible flashing light they turned on in my face. It was necessary, a test to determine my brain damage, but the throbbing light made me feel like I was in some kind of twilight tunnel.

I wondered where all the backup attendants were? Was I no longer a dangerous patient? But I didn't dwell on that thought too long. I gladly took the bathrobe, grateful to cover my naked body. Maybe the attendants and even the patients at Gatewood didn't think anything about a naked body. But to me being exposed was a loss of dignity, and I didn't think I could ever get used to it.

I stepped into the tub of warm, soapy water. I was thankful to be taken a bath, but wondered why I was allowed, if I'd been put on the afternoon list. Maybe it was procedure for getting an EEG. After I had taken my bath and my hair was washed, the attendant handed me a neatly rolled bundle, containing my own clothes. I was thankful for the slacks and pink blouse. But most of all I was grateful for underwear that hadn't touched countless other bodies.

From today, it should be eighty-seven day until I could leave. I dared not say that to anyone. I tried not to think about it too much and told myself that Dr. Cole would take care of it. *I was his patient. He would take care of everything.*

Mrs. Holt unlocked the outside door, handing me a slip of paper. "This is your appointment pass. Show it to the attendant on the bus; she'll see you get off at the right building. When you get to the EEG office, show it to the technician; she'll take care of the rest."

I stepped into the warm sunlight. For a moment I just stood on the sidewalk, holding my face into the sun, letting its warmth penetrate my skin. I closed my eyes. Without much trying I imagined I was in the garden of flowers behind my house. Years ago Mama had planted the garden. It was now a thing of absolute beauty, and so fragrant this time of year. I could almost smell the soft odors, letting the fragrances take away the lingering smell of the horrible side room.

"Hey! Miss Walker! What are you doing there? Go on and get yourself on the bus!" I opened my eyes with a start. Mrs. Holt was standing in the doorway. "Don't be lollygagging around there! Get on down there before the bus leaves you!"

I got on the bus, giving my appointment slip to the attendant.

The attendant pointed out the building, "The big brown building with the sign on the lawn that says "Jefferson" is the one. You go on in there, and the EEG people will take care of you. Here, just give your appointment slip to the people in there."

I took back the slip, got off the bus and went into the building, found a door marked EEG and knocked. A young, blond woman about my age opened the door. I handed her the appointment pass. The woman smiled. "Hi. I'm Nell. I'll be running the EEG. Come with me and we'll get you ready."

I followed her into a smaller room containing the EEG machine and a large recliner chair. And sitting nearby was the dreadful light. I hated that light and was certainly dreading it. It had never caused me to have a seizure, like I'd read it did many patients, but I'd always gotten a splitting headache after having to stare at it.

I sat in the recliner, and Nell began gluing wires to my scalp. Nell chatted as she worked, asking me about myself.

"I'm from Harper City. This is my third day here," I said, wondering if Nell knew I'd spent last night in the side room.

"Oh, I've been there," Nell said. "My Aunt Marge Slater used to live there. Do you know her?"

"Yes, I've met her. She's a friend of my older sister's. My sister lives in Cincinnati. I think I remember her saying Marge lives there also."

"Marge does live there," Nell said. "Small world. Is Mrs. Holt working today?"

"She is," I said.

"She's my older sister. Lots of employees have relatives working here. Gatewood is a beautiful place," Nell said. "A place to get well, so you can return to your home."

I didn't reply. It seemed Nell's view of Gatewood was a world different from what I had experienced on A2.

Soon, I was facing the dreadful, flashing light, telling myself to just endure and soon it would end. After the EEG had been completed, I was allowed to sit for a few minutes in the recliner. I told Nell I was getting a headache.

"It'll be a few minutes before the bus gets here, so just sit there and relax and maybe the headache will go away," Nell said.

I closed my eyes, leaning back in the recliner, wishing I could stay there all afternoon and not have to return to the ward. The thought that I might have to return to the side room sent cold shivers through me? I drifted off into a dreamless sleep, awakening sometime later to Nell gently shaking me. "Wake up," Nell said. "The bus is out there."

I stood up, thankful the headache was gone.

When I got off the bus, I stood on the sidewalk staring at the Wallace building. It really was a lovely looking building. What was upstairs, behind those gaily curtained windows? Anyone driving by would probably say the state hospital at Saberville was a lovely, serene place. Would they suspect, would they really care about the misery behind the walls? My knees shook; my hand trembled as I knocked on the outside door to A2. *Please, God don't let them put me back it the side room,* I silently prayed, as Mrs. Holt came to unlock the door and let me in.

To my great relief, Mrs. Holt didn't mention the side room. I quickly went to a corner and sat in a chair, as far away from both the patients and staff as I could get. Gladys sat at a table, flipping through a magazine and looked over at me and smiled. Remembering how she had helped hold me down the night before, I looked away. Mossie with her invisible dog in her arms walked around the room petting and talking to it. Maylene colored happily in a coloring book. Maylene just didn't color the pictures; she colored every inch of the page. Maylene stopped coloring and slowly got up from the table and began inching her walker across the floor towards the attendant at the desk. "Now, Attendant honey, you just give her a green crayon, please, attendant honey. See, my green one is all gone," she said, leaning her walker against the desk, holding up a tiny stub of crayon.

"Go and sit down, Maylene," Mrs. Holt said, not looking up from her papers. "I'll get your crayon as soon as I have time."

Maylene made no attempt to move, and said, "Now, attendant honey, the answer to your problem would be to give her a green crayon. She kept on repeating over and over, “She needs a green crayon! She wants her green crayon!” her voice screeching louder with each word, until Mrs. Holt threw her pen down and stood up.

I wondered if Maylene was headed for the side room. But Mrs. Holt, her lips tight, reached into a cabinet behind the desk and produced a green crayon. "Here! Take your green crayon and stop that screeching!"

Maylene calmly took the crayon, smiled and said, "Thank you, attendant, honey. That was the answer to your problem." She slowly moved her walker until she was back at the table. I was amazed at the determination of the little, black-eyed woman, and felt a bit of admiration for her. What had she been like before her brain tumor? Did she ever dream of leaving Gatewood? Or did she think of this place as home, content to color away her days? I shivered and sank lower into the plastic chair.

At lunch I sat at a table by myself. I was very hungry and despite the mushy meatloaf and watery potatoes ate everything on my tray.

When we got back to the ward, Mrs. Holt said, "Jordan you have an appointment with Dr. Thorpe for your physical." I didn't know why I would need a physical. I had been turned inside and out by the doctors at the clinic, but I didn't say anything and accepted the appointment slip Mrs. Holt handed me. "Dr. Thorpe's office is upstairs. Gladys will show you where it is."

I didn't want to go anywhere with Gladys, but didn't dare protest.

"Come on, Jordan," Gladys said, smiling at me. "I'll take you to Dr. Thorpe."

Mrs. Holt unlocked the outside door, "Go around to the front, that way you won't have to go through the kitchen." I followed Gladys onto the sidewalk and stood looking at the steps that led to the entryway.

"Come on, Jordan," Gladys said, starting up the steps. Looking back at me she dropped her eyes to the pavement, "I know you're mad at me for helping the attendant to fight you last night."

"Why did you do it?"

“Cause that’s my job.”

"You have a job to fight?"

"Yes, I do," Gladys said, looking into my eyes. "I'm the biggest patient on A2. The attendants always call on me to help with all the fighting patients. They couldn't get along without old Gladys," she said proudly.

I followed Gladys through the double glass doors I'd gone through the first day when the attendants and security guard had brought me to the building.

Inside the lobby Gladys said, "Come on," pointing to a stairway. "Dr. Thorpe is up there. Bet you didn't know Mrs. Holt lives up there. And Nurse Margo lives up there too. Sometimes they have to call the nurse up during the night to get the Thorazine; like they did with you last night. I think she gets mad when she has to get out of bed to give the shot."

"Does everyone get Thorazine?" I asked.

"Yep, they do when they throw a fit like you did last night. You wait. You’ll see, as you’re here longer, they’ll get the Thorazine every time, but Maylene don‘t. She can't have it. She'll blow up like a balloon, almost died one time."

I prayed I would never get another shot of Thorazine. My hip was still painfully sore, and my head was cloudy, from both the effects of the Thorazine and the EEG.

I followed Gladys up the steps until we were on the landing. Gladys stopped before a door with a brass sign, with the markings: "Dr. David Thorpe". "This is Dr. Thorpe's office," she said, knocking on the door. A petite, dark haired woman dressed in a nurse's uniform opened the door and smiled at Gladys.

"This here is Jordan," Gladys said, pointing to me. "Mrs. Holt had me to show her where the office is."

"Thank you, Gladys," the nurse said.

"I'm gonna have to go on back to the ward now," Gladys said. "Jordan's gonna have to find her own way back."

The nurse took me into an examining room and handed me a gown. "Get undressed," she said pleasantly. "The doctor will be right in. I'll be right back," she said, going out, closing the door behind her.

I quickly undressed and put on the gown. The room had an examining table and two chairs. Soon a small, white haired man entered with the nurse. He smiled kindly at me, waving me to one of the chairs. He began reading off my history from a folder in his hand.

"It says you have epilepsy."

"Yes. Dr. Cole at the clinic in Harper City told me I have epilepsy," I said. "He said he thought the new drug they are studying here could help me."

"I'm looking at the x-rays of your brain we got from the hospital where you were taken after the accident. It showed some swelling, as would be the case with the trauma you suffered. But the result of your EEG." Dr. Thorpe paused, looking puzzled, holding up a graft with wavy lines. "Hum," he muttered. "Have you had any seizures since admittance?"

"No," I said.

"What do you remember about your seizures?"

"I don't have any memory of them. Julia, that's my sister, said she saw me have several when I was in the hospital. And at the clinic, Dr. Cole said he also had observed me having them."

"We'll get the results from your EEG taken here and see what that shows," Dr. Thorpe said. "Could be you are one lucky lady and haven't suffered any permanent brain damage."

No brain damage. Could that be true? My heart soared with his words and I was filled with hope that I would soon be out of Gatewood.

"Your EEG should tell us more," Dr. Thorpe said. He tapped the graft paper and said almost to himself, "Could be a mix-up of some kind. We'll wait for the results before the evaluation for any other medications. If you are on the drug study medication, we don't really don't like to put you on any other. Could cause negative interaction."

"What other medication would I need?"

"We'll have to wait for the evaluation to see what you may need."

Dr. Thorpe finished with the exam, and I was allowed to return to the ward. As I walked back towards the ward, a nagging thought kept playing at the corners of my mind ---- What if I'd never really had seizures at all? But, no, that couldn't be. Dr. Cole and Julia had said I'd had them. Was it possible what they observed, wasn't really seizures? And the doctor had seemed evasive about the other medicine he'd said might be considered. Could be vitamins or something like that.

I knocked on the door to the ward and was let in by Mrs. Winningham. As I headed for the lavatory, Mrs. Holt called my name, waving me over to the desk. "Jordan, we need to set you up with a job. What kind of job do you think you would enjoy, perhaps working in the laundry or the kitchen?"

"It doesn't matter. I won't be here long." I said, thinking I wouldn't enjoy working at either one, but was afraid to say so, else they might think I was being uncooperative.

"Really," Mrs. Holt said.

At three o'clock, the afternoon shift came on duty. Miss. Abner and another attendant who I hadn't seen before came into the dayroom. I sank deeper into my chair. Miss. Abner had an angry red scratch above her right eye, and a long one on her right arm. *Had that happened in the fight? Was I responsible?*

"What's she doing out of the side room?" Miss Abner said, pointing to me. "You do know she attacked me!?"

Oh, God, I thought. I'm headed for that smelly room for sure. I crunched farther into the chair.

"Oh, we had to let her out to go to EEG, "Mrs. Winningham said.

"Well, if you had seen the fight we had with her last night, you wouldn't have wanted to let her out," Miss Abner said. "And how many times has one of them been let out and re-attacked in no time flat?"

"Oh, I think she's gonna be fine. Come on back to the office and let me give the report," Mrs. Winningham said, getting out of her chair, picking up the brown folder. "It's been some kind of day."

The two afternoon shift attendants followed her. Mrs. Holt was at the back of the room, busy changing a bandage on one of the patient's arms. I waited a couple of minutes then slipped out of the day room unnoticed. I wanted to get back near the office and try to hear what was being said about me in the report. I was thankful to find the hallway clear. If a patient saw me listening to the report I would be told on, of this I was certain. It seemed most of the patients loved to find something on someone else to tattle to the attendants. I could hear the voices of the attendants as I came closer to the office. Silently, I crept as close as I could without being seen, flattening myself as close to the wall as I could.

"I'll tell you one thing if that fool starts a fight this evening like she did last night, she'll get more than a shot of Thorazine." I recognized the voice of Miss Abner. "I think she should have gone back to the side room after she got the tests done. She should be on C3!"

"You know she doesn't have the standing order for C3. We'll have to wait for the doctor to write that. And without a doctor's order, we would have had to release her from the side room in twenty-four hours anyway. And she seems perfectly calm," Mrs. Winningham said.

"Miss Abner's voice rose as she angrily said, "Them damn, lazy doctors need to get up off their fat asses and write the seclusion and shot orders when they know we are going to get a new patient! We should never forget what happened to Lizzie York after she let a patient out of the side room before the patient was ready. York will never walk again. Luckily the patient got sent over to Belfort. You never know what one of them is gonna do!"

"Oh, she's new. Give her a chance. Maybe all that stuff last night was because she was scared. Being in a new place and all." Mrs. Winningham said.

"Well, the next time she blows, I hope it's you who has to fight her. You who get all scratched up! Mrs. Sullivan was right: some of you attendants cater to these patients. I say you gotta put your foot down or else they'll be running this place." Miss Abner said.

"Well, anyway," Mrs. Winningham continued. "Dr. Thorpe wrote in his report there is a possibility she may not be an epileptic; she may have had a convulsion after the accident, due to her brain swelling, but he wants more tests done. He hasn't got the report from the psychiatrist, doesn't know anything about her mental history. He's not putting her on the drug study just yet. In fact all she's on is a sleeping pill. I guess she went over there and told him she couldn't sleep. Could be Gatewood isn't the place for her."

"Well, hurray. I for one would be happy to see her go someplace else," Miss. Abner said.

I felt a wave of joy sweep over me. And I felt hope that I would not have to stay my ninety days. If I wasn't an epileptic surely I'd be leaving soon! That had to be the case. Just then I looked towards the day room to see Lee Ann standing in the hallway, staring at me. The joy that had flooded me just seconds ago was now replaced with a dark dread. I quickly walked away from my spot near the office. If Lee Ann told on me for eavesdropping I was almost certain I'd find myself back inside the side room. I was sure Miss. Abner would call up one of those *lazy, fat-assed doctors* and get the order. I went into the lavatory and Lee Ann followed. I didn't quite know how to go about pleading with her not to tell on me, and was trying to think of what to say when Lee Ann said, "Don't worry about me ratting on you. I never do that."

"Thanks," was all I could say. By then two other patients were in the lavatory.

After supper, I sat at a table with Lee Ann, as she played solitaire. "Don't be too hard on Gladys," Lee Ann said, looking up from her deck of cards. "Gladys is the muscle on this ward. Whenever, the attendants have to fight a disturbed patient, Gladys just jumps in and helps. She doesn't mean you any harm. It's just part of what's expected of her."

I felt a little better towards Gladys. I thought I would like to write to Paul, but knew I wasn't going to ask Miss Abner for paper and pen, or anything else. He hadn't answered the other time I'd written, but maybe this time would be different. I told Lee Ann I wished I had my own paper and pen.

"Oh, I'll be glad to loan you some paper and a pen," Lee Ann said, getting up from the table. I watched as she went into a small room just off the day room: it was little more than a closet with a row of lockers along one wall. Soon Lee Ann returned with paper, a pen, and an envelope. "You can buy your own supplies when you go to the canteen," Lee Ann said. "They'll give you one of those lockers just as soon as you have something to put in it. Now, when you go to the canteen, you be sure to buy one of those combination locks, so you can lock your stuff up. Things have been known to disappear out of the lockers. They say some of the patients are thieves, and that is true enough of some. But I'm guessing some of the workers here are the guilty parties when it comes to things disappearing from the lockers." Lee Ann added, whispering so only I could hear. "You don't want to get one of those locks with a key someone else could use it, if you know what I mean. You get the combination kind; then you store the numbers up here," Lee Ann said, tapping the side of her head.

I thanked Lee Ann and started a letter to Paul. Why hadn't he answered the one, I'd written in the clinic? Had he even gotten it? Although he'd said when he left he wasn't any good for me, I had wanted to tell him about the accident and had used the address I'd had for the Peace Corps, I thought I could still remember it. I didn't want to think about the possibility that something had happened to him, thousands of miles away. Or he had gotten my letter and hadn't wanted to answer. In that room full of people, I felt uncomfortable writing to the man I loved. It seemed like it had been years since I'd last seen him. But a lifetime of things had happened to me since the day when I'd said good-by to him at the airport. How was I going to tell him the woman who was someday to have been his bride had been admitted to a state hospital? Would he understand about the drug study and why I was in a state hospital? One fear kept nagging at me: what if Paul believed I had gone insane and had to be committed to a state hospital? Would he still feel the same about me if that was the case? Maybe he'd stopped loving me.

"You do know, don't you, that you can't seal the envelope when you get your letter written?" Lee Ann was saying.

"What?" I asked, looking at her.

"You can't seal the letter. No patient sends out a letter from this state hospital without the attendants going over it and deciding if there's anything in it that hadn't oughta be."

I couldn't believe my ears. "How can they do that?"

"Another one of the rules here at Gatewood. See that little basket on the attendants' desk," Lee Ann said, looking towards the desk.

I had seen the wicker basket and it had always been empty. I'd thought it was for desk supplies.

"All the letters we write go in that basket. And at night when we're asleep the night shift reads them. If there's nothing in them they disagree with, they will seal it and stick their initials right there in the corner where the stamp goes. The night supervisor picks up the letters, and they are sent on to the business office where a stamp will be put on it. Sometimes the afternoon shift will read one or two and stick their initials on them, but mostly it's the night shift's job."

"What happens if you write something they don't like?" I asked.

"Oh, you'll get it handed back to you and they will tell you that you have a problem, and you will have to correct the problem. And of course you will ask what it is, and believe you me, they will tell you. No. Never been a letter left this place the attendants didn't like. ---At least that they knew about," Lee Ann added in a whisper, winking.

"I don't think they should be allowed to do such a thing! I think that's against the constitution!" I said, feeling anger rising up in my throat.

"Honey," Lee Ann whispered, leaning across the table towards me. "The constitution just doesn't exist in this place. You'll learn, just give yourself a few days."

I didn't even want to consider that Mrs. Sullivan would be reading my most private thoughts. After all, I would be out of here soon, as soon as tests showed I wasn't having seizures. "I don't think, I'll be writing any letters after all. I'll be leaving soon," I said.

Lee Ann just smiled and said, "We'll see."

I stared at Lee Ann for a moment. Why had she said, *we'll see*. I closed my eyes as a wave of dread caused a lump in my throat. I began to take deep breaths. I couldn't afford to have another panic attack.

When bedtime came I was given a sleeping pill. I was glad to lie down and was soon asleep. I dreamed of home and Paul. And of the way things had been before his brother went to prison and committed suicide. We had been so young back then and so much in love. But in the shadows of my dream lurked a menacing, black cloud on the horizon of an otherwise cloudless day.

The next morning was bathed in gray rain clouds. Soon rain pounded the sidewalk and grass outside the picture window. I stood at the window, watching the rain, feeling that my own life was as gray as the world outside the window. Soon, Mrs. Sullivan was telling me to get on up to breakfast. Without comment, I followed the other patients towards the dining room.

About 9 o'clock, Mrs. Holt called to me to come to the desk. I hurried over, thinking she was going to tell me I was leaving this place; that freedom was waiting just outside the wall. "Jordan," Mrs. Holt said. "We have assigned you a job. Now, understand this is part of your therapy and there won't be any pay. But I'm sure the benefits you'll get from the work will be very rewarding to you."

My heart sank with disappointment. I didn't want a job at Gatewood, I wanted free of Gatewood.

"You will be working from 1 P.M. until 4 P.M. Monday through Friday," Mrs. Holt said. "You have been assigned to work in Dr. Thorpe's office. It says in your record you have excellent office skills, so it should work out great for you."

"But, I'll be leaving soon?"

"I don't know anything about you leaving," Mrs. Holt said.

I didn't say any more for fear Mrs. Holt might suspect I had been eavesdropping.

"You start work this afternoon," Mrs. Holt said.

I nodded and went and sat in the corner. I started to feel better and was looking forward to 1 o'clock when I could go to the doctor's office.

I was in for a bit of a surprise about my job at Dr. Thorpe's. I would not be doing any filing at all. The nurse explained, "All the records are confidential. None of the patients at Gatewood are allowed to handle the files in any way. You are not to enter that room at all," she said, pointing to a small room to the left of the office. Looking inside, I saw it contained rows of filing cabinets. "The patients' records are all in there," the nurse said. "You are not to go in there for any reason."

My duties were to order supplies, water the plants, clean the office and help with the patients who came in for treatments or for their physicals. It was a busy office and I was thankful to be there, away from the ward. The office seemed like a world away. All too soon 4 P.M. came and I had to return to A2.

The next morning I, an appointment slip in hand, boarded the bus. I had been allowed to go to the beauty shop. Lee Ann did my hair and nails. Why wouldn't Gladys have wanted Lee Ann to do her hair? The people Lee Ann did were much lovelier than the ones Miss Sloan did.

"Thanks, Lee Ann," I said when Lee Ann was finished.

"Making patients beautiful is my job," Lee Ann said, grinning.

When I got to Dr. Thorpe's office, the first thing I did was go up to his desk. "Good afternoon, Dr. Thorpe." I hoped my voice wasn't shaking. "Did you find out any more about my test?”

He smiled at me. “I haven’t heard any more. I'm sorry if something I said the other day got your hopes up. We don’t know yet what the EEG will reveal. These matters take time.”

Be patient. Just a matter of time, I told myself. It will work itself out. It has to.

Chapter Six

I had been told before I arrived at Gatewood I wouldn't be allowed to have any visits before two weeks. Dr. Cole had explained this was a rule in the best interest of the patient because it gave them time to adjust. Today was Sunday, the day most visitors came; the attendants told me. And my two weeks had been up last Monday. Surely, Julia was coming today.

Church services were held each Sunday at 10 A.M. in the recreation room. I'd declined to go. But today Mrs. Holt announced that the entire ward would be attending church today. I had no choice.

Lee Ann said, "This is something you won't want to miss. A preacher from one of the churches in town comes out each Sunday. The churches take turns in loaning out their ministers. Sometimes it's a Protestant, sometimes it's a Catholic. Today I think it's a Protestant, maybe from the Baptist church. They'll preach to us and tell us how much God loves us. But you watch the restroom. There'll be an attendant guarding the door to make sure no patient from the southwest side of this hospital mingles with one from the southeast side. So let us go on over there and hear how blessed we all are."

I actually enjoyed the services. The minister was a kindly man who talked about the love of God. And four singers who had come with him had lovely voices. But I did notice an attendant stood guard at the restroom door, just as Lee Ann had said they would.

After church, I could hardly wait until lunch was over. When we returned from the dining room, I took a seat next to the picture window; from there I could see the parking lot, and watched for Julia and Thomas to pull up. For the first time in my life I thought I was going to be happy to see Julia.

Dr. Thorpe said he had written Julia and requested she come to Gatewood this Sunday. I thought it would only be a matter of time before I could go home. Maybe next week would see me at home. Dr. Thorpe said there was a problem with the EEG test; it didn't print out. I'm to take one more EEG. And surely after the results, I'll be set free. The test was scheduled for Tuesday.

"Why are there so few visitors," I asked Lee Ann. I'd noticed that last Sunday, but thought it was just an off day.

"Only a few patients ever have a visitor," Lee Ann replied, her eyes sad. "Oh, Matilda's mother comes the third Sunday of the month, you can bet on her. She's old and almost blind and has to be helped up the walk, but today is the third Sunday. You watch. She'll be here."

As the afternoon wore on, I began to worry. After 2 P.M. the worry increased with each moment. Mossie's sisters had arrived and were taking her off grounds. I watched them getting into the car. Mossie apparently wanted one of the sisters to take her dog and put it into the car. She stood there holding out her arm towards her sister. Finally the sister reached out and pretended to take the dog from Mossie, putting it into the back seat. Mossie smiled and crawled into the back seat. Another car pulled up; it was shiny and new. For a moment my heart lifted, maybe Julia had a different car? But two middle-aged women got out and helped an old woman out of the back seat. The woman was dressed in a black dress, black shoes and stockings. A white straw hat was perched on a head of snow-white hair. Matilda looked out the window and began laughing and spinning around and around, singing, "Mom's a coming! Mom's a coming!"

"Matilda," Mrs. Holt said, "sit down and wait on Mom, else you're going to fall and hurt yourself." Matilda didn't sit nor tell Mrs. Holt her name was Tillie. I guessed she was too excited to care. Instead she ran to stand by the outside door to A2, and still laughing, waited for Mom to slowly make her way up the walk.

When the trio finally got to the door, Mrs. Holt let them in. Matilda threw herself into her mother's arms, shouting, "Mom's here! Mom's here!"

"How's my baby girl?" The old woman asked, holding Matilda tightly in her arms, as tears rolled freely down her wrinkled, old face. I just stare at the ancient face, thinking it must have been very painful for the old woman to have to put her daughter at Gatewood. I thought of my own mother and realized just how much I still missed her. Matilda was also taken off grounds. As time slipped away, I knew my fears had been justified: Julia wasn't coming at all.

"She's not coming today," I said, almost to myself.

"Doesn't look like it," Mrs. Holt said. "I'll bet she had car trouble or something. She'll probably be here next Sunday."

When Mrs. Holt was out of hearing, Lee Ann whispered to me, "Seems a lot of folks have car trouble on visitors' day."

I didn't reply. I knew Julia hadn't had car trouble. She could get as many cars as she wanted; new ones at that. Car trouble was the last thing Julia could use as an excuse. After a while, I asked Lee Ann when her family visited.

"Oh, I haven't seen anybody in years," Lee Ann said, with little emotion in her voice.

"Really," I said, "you mean you haven't had a visitor in years?"

"Yes," Lee Ann said, "it's been years all right."

"I'm so sorry,"

"Oh, I don't pay it any mind. I've got my Sir Lancelot. He makes up for everything, you know." Lee Ann then went towards the attendant's desk, leaving me to think about what she had just said. There was that Sir Lancelot again. Was he just a figment of Lee Ann's imagination, or did he somehow fit in, in this place called Gatewood? And I wondered just who was Lee Ann anyway: Perhaps a true romantic who had her own special dreams. And I thought if Lee Ann could find a special place in her mind to dance in the moonlight with a Sir Lancelot, then she was one of the lucky ones on the ward. But then for a fleeting moment I got a vision of my first night at Gatewood and of two shadowy figures in a gazebo, dancing cheek to cheek in misty moonlight.

Just before the afternoon shift came on duty, I approached Mrs. Holt. "Please, could I try to call Julia?"

"I'm sorry," Mrs. Holt said. "None of the patients are allowed to use the telephone unless the family has given special permission, and your record has no such permission. When your sister comes, you can ask her to sign the permission. And if she is agreeable we will set up a special time for you to go to the pay phone located near the supervisor's office, at the front of the building."

I had seen the pay phone when I'd gone to Dr. Thorpe's.

"That pay phone is run through the hospital and patients can't just dial the operator and place a collect call." Mrs. Holt said. "With that phone you have to have a dime to connect to the operator. If your sister gives the permission, an attendant will assist you when you have your phone time."

The afternoon shift came on duty, and Miss Abner walked onto the ward. How, I wished the attendant had stayed home. I sat in the corner I'd come to think of as my own. Most of the patients on the ward had a special chair or spot they claimed as their own. I had taken the chair in the corner as far away from the attendants' desk as I could get. And I was thankful no other patient claimed the chair.

Lee Ann came to sit beside me. "I heard about the phone," she said. "We'll find a way."

"What do you mean?" I asked. "How in the world could I make a call?"

"I mean, girl," Lee Ann said, looking disgustedly at me, "get some gumption. To survive you have to learn to outsmart the ones who think they're the smartest. Fool them. Let them believe you aren't capable of going against the rules, that you don't have the guts to go against the rules; that you don't have sense enough to go against the rules. You got to be a fighter to survive in this place. And you can go several ways. Number 1: fight like hell and get the Thorazine pumped into you. Then you get the side room or C3. Number 2: run and jump and do exactly what they say and never give them any problems. They like number 2 kind the best. Number 3: Now that's the kind I am. They don't know about us number 3s. They think we only come in 2 kinds. But they sure are wrong."

Before Lee Ann could elaborate on number 3, Miss Abner was making her way around the room, and Lee Ann stopped talking just after whispering, "Number 3 will get you a call home, if you dare."

The other attendant was telling us it was time to get washed up for supper.

In the dining room, as we ate, I leaned across the table and whispered to Lee Ann. "What is the number 3 all about?"

Lee Ann grinned and whispered, "Number 3 is a holder of secrets. To be a 3 you must be brave and cunning, smarter than a fox. Do you have what it takes to be a 3, Jordan?"

I didn't answer. Did I have what it took to be brave and cunning? I didn't know. I'd never had to be brave and cunning. If I looked deep enough within myself could I find something I'd never even thought about hiding there? I looked at Lee Ann. "I don't know, but I wish I had what it takes to be a 3."

“I’ve learned,” Lee Ann said, “you never know what you have until you try.”

On Tuesday, I got a letter from Julia. Not a word about why she hadn’t showed up for Sunday’s visit. The letter sounded artificial, too cheery. In fact it said little at all. But Julia had enclosed twenty dollars for canteen supplies.

The postmark on the envelope puzzled me: Harper City, where my home was. What was Julia doing in Harper City? She had told me the day she and Thomas brought me to Gatewood that they had to hurry back to Cincinnati, because there was a mountain of work she had to get done. Julia was the chief fund raiser for a political party in Cincinnati.

I knew, although I was scared to death of being caught, I had to find a way to call Julia. Why hadn’t Julia mentioned she was in Harper City, mailing letters?

Julia's letter had been opened before it was given to me. Growing up one of the things my parents had stressed was: Other persons' mail was not ever to be opened. The more I sat there looking at the envelope, the angrier I got. It took all the courage I could muster to confront the attendant. "Who opened my letter?" I asked, laying the opened envelope on the desk in front of Mrs. Holt.

"All incoming mail is opened," Mrs. Holt said, looking a bit annoyed. "It's for your own protection. All mail comes through the supervisor's office and is read there. If there is anything in the letter the supervisor thinks will upset a patient, the letter goes to the doctor and he makes the final decision. And all money in a letter must be turned into the office. It goes into an account set up for you. You get to see the money, but you must turn it in. We will give you a receipt. We can order you a canteen book. But you have to turn in the twenty dollars, "Mrs. Holt said, holding out her hand.

Realizing to argue would do no good. I took a deep breath, “Well, could I please have some change?" I asked, handing over the twenty dollar bill.

"Oh no. None of the patients are allowed to have money in their possession. That is one of the rules here at Gatewood. That is why we have the canteen books."

I just stared at Mrs. Holt, realizing I had absolutely no control over what was happening to me or anything of mine. I wanted to shout that what they were doing was against the constitution. Suddenly Lee Ann's words rang through my memory; *The constitution doesn't exist at Gatewood.* Oh, God what am I going to do? I silently asked, going to my chair in the corner.

Lee Ann came and sat beside me. "Wish I could call my sister," I said.

"I have some dimes hid away," Lee Ann whispered. "You just bide your time, and you can make your phone call."

I, at first, didn't know what to say. If I accepted money from Lee Ann and was found out then both of us would probably end up at C3. But I felt excited, too. I did so much need to call Julia and demand to know what was going on. But when was I going to be able to make the call? Even, if Lee Ann really had any dimes.

"Ok, Lee Ann," I said low, "I'd certainly appreciate the dimes, and if I get caught, I'll never tell where I got them."

"Don't think you're going to get caught," Lee Ann said, with a sigh. "Make a good enough plan so you won't get caught. Think, girl. Think. You got to use your head to get by in here." Lee Ann said, getting her things together to go to work.

After Lee Ann left, I could think of nothing but the phone call. When was I going to do it? It should be as soon as possible.

When I got to work I told Dr. Thorpe that Julia hadn't come to visit.

"Well, Jordan you did have two seizures over the weekend," Dr. Thorpe said.

For a minute I wasn't sure I'd heard right. "What did you say?"

"The two seizures you had over the weekend. How are you feeling today?"

"No! No! I didn’t have any seizures this weekend. I haven't had any seizures since before coming to Gatewood. Why would you say I had two seizures!?" I knew I was shouting, but couldn't stop myself.

"Now, now, Jordan," Dr. Thorpe said, putting a reassuring arm around my shoulders. "They said you were in denial. That you said you didn't remember the seizures, and you got upset at the mention of them. And those behavior outbursts, you have got to work on that problem. Just calm yourself."

"Who! Who said!?" I began sobbing. Thoughts ran wild through my mind: I couldn't have had seizures. Could I have had them during sleep? Why wouldn't anyone have said anything? And the behavior outbursts!? I hadn’t had any since I was put in the side room after that one panic attack. And then came the most disturbing thought of all. Was someone lying about my seizures and behaviors? But why would anyone do such a thing? And who would do it? Did this mean I'd be on the drug study? Oh, God, I'm in a terrible nightmare and I can't see any way out. By now the sobs were shaking my entire body, and I was gasping, finding it hard to breathe.

"I'm sorry you are so upset," Dr. Thorpe said, leading me to a chair. I'll send you back to the ward.

“Please don’t do that!” I begged, taking deep breaths trying to calm. “I’ll be ok, just give me a minute.”

“Ok, if you can calm. You can stay. We can’t be having these outbursts, you understand? And you will be on the drug study, starting with the night medication.”

I nodded. I forced myself to calm and the rest of the afternoon went quietly. When I got back to the ward I approached Mrs. Holt. “I never had any seizures! I know I didn’t. And I didn’t have any behaviors! Please tell me who is saying I did!”

“Now, Jordan,” Mrs. Holt said, you know I can’t tell you that. You need to take it up with your doctors. I hope we aren’t going to see a behavior out of you.”

Realizing my pleas would not be heard, and if I protested any further, I would be considered to be having a behavior, and would most likely end up in the side room with a shot of Thorazine, I retreaded to my chair in the corner. I felt trapped. *Was someone trying to fix it so I couldn't contact anyone outside Gatewood?* I tried to push the thought away.

At medicine time, I was given two, white pills. I took them without protest. The attendant said the medication was to be taken twice daily.

Later that night, after I'd been asleep awhile, I awoke and went to the lavatory. When I flushed the toilet, someone said, "Somebody is up. Miss Cody came to the lavatory doorway. *Was it Miss Cody who had reported my seizures?* "Did you see me having seizures?"

"Any questions you have about your seizures, you'll have to discuss with the doctor. Go on back to bed."

"You can't tell me anything about my seizures? What about the reports of behaviors?"

"Not allowed to discuss any of that. Anything about you seizures or your behaviors must be discussed with your doctors, your family or guardian. I'm sure you have been told this before. Just one of the rules."

Stupid rules, I thought. This whole place is so full of stupid rules. "I need a drink of water." I went to the fountain at the end of the hall and drank in large gulps. My head felt dull, my mind listless. I returned to bed and sank into a deep sleep.

The next day, I went to work without getting a chance to talk to Lee Ann about the dimes.

"I'm happy you're all better," Dr. Thorpe said.

"Could you please tell me who said I was having seizures and behaviors?" I asked. "The attendants told me to ask the doctor."

"I'm sorry. We can't discuss who writes in your record. I can only tell you what is written."

"But, but, why?" I stammered.

"It's to protect you, and the staff person. Sometimes patients' view of what happens is somewhat different than what actually evolved. And they might blame the staff who wrote the report. It's just better for all involved."

I just stared at the doctor. Lee Ann was right, patients here at Gatewood were never believed over an employee. I had to make that phone call.

In the breakfast line, the next morning, I whispered to Lee Ann, "Can you get the dimes to me at lunch time?"

"Will do," Lee Ann smiled, her dark eyes dancing with excitement.

At lunch I sat with Lee Ann. Lee Ann, after looking around to be sure the attendants were occupied, slipped a tissue into my hand. "Dimes for the call," she whispered.

"Thanks," I whispered, quickly slipping the tissue containing dines into my bra. I'd get a chance to take the dimes out when I got to work, I could use the bathroom at the doctor's office in private.

At the doctor's office, my hands shook as I watered the plants. I'd taken the dimes, (three in all) from my bra while in the bathroom, tucking them into the toe of my right shoe. Now, I was wishing they were back inside my bra. Were they jingling as I walked? Would anyone notice? If anyone found me with the dimes I'd be punished for breaking the rules. I didn't know what the punishment would be, but believed it would be harsh.

I hoped to find the entry way empty where the phone was located when I got off work. I plan to make the call then.

I got an unexpected break about 2:30. Dr. Thorpe asked me to run vials of blood down to the lab which was located on the first floor. The lab room was just down the hall from the phone booth. I delivered the blood to the lab and coming back out into the hall, nervously eyed the phone booth in the entry way at the end of the hall. No one was in sight. I rapidly walked to the phone and with pounding heart put in a dime and dialed the operator. I was shaking so hard I could barely tell the operator Julia's number. The operator said to deposit twenty cents. I put two dines in the slot. After three rings, a man's voice said, "Hello". I recognized Thomas's voice on the other end of the line. For a moment I didn't say anything. Again Thomas said, "Hello".

"Thomas," I said, and was irritated at myself for my voice shaking. "This is Jordan. I need to talk to Julia."

"Jordan?" Thomas said. "I thought you were in the state hospital."

"I am. Please let me talk to Julia!"

"I'm sorry, Jordan," Thomas said, "I guess you didn't know Julia and I are getting a divorce. She left last week, moved back to Harper City."

"What!?" I said. "What is she doing in Harper City? What is she going to do about me!?"

"She moved back into the home place," Thomas said. Just then the operator came on the line saying the time was up and more money would have to be deposited. I had no more dimes and the line went dead. I glance through the glass door at the front of the building and panicked. Miss Abner was coming up the walk. I quickly hung up the phone and made a dash for the stairs. Was it time for the afternoon shift already? All employees came to the supervisor's office to report to work. Hadn't Gladys said the office was down at the end of the hall, and way round the corner is what I thought she'd said?

I stood at Dr. Thorpe's door a wave of hot angry surged through me making me tremble. Julia had no right to move into my home. She had no right! A terrifying thought crossed my mind as I realized Julia had complete control over my very existence. There she was in my house, with control of all my finances. And here I was trapped in hell.

"Oh, God," I moaned, crumbling to a chair near the office door. I buried my face in my hands. Dear God, why, why was all this happening to me? Why was my whole world destroyed? I thought about what Thomas had told me about Julia. So, Julia had settled in my house. Was that why she hadn't come to see me? Could it be Julia didn't want me out of Gatewood? If Julia wanted me here, who could get me out? Dr. Cole? How in the world could I even get a letter to him? Who on the outside could I turn to for help? There was my best friend, Suzanne. But she had just moved to Springfield and I didn't even have her new address, and even if I did, all letters going out would be censored. Oh, God I thought in desperation. Am I in a nightmare of which there is no awakening? I held back sobs, thinking, I must gain control of myself. Taking deep, long breaths, I tried to calm my pounding heart, to steady my shaking hands, to clear my racing mind. If I was ever to escape from this hell, I would have to first think clearly, and not be breaking up at everything that came my way. I didn't know if I had it in me to fight what had been thrown my way.

Mama had told me, when I'd been a small child, that strength comes to those who reach down deep into their souls and believe they will survive whatever obstacles life brings them. Mama had been a very strong, self-reliant person since she had been a young girl. My father had told me my mother's independence had been what had first attracted him. My parents met in Saint Louis. Daddy had gone there to work on a newspaper his father had just purchased. Mother had been a reporter for the paper, a widow with a teenage daughter, Julia. My favorite story as a child had been the one my father told me of how he and my mother had fallen in love.

I managed to calm enough to finish the work at Dr. Thorpe's. And that evening after the night meal, and I'd taken my bath, I sought out Lee Ann, telling her about the phone call to Thomas.

"It sound like you got a mean, rotten sister," Lee Ann said. "Something will work out for you. I can feel it in my bones. Try to put it out of your mind. Try watching television."

I couldn't put it out of my mind. I felt despair, like a thick, gray fog, was covering my body.

A Country Music Show was on television. Matilda sat in her chair by the door, grinning and clapping her hand to the music. And many others were clapping and tapping their feet to the beat. Miss Abner entered the day room, went straight to the television, which was in an enclosed cabinet that had a glass door and a lock. Lee Ann had explained: that the television was locked up because one of the patients had gotten upset and threw it to the floor. The cabinet was mounted to the wall several feet from the floor. Miss Abner stood on a chair to reach the lock. She opened the door to the cabinet and switched channels. No one said anything, but the clapping and the foot stomping came to an abrupt halt.

"Just look at that," Lee Ann whispered. "You would think this had never happened before. They always act surprised when she does something like this. She thinks she has to watch the program on channel 2."

By now, some of the patients were sounding protest. Matilda shouted, "Nooo! Nooo!! And began biting her hand, as she stomped her foot. Another said, "Don't do that. We were watching the singing!"

Miss Abner faced the patients, her face turning bright red, and yelled, "Bedtime!"

I whispered to Lee Ann, "That woman must be one of the meanest persons on the face of the earth."

"A true devil, "Lee Ann whispered.

"I said it was bedtime!" Miss Abner shouted again. "If any of you want to see any coffee tomorrow, you'll hit your bed in a hurry!!"

I had learned in my short time at Gatewood that the threat of losing coffee was a powerful weapon. I thought some of the patients would have sold their souls for a cup of coffee. One of their biggest fears was getting their name on the restriction list: Posted on a bulletin board behind the desk in the day room, it listed all the patients who had broken a minor rule. The ones who made the list would have their coffee taken away for a day. That threat kept most of the patients in line. So, with the threat of losing coffee ringing in their ears, everyone hurried towards their beds, in hopes Miss Abner would just watch her television show and forget about them. No one dared question the early bedtime.

As I lay on my bed wondering what in the world was going to happen to me, I could faintly hear the television, and wondered why it was Miss Abner had so many rights and the patients at Gatewood State Hospital apparently had none?

Chapter Seven

I had been at Gatewood for almost two months. They did another EEG. Dr. Thorpe said it showed my seizures had increased. The drug study medication was now, three times a day. The medication left me feeling dazed for a few hours after each doze. By the time my head cleared, it was time for the medication again. But last week I stopped taking the drugs. I learned to hide the pills under my tongue then spit them down the sink. I didn't believe I was having seizures although the incident report said I did. At times I let my mind suspect that Julia and someone inside Gatewood were conspiring to keep me forever a patient at Gatewood: That thought terrified me. Each time I tried to talk to Dr. Kelso or Dr. Thorpe about my suspicions that someone was reporting false things about me; they just explained that I was in *denial*. The one person at Gatewood who believed me was Lee Ann.

"Honey," Lee Ann said, "you just hang on, something will come through for you. I know you don't belong here at Gatewood."

I got a note from Julia. She wrote that she'd left Thomas and was living in the old home place to be sure my interests were looked after. I didn't believe for one moment that she was concerned about my interests.

I wrote Julia back, begging her to come and get me. I reminded her that my ninety days were almost up.

Julia wrote back. In her letter, she said she had discussed the situation with Dr. Cole and he agreed it would be in my best interest to not see anyone from home just yet: That they believed it would only cause me to place my attention on the things at home and take away from me concentrating on getting my seizures and behaviors taken care of. She wrote that they had discussed it and decided that it would be in my best interest to not be writing or getting letters for a while. But just as soon as everything was under control, she'd get in touch.

My, God! I thought in despair. What am I going to do!? My sister is in control of my very existence! I almost had a panic attack realizing that I might be trapped in this state hospital for who knows how long. I took deep breaths. I couldn't let myself lose control. I had to stay out of that smelly side room.

Sometimes I thought that the despair, and the hopelessness, I felt were surely destroying me, but I tried not to let it show.

According to the report Dr. Thorpe was always referring to, my seizure were a couple of times a week.

Who was in charge of the report? Everyone who carried a key became a suspect to me. And I knew if I ever got to tell someone on the outside about a mysterious report they wouldn't believe me; they would think I was indeed a loonie or lunatic. The word wouldn't matter one bit, either way they looked at it, I'd be considered crazy.

One day the thought that Julia was behind it all was so great I just allowed my thoughts to run wild. And considered what if? If it was really Julia, who on the inside of the hospital would want to help her? Was it Miss Abner who was writing down the false lies in the incident book? Was it the hateful Mrs. Sullivan? Could it be Miss Jones, Miss Cody, Mrs. Winningham or Mrs. Holt? Maybe even Nurse Margo? But why? And how would Julia have gone about getting them to do it?

Somehow, I had to find a way to get into the office and look at my chart and find out who was recording the false seizures, and reports of behaviors: Such as talking to an imaginary person. At each session with Dr. Kelso he tried to get me to tell him about this person. And when I denied it, he always told me I was in *denial.* God, how I hated hearing that word and knowing if I protested he would only tell me, "See, this is what I'm trying to explain to you." At other times I asked myself what if I had actually gone insane. Was an insane person aware of anything that was reality?

I felt I was in a nightmare of which there was no awakening. And I dared not trust anyone, except of course Lee Ann. I told Lee Ann I thought someone was trying to make it appear that I was insane, and I added that I wasn't even sure if my mind had not taken a crazy turn, then I asked if she had ever seen me having seizures or crazy behaviors.

She stared at me for a moment then said. "No. I've never seen seizures or crazy out of you. Listen girl, you are not crazy. I've seen plenty of crazy in my time. You are not one. Some people may be out to make it seem so, but I know different. Don't let them do this to you." Just then Mrs. Holt was walking near and told Lee Ann it was time to catch the bus for work. I watched my friend walk out the door. Dare I take comfort from this person who herself admitted was sometimes crazy?

Everyone on the ward was excited about a big celebration scheduled to take place the next day. "It's the same thing every year," Lee Ann said. "The whole hospital celebrates. It's a picnic. Charity groups from in town always come and put on entertainment. And there are games and you can win prizes. It's really rather nice. I think most of the patients enjoy it. Everyone goes, even the ones who are in wheelchairs and crib beds."

I found myself actually looking forward to the next day if only to get outside for a little while. To go anywhere outside the wards at Gatewood was closely regulated. If one was not at a designated place at a certain time, then someone was sent to find out why. And if the offending party didn't have an excuse that suited "*the powers that be*," then that party was subjected to what was deemed suited punishment, such as not being allowed to go anywhere alone again, or maybe the side room, or even C3. So far I had escaped being charged with the offense of not getting to my destination on time. Although, at times, I certainly was tempted to just flee and run for freedom over the rock wall. As I walked to my job at Dr. Thorpe's the temptation to run was almost a daily occurrence, but I was more terrified of what might be on the other side of the wall than what was inside it, and this knowledge about myself both confused and scared me. Sometimes I wondered if I was somehow becoming institutionalized. And I wondered how long I could keep my sanity, if I hadn't already lost it.

Lee Ann said most of the town's folks looked on the Villagers, as the patients at Gatewood were called, with fear and suspicion, and someone always called the police if one was seen on the streets of the town.

Sometimes I daydreamed of having the courage to scale the wall: "*Going over the wall"* was what the patients on A2 called running away from Gatewood.

"They always find you," Lee Ann said. "And the penalty for running away is a two week's stay on C3. I went over the wall, one time," Lee Ann whispered, leaning close so only I could hear. "I found my Sir Lancelot that day, out there beyond the wall and into the woods." Lee Ann had a faraway look on her face, and I wondered if she was telling an actual story or if it was just something she had dreamed up.

If I could have had one wish at Gatewood other than to go home, and have a look at my own chart, it would have been to read the history on the other patients, especially Lee Ann. The little room off Dr. Thorpe's office held files on all the patients at Gatewood. And of course the charts in the attendants' office would surely have histories on everyone on the ward. I had stood at the door to the office on A2 and gotten my appointment slips many time from the day shift attendant. Inside the office, above the desk, was a chart rack. I had looked at the chart rack with all the metal charts sticking out of the alphabetized slots, and knew one contained a workup on myself and believed surely it must contain a write up about the false seizures and the so called behaviors. If only I could come up with a way to get into the office.

And then I learned of all things, Lee Ann had a key to the office. I confided to her that I longed to get into the office and have a look at my chart.

Lee Ann looked at me thoughtfully for a long moment; then looked around the ward to be sure no one was in hearing distance and whispered, "I have a key."

"Are you kidding!?" I asked, astonished that such a thing might be possible. I knew the keys were passed from shift to shift and each key was accounted for, so how was it possible Lee Ann had a key?

"I'm not kidding," Lee Ann said, a beginning of a smile forming at the corners of her mouth.

"But how did you get it? Where did you get it, and where is it now?"

"I stole the damn thing," Lee Ann said, the smile turning into a full pledged grin. "I've had it for almost four years. That damn Miss Abner left her key in the door to the clothing room one night and went into the day room to watch television. I saw my chance and grabbed the key." Lee Ann now had a glint of triumph in her eyes as she continued. "I knew if I was ever found out to have taken the key I would most likely be a permanent patient on C3. Oh, I was a suspect. They searched my room and turned this ward upside down. But they found nothing. Let me tell you this," Lee Ann said grinning broader, "Old Miss Abner got in deep shit over losing her key. She even had to write a letter to the superintendent explaining her carelessness. I heard her telling all this to one of the other attendants. She said she told the superintendent one of the patients had stolen it and flushed it down the toilet. She picked one of the lower grade patients who couldn't own up to it if they had wanted to. I still think she suspects I had something to do with it though. I've been here longer than any of them and I know things they will never find out. I don't give a diddly damn what they have written up on me in those damn charts, but if you want to see yours, I'll help."

For a moment, I just stared in wonderment at Lee Ann. What she was telling me was almost unbelievable.

“I use the key to go see my Sir Lancelot." Lee Ann said, placing her chin on her hands and getting a faraway look in her eyes. I unlock the storage room, just down the hall from my room. And Abner’s key isn’t the only one I have either.”

“What! What other key?”

“Well the other key. You may not know this but when this place was first built this building had a tunnel underneath it, still there too.” I stared in awe as Lee Ann continued with her story, thinking if she wasn’t telling the truth then she sure was a whale of a story teller. Lee Ann continued, “The tunnel used to have pipes for heating when they had a large coal furnace somewhere nearby, and also pipes that took waste out of here. They changed the system years ago. Anyway there is a door inside the storage room. The door is behind a wood panel and even I would never have known it was there. But a nosey maintenance man found it and unbeknown to him I was watching. His key worked and he went in there leaving his key in the door. I don’t know how long he was in the tunnel but when he came out his key was gone.” Lee Ann chuckled. “And I believe he would never admit to losing a key. I was in the dayroom with everyone else when he came out. Later that day I went back to the closet and the paneling was back in place and the door to the tunnel was locked. Guess the man had another key. Anyway I go through the tunnel to the outside. Once I get out, I head for a patch of evergreens. Beyond the trees is an old gazebo." Lee Ann said. “And every time my Sir Lancelot is there.”

I stared at Lee Ann for a few seconds. Was all this possible? “How do you get out without the attendants checking and finding you gone?” I asked.

“I put pillows in my bed and cover them so they look like my shape. They seldom venture back where my room is,” Lee Ann chuckled. “It all has to with their fear of the ghosts that are supposed to wander this place. Don’t believe in them myself, butttt that don't stop me from telling about the one that roams the hallway outside my room." Lee Ann was now almost laughing out loud. "Sometimes I like to see how a rumor which in the beginning can be small and as it spreads will turn into a life all its own."

"Did you start the rumor that ghosts roam the grounds and the old building that used to be a morgue?" I asked, remembering what Rosa had told me on my second day at Gatewood.

Lee Ann nodded, "As I said I like to see how a rumor will grow. And I have been here a long time; have to have something to keep me entertained. The only person who isn't scared of ghosts is Nurse Billingsly. She's the nurse for the lock-up wards both for the men and women. That old buzzard isn't afraid of anything. I think if she met up with the Devil, she'd whip his ass. When you're ready, we'll figure something out." Still chuckling Lee Ann got up from the table and headed towards the hallway, leaving me wondering if I dared believe what she'd just told me.

Nurse Margo, the nurse for all the wards on the Wallace building, had a rule: all lockers were to be opened the day before canteen day, and all food items were trashed; because, she said, there could be an ant problem. I hated the day before canteen day. I've seen many of the patients become upset because something was thrown away they desperately wanted to keep.

I wondered why have the lockers at all, but had by this time learned not to openly express my views. I had vowed to myself, when I had first witnessed the cleaning out of the lockers, I would only purchase items that weren't trashed, such as writing paper. I had bought some on my first trip to the canteen, but I had yet to write the letter I dreamed of. I had been thinking about Paul a lot lately. I read in my hometown newspaper--Dr. Kelso said it was a great idea I get my hometown newspaper to keep up with current events—I read that Paul had returned from the Peace Corps and was back practicing law at the old firm. I marveled at the fact that just his name on a printed page could still make my heart skip a beat. *Did I ever cross his mind? Had he tried to find me? Did he know I was in a state hospital? Would he even care?*

On the society page, I read an article about Julia hosting parties at my house on Hickory Lane. That article just about got me a trip to the side room. I became so upset that Julia was passing the home place off as her own that I yelled, "Damn that woman!" And in frustration threw the paper across the room. I felt so helpless, so hopeless, so trapped I thought I was going to explode.

Mrs. Holt sitting at the desk had sternly told me I was to, "Calm down, now!"

I knew if I let myself act on my anger any further, I'd be seeing the inside of a smelly room. So, with the rage and anger and hate I now felt for Julia, burning deep inside me, I just sat in my corner and vowed I would not cry for the life I had known and lost. I feared for my future and knew I was going to have to find a way to get out of Gatewood: I had to find a way.

The next day (picnic day) dawned with a glorious sunrise. As I stood looking out the window of the dormitory at the beautiful colors of red, purple and gold, a deep sadness sweep over me. I longed to just have the freedom to run across the well-kept lawn in the early morning light. Ah "Freedom:" What a beautiful word. I thought now I fully understood what it meant, and wondered if I was ever to feel it again in this life.

Soon, the night shift attendants were in the dorm telling everyone to hurry along, a big day was at hand. The bath bundles contained the next best clothing each patient owned. "Everybody is gonna look extra pretty today," Gladys said, pulling on a bright red dress with large yellow flowers. "My sister, Eva, give me this dress. I think it is awful pretty. I thought they might save it for my burying bundle, but they picked my blue one for that." Gladys looked thoughtfully at me and said, "Do you guess my blue dress will be awful old before I wear it?"

For a moment I didn't answer, I hadn't thought that Gladys was capable of thinking such thoughts. Perhaps she wasn't as retarded as everyone thought. "I'm sure your blue dress will be just as pretty years and years from now," I said, smiling at the big, red haired woman.

Gladys smiled happily at me, "It's gonna be a great day."

As I ate breakfast, I looked around the dining room at the brightly dressed patients, a striking contrast from some of the drab gray clothing many wore every day. I thought the hospital was brightening them up for the town's folks who Lee Ann said would be attending this shindig. "Oh, the town people don't want us patients on their streets or in the stores, but some of them come out here every picnic day and put on a charity show. I guess it's their good deed for the year."

I remembered many times just before Christmas my mother and I would buy gifts and go with a group from our church to the orphanage just outside of Harper City. It always made me feel good to see the smiles on the children's faces. I now remembered with a pang of guilt that I had soon forgotten the children until the next Christmas.

Just before the green bus came to take us to the school yard where the picnic was to be held, Nurse Margo made a speech. She stood in the day room of A2, in her starched white uniform, her hair newly bleached blonde, and said, "I expect all of you to be the best behaved patients at the picnic. Remember, I will be watching," she said, smiled and turned on her heels and marched out of the room. "Makes that same damn speech every picnic day," Lee Ann said.

When we got to the school yard, I was surprised to see how well the event was organized. There were booths where patients could knock down bowling pins, or shoot a ball through a hoop, or maybe ring a peg. The most wanted prizes were jars of instant coffee. I had never understood the patients' attraction for the coffee. They were only allowed to make it with lukewarm water. I tried it once and it tasted awful, but most of the patients waited in line for their coffee. Lee Ann said it was an acquired taste.

There were about six hundred patients at Gatewood ranging in ages from six months to ninety-three. John Brentwood was the ninety-three-year old. They had him sitting under a giant maple tree, wearing a bright red shirt. As I looked at the old man with the head of snow white hair, wrinkled face and hands, and cloudy, blue eyes, I wondered how long he'd been at the hospital. "Been here since this place was first built," Lee Ann said. "They always put him up there under the maple tree. They said he used to run the farm building back when this place was self-supporting. They said he was a very smart man in his younger years. Just unlucky because he was born with seizures," she said, shaking her head.

Some of the families of the patients were present. "Some come for this event," Lee Ann said, "especially the families of the younger patients."

"Do you ever have anyone come?" I asked.

"No," Lee Ann said. "Haven't been any of my people here since before Mama died. Didn't you ask your sister to come?"

"Said she couldn't make it," I said.

A social worker had come on the ward and told me that she had called my sister and invited her to the picnic. My sister told her she had to be out of town, but was very concerned about my mental state. The social worker said I should see Dr. Kelso as soon as possible and she had set up an appointment for next week.

I had tried to tell the social worker someone wanted me kept at Gatewood and the reports of me having seizures and behaviors were false. The lady had patted my arm and said, "I understand your denials of your problems. If you would just admit to them, I think your treatment would go better." I hadn't answered. I knew it was useless.

At the east end of the school yard workers had set up a large tent. It sheltered the patients who were in wheelchairs and stretchers. There was a stage in the center of the yard where groups were playing music and singing. And rows of picnic tables were off to the west end where chicken dinners were served. I ate with A2's patients who didn't have family in attendance. The attendants were Mrs. Holt and a Mrs. Stevens, and several attendants from different wards and cottages. Also, Miss Jones and Mrs. Sullivan were working overtime.

After lunch, the patients were allowed to visit the booths. Cola was plentiful as was lemonade. About mid-afternoon The Saberville Lions Club set up their tent. The treat at that booth was hot dogs. Maylene had been telling Mrs. Holt, "She wants a hot dog. Please attendant, honey." Mrs. Holt was watching a play the ladies' club from Saberville was putting on. "You just wait a few minutes, Maylene," she said.

"No. She can't wait, attendant, honey," Maylene said, tugging on Mrs. Holt arm. "The answer to your problem is to get her a hot dog, a good one, with mustard on it."

Mrs. Holt sucked in her breath. "Lee Ann, you and Jordan take Maylene to the hot dog booth. She's not going to hush until she gets that hot dog. I don't want her to start screeching."

Maylene happily inched her walker towards the booth accompanied by Lee Ann and myself. The booth was attended by a large, burly man with a bushy beard. He already had about a dozen hot dogs prepared and had put mustard and ketchup on them. Maylene smiled sweetly at him and said. "A hot dog, please, with mustard."

The man smiled pleasantly and tried to hand Maylene one of the hot dogs. Maylene looked at the man, smiled, cocked her head to one side and said, "Give her one with mustard."

"How about if I just scrape the ketchup off?" The man said, preceding to try to remove the ketchup and again tried to give Maylene the hot dog.

Maylene pushed the hot dog back to the man and said patiently, "Now, Honey Man, the answer to your problem would be to give her a hot dog with mustard." The man sighed, and soon Maylene was happily eating a hot dog with mustard only.

"Maylene believes if she is persistent long enough she will eventually get what she wants," Lee Ann whispered to me. Then she smiled thoughtfully and said, "You know, I can't think of one time she failed in all the years I've known her."

Male and female patients were allowed to mingle under the close supervision of the attendants. The school was opened up for the use of the restrooms, with an attendant standing guard at each door.

"Sir Lancelot might be here," Lee Ann whispered to me. "But I wouldn't dare tell even you. I have to keep him top secret."

This left me to wonder if he really was real: If he existed, could he be an employee, or someone from in town?

It was late afternoon by the time the picnic was over. After a supper of soup and sandwiches, the patients who said they were tired were given special permission to go to bed an hour early. Miss Abner wheeled the medicine cart into the day room and gave the bedtime medication early. I overheard her tell the other attendant she was glad to see the day end.

Much later, I lay on my bed in the dim shadows, listening to the breathing of the other patients as they slept. I find myself remembering picnics in my past. One particular happy one was when I'd been about ten and Daddy and Mama had taken me to the cottage on Lake Michigan. Daddy had taught me to swim that year. But that had been a lifetime ago.

Chapter Eight

I survived day by day at Gatewood. Sometimes the despair and fear that I was forever to be a patient in a state hospital was so great I thought surely I would go insane, if I hadn't already. But something deep inside me kept me hanging on. Perhaps it was a basic instinct; maybe it was the inherited spirit of my great-great grandmother who had landed in Boston Harbor almost a hundred years ago. I had been named for her: Jordan O'Shannon, a spirited redhead from Ireland.

The story went that Jordan O' Shannon arrived in Boston in the year 1870 with only the clothes on her back and fifteen cents in a handkerchief tucked in her bosom. Great-great grandmother's belongings had been stolen on the ship. I tried to imagine what it must have been like for my ancestor to have just landed in a foreign country, being a woman besides. I thought Jordan O'Shannon must have been frightened. But she surveyed her circumstances and decided she had a few choices: she could walk the streets and beg, she could become a lady of the night, or she could find work. She found work. She became a cook and served drinks to the patrons in a tavern on East Bower Street. The story goes that she took nothing off the boisterous, Irish men who frequented that tavern. In two years Jordan O'Shannon owned the tavern. In three more years she owned one of the finest restaurants in Boston. She soon married Henry MacKaye, a surgeon. A favorite memory from my childhood was of my father who had told me about that ancestor: We were looking up into a star-filled night. He'd pointed to a bright star and said that it was Jordan O'Shannon: Our eye in the sky. A painting of the lovely redhead hung in the foyer of the home I grew up in, the home Julia was now calling home.

I hoped I could draw on some of the strength that had been in my ancestor, to get me through my terrible nightmare. What could I do? What would the spirited Jordan of years past have done? I thought my redheaded ancestor would have gone over the wall, probably on her first day at Gatewood.

The only bright spot in my existence was my job at Dr. Thorpe's. As I worked setting up appointments and ordering supplies, I often looked longingly at the little room which held the patient's files. If only I could find a way to get to my file. But I was never alone in the doctor's office. However on a rainy day in early August my chance came. I had just arrived at work and was in the entrance hall hanging my raincoat in the closet. I heard Dr. Thorpe's nurse, Nancy Brown, talking urgently to Dr. Thorpe, "There's an emergency down on Al! Patient has stopped breathing!" I saw the nurse grab the doctor's bag. In an instant I stepped into the closet, pulling the door shut. I heard the sound of running feet go by, then the door slamming shut. I was locked in the office.

For a moment I stood there in the dark closet, my knees trembling. I slowly opened the closet door and went into the office. The door to the file room was open and I quickly went into the room. The room contained rows of gray five-drawer filing cabinets. "The secret to why I'm here and who has been recording the false reports on me is in one of those cabinets," I whispered as I stood before the cabinets. With shaky fingers I opened the top drawer on the first filing cabinet. Realizing my file would be near the last, I shut that drawer and went to the last filing cabinet, searching through the W's until I located Walker. But to my dismay it wasn't a file on Jordan Walker, it was on a Ted Walker. It has to be here, I thought, frantically flipping through the remaining W's. All sorts of things flashed through my mind as I continued to search. Could there not be a file on me? Perhaps someone wanted it to appear as though I had never existed! That thought sent shivers of terror through me. As I stood there with panic seizing me, I saw a clipboard on a nail in the wall next to the cabinets. I stared at the clipboard: My name appeared in bold handwriting on a sign-out sheet attached to it. Pulling the clipboard from the nail I read my file had been signed out by Dr. Kelso's secretary. Dang, I wouldn't be seeing my file, but at least there really was one.

I stood there in the silence of the doctor's office and thought of what I should do. I should get out of there quick and wait outside the front door for Dr. Thorpe to return. If I were found in the files, drastic action would be taken; still I stood there, staring at the cabinets. Somewhere in there was a file on Lee Ann, and I couldn't resist looking for it, hoping to find out what this hospital thought Lee Ann was all about.

I found the file, near the back of the D files, bulging out of its folder. I sank down in a straight-back chair near the filing cabinet and began to read. Stamped in red on the first page in large letters was the word Voluntary: *Could Lee Ann leave at will?* I flipped the page and became fascinated at what was written in the thick file, yet, I felt a pang of guilt that I was looking in on someone else's private world. Still, I read on. According to the file, Lee Ann had been sent to the *"Village for Epileptics,"* as a twenty-four-year-old. The seizures started when she had been a college freshman, cause unknown. She was the daughter of a wealthy physician who was also, at that time, a state senator and a close friend of the governor who just happened to have been superintendent of the Village and would most likely return to that job where his term as governor was up.

I read on, engrossed: At first it was hoped a cure could be found for the seizures. But as time went on and no sign of a cure loomed on the horizon, Lee Ann became an embarrassment to the family. Lee Ann's aunt was a beautician and had allowed her niece to help out in the beauty shop, until Lee Ann's seizures caused the aunt considerably distress, then Lee Ann had been sent to the Village to be with, "*her own kind.*" Her father had donated large sums of money to the hospital on the condition Lee Ann was to have a private room. He had agreed she was to follow all the other rules of the hospital, but it was his wife's insistence their daughter have her own room. So the state had agreed.

I stopped reading for a moment and thought about what Gladys had said about Lee Ann being too mean to be in the dorm with the rest of the patients. I was glad Gladys was wrong about the reason for the private room. While in college Lee Ann had dreamed of being a playwright, had even gotten one small play published and had studied Medieval History. The psychological workup on Lee Ann stated she was also mentally ill, at times could appear completely sane, but was delusional and known in recent years to tell a story about a fictional lover named Sir Lancelot. The psychiatrist didn't know if Lee Ann believed Sir Lancelot existed, or if she was telling the story to try to impress someone. He wrote Lee Ann was quite cunning.

I felt deep sadness as I read on. I understood what it must have been like for Lee Ann to have suddenly found her world falling to pieces, and the realization that there wasn't a thing she could do about it. The report read that Lee Ann had spent a great deal of time in the "*lockup"* when she first came to Gatewood, but she had calmed down considerably in the last few years.

I was so absorbed in the file I hadn't heard the door to the office open. I jerked upright in fear and despair when Dr. Thorpe said, "What the hell! Jordan, what are you doing here!?" Seeing the file in my hands, he angrily raced across the room and ripped it from my hands. "You're in a mess of trouble, young lady!"

My heart sank to my knees. I knew all too well that I, indeed, was in a mess of trouble. I thought about pleading with Dr. Thorpe, but didn't know what to say. What excuse could I offer for being in the files when he had plainly told me I was never, under any circumstances, to touch them? Numbly, I watched as he went to the phone, shaking his finger at me, telling me not to move. His voice seemed so far away as he bellowed into the receiver, "Send security over here to Dr. Thorpe's office! A patient has broken into the files. Tell them to get an attendant up here, too!" Dr. Thorpe put down the receiver and demanded to know how in the hell I had gotten into the office?

I didn't say anything. I knew it would do no good to try to explain, for me there was no explanation. I was aware Dr. Thorpe's nurse, Nancy Brown, was in the room staring at me.

"Broke in here and helped herself to the damn files!" Dr. Thorpe said to his nurse. "This is the last one I'm going to let work here. To hell with the work program!"

Soon two security guards and Mrs. Holt were in the room. And the doctor was telling them that I had broken into his office. Mrs. Holt faced me. "I guess you know this little caper means a trip to C3!"

As the security guards came to take hold of my arms, I felt fear of what lay ahead on C3. I thought about begging Dr. Thorpe and Mrs. Holt to give me another chance, but realized it would be hopeless: rules here at Gatewood had to be obeyed, and I had just broken a biggie.

I fought back tears as I was led out of the office, down the stairs, out the door, and into the rain-splattered pavement to a waiting security car. I sat between Mrs. Holt and one of the guards in the back seat as the other guard drove to a large, brick building sitting high on a grassy hill.

As I was being led inside, I looked to the deep woods behind the building. Oh, how I wished I could break free of the security guards' hands holding my arms and run for freedom into those dark, green woods. I almost panicked as the thought came to me that I might be spending forever in this place called C3.

The inside was dark and dreary. The walls were a dark brown brick. I was led down a long hall to a door marked C3 in bold yellow letters. Those yellow letters were the only bright color I'd seen in the building. One of the guards unlocked the door.

When we were inside the door marked C3, the security guards and Mrs. Holt led me down a long hall. On each side of the hall were rows of doors. Each door had a tiny window just like the side room back on A2. In almost every window was a face. Some of the faces smiled at me. Some stared blankly and others yelled at Mrs. Holt. "What are you doing here, Holt? Are you coming to work here?"

I guessed they knew the attendant's name because she had probably escorted countless others patients to this dismal place.

At the end of the hallway, to the left, open doors lead into a large day room. Three attendants were sitting around a desk at the far end of the room. Several patients in drab, gray clothing were milling about the room.

A dark haired woman with a name tag which read, F. Voiles smiled and said hello to Mrs. Holt. "So, you can't keep your patients in line, huh, Holt?"

"As they told you on the phone, this one broke into an office," Mrs. Holt said.

"Now, why did you go and do a thing like that?" attendant Voiles said, looking me up and down.

I didn't answer. My knees were shaking but for some reason I didn't want the attendants to know how afraid I was. Some of the patients had come to survey me, and the attendant told them to get on away if they knew what was good for them. Every one of them hurried to the other side of the room. Attendant Voiles said to the two attendants sitting at the desk, "You two go on and get her into the side room, and I'll do the paperwork."

The two attendants got up, and the tall one with dark hair pulled into a bun on top of her head said, turning to attendant Voiles, "You want her in two or eight? Everything else is filled up."

"Put her in two. That way it will be easier to keep an eye on her."

"Come on," the tall attendant said, waving me into the hallway. "Get on in here and get yourself stripped down."

The other attendant took my arm and we followed the tall attendant into the hallway and stopped when she stopped before a side room door. I obeyed the attendant's command and stripped my clothes off and stood naked, trying in vain to shield myself with my hands. In the long, dim hallway the attendant's keys jingled as she unlocked the side room door. "Get on in there," she said. "You behave yourself, and your stay here will be more pleasant for you."

I obediently walked through the door, wondering how I was to survive in that smelly side room much like the one on A2. The attendant pushed the door closed and I heard the jingle of keys as the door was locked from the other side. In the side room on A2 I had been lucky and had only had to stay a night and part of a day. Now, I could hear Lee Ann's words ringing in my ears, *"Getting sent to C3 means at least a three week's stay in that hellhole. You don't wanna go there*!""

I shivered and walked to the tiny, barred window, stepping over the ugly green mattress lying on the floor. As I looked at the world just inches beyond the window, I knew it might as well have been hundreds of miles away. The rain had stopped and golden sunlight danced on wet, green leaves as they fluttered ever so lightly in the soft, summer wind. Tears blinded my eyes and I quickly wiped them away, thinking I must stop this self-pity. I must reach deep within myself and search for a spark of who my great-great grandmother Jordan had been. If I could find within myself a thread of what my ancestor had been, I might somehow find the strength to survive in this place. I was somehow feeling stronger as I stood there in that stinking side room on C3 and vowed to somehow find a way to get out of there and even beat Julia. I realized that I was going to have to depend on myself totally to get out of there. I was still afraid I might fail. But I vowed to the world outside that barred window: I sure as hell was going to fight!

The first thing I was going to have to do was to survive my time on C3. I sat on the bare mattress in that side room that ranked with the smell of old urine and asked myself if I thought I could stand it? Yes, I could stand it, knowing full well I had to stand it; I had no choice. But it made me feel better to say I had the power and the will to stand it.

I was allowed out of the room to go to the toilet just before supper. Two attendants from the afternoon shift stood guard. What did they think I was going to do? There was no way I could have escaped. I guessed guarding patients was one of the rules on C3 and the attendants were just doing their job. I smiled and said thank-you as I was being led back to the room. One of the attendants, a blonde haired woman with bright blue eyes, stopped talking to the other attendant and looked at me as if she was seeing me for the first time.

I went on inside the side room. Another attendant was occupied with a patient who was screaming and spitting out the tiny window in the room two doors down. The blonde attendant smiled at me. "You just obey the rules and don't cause any trouble like that fool down there, and you will work your way out of the side room and can spend the rest of your time in the day room. That sounds better. Doesn't it?"

Remembering the drab looking patients I'd seen in the day room I wasn't sure it would be better, but I smiled and said, "Yes, it does sound better than having to stay in this tiny room." The attendant closed and locked the door.

Much later, an attendant opened the door. "You stay on that mattress while I put your food down," she said, eyeing me as she set the plate of food on the floor. *Does she really believe she might get attacked?*

Supper was served on a large, gray, metal plate: a rectangular mold with five different sections for the food. Three of the sections were filled with food: beans, a large helping of greens and a piece of cornbread. Milk was in a metal cup made out of the same material as the plate. And a large spoon was sticking in the beans.

As I sat on the mattress and dug into the food, I thought about how a few weeks in this place had changed me. I thought of what my reaction to eating in such surrounding would have been when I had been living at home and eating off fine china and linen table cloths. Back then I couldn't have imagined the possibly of enduring such accommodations. But, I reminded myself, things had changed.

I was given the drug study medication. One attendant handed me the pills another stood nearby. I put the pulls into my mouth, slipped them under my tongue; and then took a quick sip of the water the attendant handed me. After the attendant closed and locked the door, I quickly removed the pills and placed them on the narrow edge of the windowsill at the back of the room. From then on when I was given the medication, as soon as possible I removed the pills from my mouth and placed them on the windowsill. Then when my meals were served, I removed the pills used the spoon to scrape the partly dissolved pills off the windowsill. I placed the medication into a bit of food on my tray. I then poured milk onto the mixture. Later the attendant picked up my tray and sent it to the kitchen. I prayed it would all go into the garbage.

I learned while I was in the side room, that like on A2, I would never be allowed to have any form of clothing, including bed clothes. The reason for this rule was patient protection. It had come about because a patient hung herself while in the side room with strips torn from the sheets, or from the patient's own clothing. I learned that from Cordelia, a bushy haired woman in a side room across the hall.

I had been laying on the sticky mattress trying to figure out a way to get myself out of the state hospital when I heard a horrible voice screeching cuss words at the attendants. "You, low-life, fat-assed, two-bit whores, I've been in and out of C3 for twenty years and I never attempted to hang myself! So give me some damn sheets and a blanket. I'm cold!"

I got up off the mattress and went to the window. Two attendants stood by the room across the hall. "You had better calm down, Cordelia," a tall attendant said, twirling her key, which was tied on a long brown shoestring.

"You know the rules around here, Cordelia," a little blonde attendant said. "You get in the side room on C3 and there is to be no clothing what so ever."

"Well, it's a stupid-ass rule!" Cordelia yelled. "It's cold in here, and I want a blanket. Just because dumb-ass Peggy Moore up and hung herself, don't mean I wanna do it too. Besides, why in the hell would anyone care if I did?"

I could see that the bushy haired person called Cordelia was not going to shut up, and some of the other patients were beginning to follow her lead and were starting to yell for blankets also. The tall attendant with the dark hair said, "Go on and make up the shot, and I'll call security. We'll just go ahead and give her the Thorazine. She ain't gonna shut up till we do, and some of the others are getting upset." The other attendant threw her hands in the air in disgust and started walking towards the day room.

The attendant sighed as she looked at Cordelia, "You are just a plain, old trouble maker, Cordelia. You know we have to go by the rules, and you make our job harder by throwing a fit every time you come to C3."

"Well, I don't aim to be one of your model prisoners. And who gives a holy shit, anyway!" Cordelia screamed through the tiny window, spitting at the attendant.

The attendant shook her finger at Cordelia, saying, "That will get you an extra three days in this side room, without a blanket, too."

"Who in the hell cares?" Cordelia screamed as the attendant rapidly walked back toward the day room. I wondered if Cordelia was going to get an extra-large shot of Thorazine. Cordelia continued to scream and bang on the door.

Soon the two attendants were back with two security guards. The small attendant held a needle in her hand, no doubt filled with Thorazine. Cordelia stood her ground as the other attendant unlocked the door to the side room. "You think I won't put up a fight, missy. You got another think coming!" Cordelia screamed, lunging for the attendant.

"Grab her! Get her!" the attendant holding the needle said, stepping back out of the way as the two guards and the tall attendant grabbed the fighting Cordelia. Soon, the three had pinned Cordelia to the floor. The other attendant raced across the floor and quickly jabbed the needle into Cordelia's hip. But Cordelia still tried to fight. She managed to fling the attendant and one of the guards off her and was up on all fours before they pinned her again. Screaming and spitting all the while. The attendant, who had given the shot, quickly placed the syringe in the hallway near the side room then grabbed Cordelia's legs. The other attendant's hair that just minutes ago had been in a neat bun, now hung in long tangled strains.

"You girls get on out the door!" one of the security guards panted, his breath coming in harsh grasps, as sweat rolled off his forehead. "Hold the door open and Jake and I will make a run for it before she can get up!"

I watched as the attendants on a "One, two, three," quickly let go of Cordelia; then ran out the door. They stood just outside the door while the security guards poised to let go of Cordelia and make a run for it, before Cordelia could get to her feet. {I thought by this time the Thorazine would have started to take effect.} One of the guards panted, "One! Two! Three!" and on the count of three, both let go and then ran through the door. The attendant swiftly slammed the door and turned her key in the lock.

"Damn son-of-bitches," Cordelia screamed. I wondered if soon C3 would have heard the last of Cordelia for one night. The attendants and security guards went out of sight towards the day room and suddenly all the other patients in the tiny, smelly rooms on C3 were quiet. I thought a battle had been fought and Cordelia had lost, and I wondered if anyone had really won.

I sat back down on the mattress and listened to the quiet of the gathering darkness and tried to figure out what I was going to do. The first order of business was to get out of the side room. "*Work her way out*," like the little, blonde attendant had said.

When darkness came, I lay on the bare mattress shivering, with thoughts of my own lovely room at home. My thoughts were not if I was ever to see my room again, but when and how I was going to go about doing it. Help would have to come from somewhere outside the hospital. I knew better than to try to voice my true feeling with any of the doctors inside the institution; they would only again tell me I was in denial. After all, they could point out the proof that I was still having seizures and besides, now they would be saying my behaviors had increased and I couldn't be trusted. I realized as I sat on that cold mattress in the shadows of the side room in the state hospital my situation looked mighty grim.

I remembered something my great-great grandmother Jordan had written many years after she had arrived in America. *'I sat there in the loneliness of Boston Harbor; long after every other passenger had found their families and had gone to their new homes. I sat there in the stillness of the night and watched a lighthouse beacon shining out there in the darkness and thought surely there was a light for me out there somewhere in the darkness if only I had the courage to look. So I took all the strength I possessed and marched into Boston not knowing what lay within.'* I had always admired the tales of the strength of my ancestor of so long ago, never dreaming I would be in a position to test if I had the same strengths. Fear was still like a large knot in my stomach, but I knew I was going to try to get out of my horrible situation. I just hoped the spirit of Jordan of old would be with me, for I knew a very rough road lay ahead and I was going to need all the help I could get. And the only one in this whole state hospital I dared to turn to was Lee Ann, who, by all recorded accounts, was mentally ill. But then, couldn't the written words about Lee Ann be false also? After all, look at what has been written about me.

Chapter Nine

I survived on C3 by trying to visualize the day my ordeal would be over. I caused no problems and did my best to cooperate with the attendants. Most of them were friendly and seemed to like me.

The day shift attendants went to bat on my behalf and got me out of the side room and into the day room in just four days. I hadn't thought getting to the day room was any big deal when I first came there and saw the bare drabness of the room. But after spending a time in the side room, the idea of making it to the day room became more and more desirable.

When I was given my clothes, a rolled up bath bundle, and told I could take a shower and would be given a try at the day room, and would be sleeping in the dormitory if I behaved myself, I almost cried with joy.

Cordelia yelled, from her little window, "You're the attendants' pet. You're a puppet. You do anything they say. You're a egg-sucking traitor. You ain't got no guts. And it won't be no time until you'll be right back in here with the rest of us fools!"

I wondered exactly what an egg-sucking traitor was, but made no comment as I walked past Cordelia's door, out of the hallway into the day room. I prayed Cordelia was wrong about me being back here in no time. Lee Ann had been right; this place called C3 was indeed a hellhole. As I'd lain at night, shivering on the old mattress, I had listened to the sound of the other tormented souls in the other side rooms. There had been Cordelia cussing, using her own style of phrases. Some of the others were crying; some talking about weird things, like devils being outside the door. I thought those sounds would be forever etched on my mind.

Late in the afternoon, security and two attendants I'd never seen before brought in Rosa, the woman I had met on the bus my second day at Gatewood. I remembered the woman had said her husband was a doctor and had signed her in to the institution. The woman was in tatters: Her clothes were ripped almost off her body, and her face and body were covered with scratches. One of the security guards was in almost as bad a shape. His uniform was also torn in several places and he, too, had scratches on his face and hands. His face was flushed with anger as he told the attendants on C3 to get "*that*" locked up and out of his sight.

Miss Voiles (who was working a double shift) laughed in his face, saying, "Well, well, Jake, looks like you either met up with a wild cat or a briar patch." That only made Jake all the angrier: He began waving his arms and shouting, "That damn fool ran right through a briar patch! The boss got a call from the sheriff in town that someone had better get in there and take care of Gatewood's patients, said they didn't have time to go chasing loonies. When she saw me coming after her, she darted into a field and ran right into a briar patch. I had to catch her, so I got all scratched too. I felt like busting her chops, but you know the law, can't hit one of these fools. No matter what they put you through. I tell you right now the state don't pay enough to work here! You get bit, hit, and spit on and have to chase them through fire and briar patches, or anything else they happen to be headed for. Tomorrow, I hand in my resignation!" Jake turned on his heels and angrily stomped off.

The attendant, her mouth gaping, looked at the other security guard. "Is he serious?"

"He's dead serious," the other security guard said, shaking his head. "I think today was the last straw. Remember last year when he almost got his ear bit off by a patient over on B4. He almost quit after that. Tomorrow, that boy will be looking for a safer job. And I may not be far behind."

"I sure do hate to see him go," the attendant said, the smile gone now from her face. "I always liked Jake. We could always count on him to help with a disturbed patient. I hope I didn't make him mad by laughing. I didn't mean to upset him."

"Oh, it ain't anything you done, Voiles. He's just fed up. Well, good luck with the fugitive from the briar patch," the security guard said. "Don't look like you'll be needing any help in getting her to the side room. So, I guess I'll go on and see about Jake."

"She won't be any trouble," Voiles said. "But I guess I'll have to call the nurse and see about getting all those scratches taken care of. I sure hope she's not bad enough to call out Dr. Thorpe, he gets all upset if he has to come out after hours."

I felt sadness as I looked at the ragged woman with the scratches all over her body. I remembered the day on the bus when I'd met the woman. Rosa had said her husband had put her in the state hospital and she would be staying forever. What had happened to change her mind, to make her run?

The attendants were busy cleaning up Rosa and paid little attention to me and some of the other patients standing nearby. They took Rosa to the shower room at the far end of the hallway. I, along with several others, followed. For a moment, I felt a bit uncomfortable that we weren't giving the woman privacy, but the need to see what would happen next overpowered the fleeting feeling. Maybe, I was becoming one of *them*? I watched as the attendants stripped Rosa's torn clothes from her body.

I felt like crying for the woman: She looked so wounded and frail, standing naked in the shower room waiting as the attendant turned on the water. I thought she looked like she was in shock. When the attendants got Rosa cleaned up, they decided she wasn't as bad as they had first suspected. Another attendant came into the hallway. "The nurse is on her way. She's not too happy she got called over here."

"Well, that is just toooo bad," one of the attendants sniffed.

"Rosa," attendant Voiles said, looking at Rosa and shaking her head. "What in God's name were you thinking, running away? And why did you run through a briar patch?"

Suddenly, Rosa, who was now wrapped in a towel, her eyes wide and fearful, grabbed Voile's hand. "Miss Voiles, you know I haven't ever done anything to get sent here to C3 in all the time I've been in this institution. Please! Please don't let them put me in the side room!"

"I know you've been a good patient, Rosa," Voiles said, and I could see the genuine caring in her eyes. "You've been working good for us here on C3 every day, helping to take care of the ward and all. What in the world made you run away? You know what the punishment is for running."

"I think I was having one of the running kinds of seizures, like I had before the hard ones started. The kind I had before *he* sent me here. I was on my way over here to work, and suddenly I thought I was at home and my little girl needed me. And I started running. I thought I was trying to get to her!" Tears were now running down Rosa's face.

I thought all of Rosa's pleading would do absolutely no good and she would be seeing the inside of one of those smelly side rooms before the night was over. Rosa had broken a rule. And broken rules were always punished, period. I felt deep anger that this woman would face harsh punishment for something she couldn't help. But I also knew I, least of all, was in no position to do anything about it.

Nurse Billingsly was a large woman with red hair and flaming red lipstick. She marched onto the ward. I stared at the big woman knowing I was looking at Lee Ann's *fearless, ass-kicker Devil- whipper.*

Nurse Billingsly was a no nonsense type person and was proud of it. She came onto the ward snapping, and she expected attendants as well as patients to snap to attention. "Get these other patients out of this shower and out of the hallway!" she snapped. I and all the other patients made a speedy retreat to the day room.

I longed to have the power to change the way things were, to give understanding and comfort to Rosa. Most of all I would have liked to have given the woman a warm, comfortable bed to sleep in. Instead I knew she would be lying cold and naked on the sticky mattress in the smelly side room and that thought made a deep sadness fill my heart.

The nightmare of C3 ended for me just before super time. The security guard who had helped Jake bring in Rosa was there to help an attendant from the afternoon shift take me back to A2. As bad as I had thought A2 had been, I was happy to get to go back there. After what I had seen and experienced on C3, even old Miss Abner was going to look good.

When we arrived on A2, all the other patients were getting in line for the dining room. "Well, did you have to bring her back right at super time?" Miss Abner said, looking very disapprovingly at the security guard and the attendant from C3.

"Well, excuse us!" The attendant from C3 said.--She was one I hadn't seen before this afternoon, an older woman with short, white hair. *Surely she was almost ready to retire.* "You might as well have her as us. And the order was to send her back tonight. We're all filled up! We had to release someone, so we could have room for another. If you people on the outer wards would teach your patients right in the first place, then we wouldn't be getting them on our ward!"

Miss Abner just stood there squinting her eyes at the other woman for a moment. "Oh, Miss Tanner, don't go getting your feathers all ruffled. I didn't mean to get you upset. Voiles called earlier and said we'd be getting her back today, but I thought she would have sent her before our busiest time."

I stood there, knowing full well I wasn't wanted on either C3 or my home ward and they were referring to me as *"her"* and not really seeing me as a real person. I wanted to shout I had a name. I wanted to say I am Jordan, not just *a her*.

Miss Abner turned to me. "Well, go on! Get out there in the hallway and get in line with the other patients for supper." I did as I was told. I had been amazed since my first day here with the waiting line, that mostly happened on the afternoon shift. The attendants told the patients to lineup for meals several minutes before time to eat. The patients had to stand in line along the hallway and wait. I thought that was so silly, but didn't dare say anything.

Lee Ann smiled at me and came to stand in line beside me. "So you survived old C3, did you? Glad to see you made it back all in one piece," Lee Ann said, affectionately patting me on the shoulder. "Told you, it was a hellhole up there. Didn't I?"

"Yes, you did. I never thought this ward would look good."

"Well, from now on, just stay out of trouble," Lee Ann advised.

I looked over the line of patients. All seemed about the same as when I left. Maylene was down near the office door saying, "Attendant, honey, just give her the napkin with her name on it! Please attendant, honey!" She shrieked this over and over again, until Miss Jones rushed out of the office and threw a pillow case over the bar of Maylene's walker. Maylene picked up the pillowcase and after seeing *her name* was printed on it, smiled and said, "That was the answer to your problem, attendant honey."

Miss Jones just stood looking at Maylene for a moment, finally through clenched teeth she said, "Someday, Maylene. Someday!"

I smiled at the determined, little, black-eyed woman. Maylene returned the smile and said, "She's back."

Matilda had gotten tired of waiting and sat in the floor. Miss Abner came out into the hallway and said, "Matilda get up off the floor."

Matilda stood up, but began to bite her fist and stomp her feet, shouting, "Her name is Tillieee! Mom calls her Tillieee!"

"If Matilda wants any supper, she'd stop that racket," Miss Abner said. Matilda shut up, but still bit her fist and violently shook her head.

I had been wondering since I came to Gatewood just why, if it made Matilda happy, didn't they just call her Tillie? I whispered this to Lee Ann.

"Oh, honey," Lee Ann said, shaking her head. "There aren't any nicknames allowed here at Gatewood."

"One of the rules?" I said.

"Right," replied Lee Ann. "The attendants have to go by the rules. If they get caught calling one of the patients by a nickname or a pet name, they're in big trouble."

Gladys standing in line a few patients ahead of me looked around at me, and with a silly grin on her face asked, "Did you learn your lesson up there on C3? Are you gonna mind the attendants now?"

Before I could say anything, Lee Ann snarled, "Shut up, Gladys! And mind your own business."

"Miss Abner! Miss Abner! Lee Ann is telling me to shut up!" Gladys yelled.

Miss Abner rushed out of the office and stood with her hands on her hips glaring. "I'm telling all of you right now! If you don't quiet down, there will be no supper for anyone this night!

Suddenly all was quiet. Would Miss Abner carry out her threat if anyone spoke a word? I believed she would and guessed all the others believed it too. No one spoke another word and soon the attendants came out of the office, locked the office door, then unlocked A2's door, and everyone marched in a line to the dining room.

After supper, when the baths had been given, everyone sat in the day room waiting for bedtime. Some of the patents were watching television, a few were playing cards, and Maylene was coloring in her coloring book. I sat next to Lee Ann. I thought about what I had read about Lee Ann in the record in Dr. Thorpe's office. And I thought a very talented person had been lost to a state hospital, and the thought filled me with sadness.

"Why the long face?" Lee Ann asked.

"Oh, I guess it's just being here in this state hospital and not wanting to be," I said.

"Well, I have known since you arrived here you didn't really belong."

"I appreciate that, Lee Ann," I said and began to tell her about the doctors insisting I still had seizures when I knew I did not. And about the behavior problems they insisted I was having.

You can't stop what they write. They have all the power."

"That they can write what they want and we have no say is so unfair."

"I know. We'll find a way to get you out of this institution," Lee Ann said, patting my hand. "I promise, we will find a way.

I felt lower than ever as I watched Lee Ann walk out of the day room and disappear down the hallway towards her room. How was I going to get out of this place when the only person in the world I could count on for help was a person who believed she had a lover named Sir Lancelot?

Miss Abner stood up and turned off the television and announced, "Bedtime."

Long after all the other patients had been sleeping, I got up and looked out the window. In the distance, when the wind blew tall evergreens causing them to sway, I thought for an instant I saw what remained of a gazebo. Were two figures dancing in the misty moonlight? No. I thought. It's just the shadows from the trees as the wind blows the branches. Still, the movement was more than what the shadows from the tree would have made. Could Lee Ann be out there, if only in her dreams?

The next day I timidly went up to Mrs. Holt. "Is there any chance I could go back to work at Dr. Thorpe's?"

For a moment Mrs. Holt just stood there at the desk in the day room on A2 and stared at me as if she couldn't believe what she had heard. "Do you mean to tell me you think you should have your job back after what you have put us through!?" Mrs. Holt said, shaking her head. "No, Miss Walker. There is no chance, what so ever, of you ever getting to go back to work for Dr. Thorpe, nor will you be permitted to work in any office in this institution. You are not to be trusted. You have been assigned to work on A-l. You will be helping feed and change the patients over there. You are to work from noon till two, Monday through Friday, starting today." Mrs. Holt briskly turned away and walked off towards the office, leaving me standing there with my mouth open.

Gladys, who had taken it all in said, "So, you're gonna be working with me. Don't worry, I'll teach you how to feed um."

I didn't say anything. I just walked away and went to look out the window. I didn't want to go to work on Al. God, that awful smell that came out of there when an attendant opened the door when I'd passed there on the way to meals. The smell was something dreadful, yet indescribable. It was the smell of something which had soaked into the ward that no amount of cleaning could remove. I felt nauseous just thinking about it. And now I was to have to spend two hours a day in there! God, how in the name of heaven am I to stand this? Yet I knew I must stand it, I had to stand it. So later, after Gladys and I had eaten an early lunch at 11:30, I found out just what besides the smells lay across the hall, in that ward called Al.

When we came back from lunch, Gladys knocked on Al's door. A tall attendant with short brown hair came to unlock the door, letting us in. "Hi, Miss Gray," Gladys said. "This is Jordan."

"Great," the attendant said absently, going out the door, locking it behind her.

"She's going to lunch," Gladys said.

I had seen patients in the hallway of Al when I had looked in at the door, and I'd assumed all of the patients were much like those. I was wrong. Only a few were able to walk around on their own. The rest were in wheelchairs, or walkers that had a seat and wheels, or in cribs in the dormitory. For the patients in the cribs their beds were their total existence, they were fed, changed, bathed and doctored in there. The other beds in the dormitory were low like the ones on A2, and those beds were for the ambulatory patients on the ward.

I tried to push back the feeling I was going to be sick. "What is that smell?" I asked Gladys.

"What smell?" Gladys said, looking at me and raising one red eyebrow.

"Oh, never mind," I said and let Gladys lead me into the day room.

"This is Jordan," Gladys said to three attendants who were standing beside a large food cart. "She's mean, just got out of C3, but she can feed the babies. Want me to learn her how?"

"That won't be necessary, Gladys," a short, fat, blonde attendant with a smiling face said. "You take this tray and go on and feed Jane. We'll see Jordan does her job." Gladys stuck her lip out pouting, but took the tray and went towards a small, dark haired figure crumpled up in a chair in the corner.

The blonde attendant with a name tag that read, "Mrs. J. Pointer," handed me a tray and picked up another for herself. "Follow me," she said, smiling at me. I followed her into the dormitory. "You can feed Mandy," the attendant said, pointing to a crib bed against the wall. A small figure, with bright blue eyes and blonde hair pulled into a pony tail atop her head, was propped on a pillow. "You have to feed her slowly, but she's a good eater," the attendant said.

My hands shook as I set the tray on the bed. I knew nothing of feeding handicapped people. What if this patient choked? What was I to do then? Mandy was looking at me as if to say, *"Bring on the food."* I picked up the spoon and slowly began to feed her the ground up food.

The two hours were up before I knew it. The attendants said I had done a good job and they were glad to have my help.

When I got back on my ward, I found out I had an appointment with Dr. Kelso at four that afternoon. I got on the bus wondering what Dr. Kelso would be asking me today. I was not going to tell him someone was recording false seizures in my record, nor about the behavior reports. He would tell me: I was still having the seizures, my behaviors had been recorded, and I was still in denial. As the bus went by the cottage where Rosa lived, I felt sadness knowing the little woman was most likely still locked in a C3 side room.

Dr. Kelso was ready to see me as soon as I got into the building. "Good afternoon, Jordan. Please take a seat, he said, smiling, motioning to a chair in front of his desk. "How are we doing this fine day?"

I sat down and smiled. I had decided I was going to tell the doctor all was well in my world, although I knew my whole life was in shambles. Dr. Kelso looked from me to a paper lying on his desk, tapping the desk with a pencil.

I found myself counting the beat of the pencil. One, two. One, two, three, one two.

Finally Dr. Kelso looked up from the paper, laid his pencil aside, folded his hands on the desk, and leaning forward smiled. "Well, looks like we've been in a bit of trouble since the last time I saw you."

I knew he was referring to my trip to C3. *How would great-great grandmother Jordan handle this?* Suddenly a thought ran through my head: *Tell him what you think he wants to hear.* "Dr. Kelso, I really am ashamed of myself," I said. "I know I did wrong to get into Dr. Thorpe's files, and I hope the good people here at Gatewood will find it in their hearts to forgive me." Dr. Kelso was leaning forward anxious to hear more of my repentance.

"Good. Very good, Jordan. It is very important for us to recognize and admit our mistakes." He leaned back in his chair, folded his hands behind his head and smiled. Leaning forward again, he asked, "Is there anything you can think of you want or need?"

I wanted to scream, Of course there are many things I want and need. I need most of all for someone to believe me, and to see me as a real person. I need to get out of this place! But I didn't voice any of those thoughts. I knew better. Instead, I smiled at the doctor and said, "I really am doing better."

"I see here you are still having seizures," Dr. Kelso said.

It was all I could do to keep from screaming: It was all a lie. Someone was out to keep me in this hospital forever. But I forced myself to smile at the doctor. "I do so much want to get well. So I can go back home, Dr. Kelso. I just don't remember having the seizures. Is it common to have them and not remember?"

"Oh, yes. Absolutely. I am so pleased to see that you are working on your denial. Now, maybe we can begin to work on both your seizures and your mental condition."

I just sat there across from the doctor and listened as he explained to me what I was feeling and why I was feeling it. It would do no good to try and tell him what he was saying wasn't at all what was in my mind and heart. He would say my thoughts were all due to my **"denial."** God, how I'd come to hate that word. I wanted to say, *"Look, Dr. Kelso, Julia is somehow conspiring with someone inside this state hospital to keep me here. I understand full well what her motives are. Greed is the great motivator: To keep me forever behind this wall will enable her to always remain my guardian and to have full access to all my finances.* But I kept my mouth shut; believing to keep my innermost thoughts to myself would be in my best interest.

Dr. Kelso said, "I talked to your sister on the phone and got a full history on your background." The doctor leaned back in his chair.

I felt a wave of helplines sweep across my insides.

"I see here you have had a couple of disappointing love affairs," the doctor said, looking closely at me over his glasses which were perched halfway down his nose. "Your sister said you have always had a feeling of people rejecting you."

"But that is an absolute lie!" I said. "Why is Julia telling this?!" I knew my voice was raised, but I couldn't help it.

"Now, now." Dr. Kelso said. He held up his hands as if to calm me. "Don't go back into denial. We can work through this. It will do no one any good if you become upset."

"Sorry! Sorry." I managed to say. My God, I thought. He thinks I'm totally insane. And nothing I say or do will change his mind.

I felt like crying. I wanted to slap the doctor up the side of his head. Why couldn't he see I was the same bright woman I'd been before the accident? That I'd had a head injury causing me to have a few convulsions, but my brain was healed now. And the reason I was being kept prisoner in this institution was all a conspiracy on the part of one Julia Bristol. Why couldn't he see? But I sat there, as the doctor continued to explain to me what I was feeling.

I listened as Dr. Kelso told me of Freud, and of my id, and ego, and superego. "We will continue to work through your denial. Don't be too disappointed with your progress. Setbacks are common. Sometimes it takes years to understand it all."

Years!! That word sent terror through me, but I tried not to show it. Did he really think I was going to be here for years!?

Shaken, I left Dr. Kelso's office. This had been the most disturbing session I'd had with him.

I headed down the walk towards the shuttle bus. The sun was shining, spreading golden light on the world, but all I could see was gray and cold. To my left was the ugly rock wall. I stopped on the sidewalk and just stood there staring at it, realizing I hadn't thought it as being ugly before. It hadn't changed, had it?

The bus was waiting at the end of the walk, with the attendant standing in the doorway staring at me. I felt the urge to just run and scale the rock wall and search for freedom on the other side. I almost started running for it. Then a picture of Rosa flashed across my mind. I saw the woman all ragged and scratched, shivering in a shower room on C3. I realized to go over the wall would find the same fate waiting for me. "Jordan Walker, you get on down here, and on this bus, right now!" the attendant yelled. I walked to the bus and climbed aboard.

As the next week went by, I went to my job across the hall on Al for two hours each day. I was beginning to like the work. I believed I was in some small way helping the patients.

I had a burning desire to, first get the hell out of this place, then go back to school and work on a degree which would help me to be an advocate for people who found themselves in a spot such as me. But my foremost thoughts were to find a plan to get out.

The next Friday afternoon as I was reading over my weekly paper, my heart began beating faster as a name beckoned to me from the printed page. I read that Paul had set up his own law practice on Cornwallis Street and was a public defender. The article hadn't said anything about a wife. I was thankful for that. For I still loved him, I had never stopped. But for the last few months there had been thoughts that kept tormenting me, thoughts I'd tried to press deep into the recesses of my mind: What if Paul had found someone in the Peace Corps? Had he tried to contact me? What kind of story would Julia have told him?

I had loved Paul from afar since I had been thirteen years old. He was a high school basketball super star. I don't think he knew I existed back then. But a few years later, everything changed when I returned home from college and he was working his first job with a law firm. We connected through a friend and fell in love. A lifetime of things had happened to me since the October day when I'd said good-by to him at the airport. I closed my eyes, letting my mind take me to that day. It had been a beautiful autumn day, and the Midwest countryside had been ablaze with the beauty of nature. And the sky had been a crystal clear blue. No clouds had dotted the heavens. Paul had said, his handsome face filled with sadness, he still loved me, and would always love me, but he had to go away, to be alone; he had failed his brother. He had to get away from all the things reminding him of his failure.

I didn't think I could let him go. I was overwhelmed at his depression and didn't know what to do to help him. In the last days since the trial, he had become almost a stranger to me. I had watched as his plane carried him away and felt surely my heart was breaking into a million pieces. Paul, just out of law school, had taken on his first big case and had tried to defend his brother who had been charged with embezzling a million dollars from the company of which he was president. Paul had taken the case; sure he could prove his brother innocent. That didn't happen, and his brother was sentenced to ten years in the state penitentiary. Paul blamed himself for not being able to get an innocent verdict. Later, his brother confessed to the crime, then committed suicide.

On the next page of the newspaper, I read about Julia. There was her picture all smiling beautifully as she hosted a charity function. Frustration churned deep in my gut. Julia was going on with her life just like she didn't have a sister trapped in a state hospital.

The next few days, my thoughts were more and more about Paul. I longed to write him, telling him about my imprisonment in the institution. Since Julia had fixed it so I wasn't allowed to write to anyone, I didn't see how writing to Paul was possible. I tried to think of a way I could slip a letter through. But with the way things were set up at Gatewood, I didn't see a way. It was Lee Ann who came up with a plan.

Lee Ann was the only person I trusted. She was the only one, when told there was a conspiracy, who didn't try to tell me I was in denial. I told her all about believing Julia had gotten someone inside Gatewood to conspire with her to keep Dr. Kelso and the others believing I was still having seizures, and most likely insane. And that I wanted to write Paul, that I had read he was a public defender, and I wanted to ask him to help me, but felt there was no way a letter would get through.

"I believe you," Lee Ann said. There was no, why do you think your sister is out to get you? No, you must be imagining things. Just simply, "I believe you." Her saying that meant the world to me and endeared Lee Ann to me forever.

"We can get your letter out of here," Lee Ann whispered. "This evening after supper there is a special program to be on television. I know most patients want to see it and the attendants will want to watch too."

"You write the letter. I'll see it gets out."

I didn't ask how she was going to get a letter out of the hospital. I just got my paper and pen. And when the program came on television I sat at the long table in the day room on A2 and stared at the blank paper lying before me. The only letter I'd ever written to Paul was the one he hadn't answered. How was I to begin? I tried to picture his handsome face as he would open my letter. When he found out I was in a state hospital, would he think me insane, and my writings the words of a crazy person? Would he think my suspicions of Julia were something I had concocted from a deranged mind and were just the ramblings of a patient in a mental hospital? I had almost backed out of writing to Paul when Lee Ann walked by and seeing the blank paper said, "Good Lord, girl you had better get with it and get your letter written and to me before this show is off television. We may never get a chance like this again. Hurry up. You don't want to spend the rest of your life here with me and the rest of them. Do you?"

I began to write. Dear Paul. I longed to write that I loved him, and was constantly remembering those long ago days we had spent together, planning our future. But I didn't know what was in Paul's heart now. I could only hope for the sake of the love we had shared he would believe my words and try to help me.

If I were caught trying to sneak a letter out of the hospital it would automatically mean a trip to C3. The thought of having to go to C3 sent cold shivers down my spine. But I had survived it once and could again, if need be. Rapidly I wrote, telling him I was being kept against my will. That I knew how bizarre my accusations were sounding to him, but he must remember the kind of person he had known, and to ask himself if something like this was possible. I warned him not to let Julia know I had written. That I suspected Julia and someone inside the institution were conspiring to make sure I was forever a patient at Gatewood State Hospital. I told him I had read he was a public defender and I was in desperate need of a defender. I explained about the rules for letters going outside the hospital and this letter was being smuggled. I dared not mentioned Lee Ann, for fear if the letter didn't make it Lee Ann as well as I would be seeing C3. I signed the letter simply, Jordan. I longed to put sent with love, but decided against it. Suppose he no longer had the same feelings for me? What if he had a new love? I didn't want to think about that. I had an extra sheet of paper with scribbles on it, in case the attendant should see me with pen and paper.

I copied Paul's address from the newspaper onto an envelope. I sealed the envelope and slipped it to Lee Ann as she returned from the bathroom. Lee Ann tucked it into her bosom and went to sit beside Miss Abner, who was sitting in a chair at one of the tables near the front of the room. I shut my eyes. What in the world was Lee Ann doing, taking a chance like that!? I didn't like the idea of my letter being close to Miss Abner. I could just see her hawk eyes being able to see my letter through Lee Ann's blouse.

I was able to breathe a little easier when Miss Abner stood up, turned off the television and announced it was time for everyone to go to bed. I almost fainted with fright when Gladys stood up and said in a sang-song voice. "I know something that Lee Ann's got. I seen Jordan giving her a letter." Then she smiled first at me, then at Lee Ann.

"Shut up your mouth, tattletale fool!" Lee Ann said, her face flushed red with anger, and I thought Lee Ann was going to attack Gladys who was standing with her hands on her ample hips looking smugly with a half-smile on her lips.

"Both of you cut it out, now!" Miss Abner said, looking from one to the other. "Lee Ann if you have a letter belonging to Jordan, hand it over," Miss Abner said, holding her hand out to Lee Ann.

I sucked in my breath, thinking, oh God; I'm heading for C3 before this night is over. Everyone's eyes were on Lee Ann. I was aware of the silence of the other patients as I waited. Everything seemed to be in slow motion.

"Come on, Lee Ann," Miss Abner said impatiently. "Give me the letter!"

Lee Ann reached into her blouse and pulled out an envelope. "Here," she said. "Miss Abner, I just borrowed an envelope from Jordan. I didn't know that was against the rules."

I held my breath as Miss Abner examined the envelope and finding it empty returned it to Lee Ann. Glaring at Gladys she said, "Gladys you're going to have to learn to start minding your own business. You almost got this ward in an uproar. Now, go on to bed, all of you." Gladys dejectedly hung her head and shuffled towards the dormitory. Lee Ann looked at me and grinned, then spun around on her heels and marched into the hallway towards her room.

I was still shaking. Lee Ann had to have put two envelopes in her blouse. She had anticipated maybe Gladys or someone telling.

I found it impossible to sleep. I rose upon one elbow and looked around the dimly lit room. Everyone appeared to be sleeping. Gladys had refused to look in my directions as we had prepared for bed. Matilda was sleeping with her thumb in her mouth. Just before she had gotten into her bed she had come up to me and whispered, "Her name is Tillie. Mom calls her Tillie." I whispered back that I knew her name was Tillie. Maylene was happily sleeping on a pillow with a pillowcase which was stamped, in bold black letters, *"Gatewood State Hospital"*.

I was still awake when the night shift came on duty. I closed my eyes as Miss Abner and Mrs. Sullivan made their rounds. They stopped beside my bed. "Gladys tried to get Lee Ann into trouble," Miss Abner whispered so low I could barely hear. "Said Lee Ann had a letter belonging to Jordan. I don't think she really thought she had a letter, I think she wanted to make Lee Ann mad enough to hit her so Lee Ann would get a trip to C3. You know how Gladys is, happiest when one of the other patients is in trouble."

I lay there until they had gone. I then got out of bed and quietly made my way to the dayroom and stood at the desk. The wicker basket was empty. I could hear the muffled voices of the attendants down in the office as the report was being read. When was Lee Ann going to get the letter into the basket? I tiptoed back towards the dormitory. Just then I heard Lee Ann's voice. Looking down the hallway I saw her standing at the office door. "I'm just going to go to the bathroom and then to bed for good, Miss Abner."

I stood in the shadows of the doorway to the dormitory as Lee Ann came swiftly up the hallway, she didn't even slow down at the door to the lavatory. She came straight into the day room and went directly to the desk and dropped an envelope into the basket. I wanted to call out to her, but could hear the attendants talking louder down in the office and thought the afternoon shift were coming out of the office to go home.

Lee Ann barely made it back to the lavatory when the attendants came towards the day room ready to go home, leaving through the day room. One of the night shift attendants was with them to unlock the door and let them out. I didn't have time to make it back to my bed before they passed the dormitory door. I flattened myself against the wall by the door, hoping the attendants would not look into the dormitory and see my empty bed. Luck was with me and they went on through the day room and I heard the keys in the lock.

When I heard the jingle of those keys, I thought I would have enough time to get to my bed before the night shift attendant made it back past the dormitory door. I swiftly made the length of the dormitory and was under the covers when a white blur went past the dormitory door. I lay there for a long time worrying about my letter. Lee Ann had told me she would put Miss Abner's initials where the stamp would be placed. And the supervisor would pick it up when she made her rounds. If all went well, no one would question the initials and the letter would soon be in Paul's hands. Still I was awake until the wee hours of the morning and heard the supervisor come on the ward and leave. I could only hope my letter went with her.

Chapter Ten

The next morning my stomach was in knots. I expected any moment for someone to tap me on the shoulder and tell me I was headed for C3. When we were in line for breakfast, Gladys sauntered over to Lee Ann and smirked, "You did have Jordan's letter. I know it. And I'm gonna tell Nurse Margo. She'll believe me."

"Shut up, tattletale! All you know how to do is, tell, tell, tell!" Lee Ann hissed.

Suddenly Mrs. Sullivan appeared in the office doorway. Shaking her finger at the line of patients, she yelled, "If I hear any more of this fussing, somebody is going to be in big trouble!" Lee Ann flattened herself against the wall, and Gladys quickly found a place in line and turned her face to the wall pouting.

As the week went by, I began breathing easier. I kept a belief in my heart Paul would find a way to help me, and that he would want to. One morning at breakfast, Lee Ann whispered, "I can feel help coming for you. You don't belong here, Jordan. You know it and I know it. We know it's your sister's greed keeping you here. Someday you'll be free like the birds," Lee Ann said, fluttering her hands and fingers above her plate.

"When I get out of here," I whispered, leaning over my plate towards Lee Ann, "I will help you get out, too."

"No! Absolutely not!", Lee Ann said, startling me. "I've told you before I don't belong out there; I have to be here for my Sir Lancelot!" She didn't say anything for a few more minutes, leaving me to wonder why in the world would she want to be in a state hospital! Finally Lee Ann looked at me again and whispered, "If you want my help, you will stop saying anything about me leaving. I'm willing to help you. But, now listen to this good, I'm not going anywhere. This is the only home I've known for more than half my life. So get off my case!"

I was stunned. The last thing I wanted to do was alienate Lee Ann, the only friend I had in this confined world called a state hospital. I gently touched Lee Ann's arm. "Sorry," I whispered.

"Enough said," Lee Ann smiled, looking like her old self again. Suddenly Mrs. Sullivan was at our table. "What's going on?" she demanded. "What's all this whispering about?"

"Oh, we were discussing Gladys' hair," Lee Ann whispered to the attendant. "Do you think she combed it this morning? Look at it, all standing on end."

Mrs. Sullivan glared at us. "Gladys's hair is none of your business", she said curtly. "You had better hurry up and eat or you'll be leaving the dining room without breakfast." But she went directly to Gladys' table and I heard her say Gladys was going to have to comb her hair before coming to breakfast from now on.

Lee Ann leaned forward and whispered, "I get a kick out of seeing how the attendants work. If I hadn't pointed out the hair, she wouldn't have noticed."

By Thursday night, I was feeling much better, believing my letter had made it out of Gatewood. And when Miss Abner announced, "Anybody who wants to go to the dance raise your hand." I put my hand up. Each Thursday night a group of retired business women, called the "Gold Ladies of Harden County," came to Gatewood and hosted a dance in the recreation building.

Lee Ann and several of the others always went. So far I had declined to go. But tonight I thought I'd find out what it was like.

Lee Ann smiled and said, "I'm glad you're going. The only reason I go is to keep in practice for my dancing with Sir Lancelot."

Gladys was dressed in her brightly colored dress she'd worn to the Picnic. And Maylene was telling Miss Abner, "Attendant, Honey, she'll go to the dance if you give her a party dress with her name on it."

"Maylene," Miss Abner said. "There's no party dress on A2. And besides, the bus isn't running tonight. Everyone will have to walk, and you can't make it on your walker."

Maylene began screeching, "The answer to your problem would be to get her a party dress with her name on it!"

Miss Abner stood with her hands on her hips, glaring at Maylene. I thought the attendant would have liked nothing more than to throw Maylene into the side room. Instead, Miss Abner sighed, threw up her hands and matched off towards the clothing room.

Maylene continued to screech, "Give her the party dress! Give her the party dress!"

Soon Miss Abner returned with a brand new state gown which was boldly stamped with ***Gatewood State Hospital.*** "Now, look at this, Maylene," Miss Abner said, holding out the gown. "A beautiful, new gown, and look, it has the name stamped on it. Now if you calm down, you can sleep in this tonight."

Maylene stopped squawking right away and grabbed the gown, examined the bold printing, smiled at Miss Abner and said, "That was the answer to your problem, attendant, honey."

"They always give in to her," I whispered to Lee Ann.

"They can't stand her yelling. It just grates on their nerves something awful. Maylene is the only one who can get to them like that. When she first came here they tried throwing her in the side room, but she still screamed for hours. All the rest of us would have either given up with exhaustion or our voices would have given out on us, but Maylene doesn't know the meaning of giving up. They tried the Thorazine, but she's allergic and almost died once. So they just try to pacify her, and I for one am glad they don't put up with that terrible screeching." I was glad too.

Later I dressed for the dance, putting on a light blue dress the attendant got out of the clothing room for me. This had been one of my favorites, back when I cared about clothes, back when I'd had a life. Lee Ann looked me over saying, "You do look pretty. You will enjoy the dance, if only for the refreshments served. They always have soft drinks and little cakes, and best of all coffee."

Miss Jones was to escort us to the dance. I was thankful Miss Abner was staying behind. In all, ten of us patients walked with the attendant to the recreation building, a few blocks from the Wallace building and past three of the cottages. As we passed Rosa's cottage, I wondered if the little woman was back on the cottage or still locked inside a side room on C3. In the early twilight, a soft, warm wind gently rippled the leaves on several trees lining the walkway. I breathed in the fresh air. How peaceful this place must seem to anyone just driving through these grounds. All the patients seemed in a jovial mood, and Miss Jones joked with some of them about the boyfriends they would be seeing at the dance.

A band from the local high school provided the music. The Gold Ladies tried to get every patient to dance at least one dance. I was asked by several of the male patients to dance and accepted all their invitations, whether I wanted to or not. Some of the patients were obviously retarded. Many others were normal looking and carried on a normal conversation. Lee Ann had said there were so many different levels of intelligence at Gatewood. That the only requirement to get in there was to have someone sign you in and you have a history of seizures: but she'd added, someone has to sign you out, unless you were a Voluntary.

After countless dances, the bottoms of my feet were beginning to get hot and I was out of breath. "I'm going to have to rest awhile," I told my partner, an older man of about fifty.

"Well, missy, you just take a rest if you're tired. I'm gonna dance till the Gold Ladies run me off," he laughed, letting go of my hand. I watched as he headed for a teenager in a pink dress. As he took the girl's hand, he looked back at me and smiled. I smiled and waved, then sank into the nearest chair. It had been years since I'd danced so much.

"Hi, Miss." I turned. A young man in a wheelchair had rolled beside me.

"Hi," I smiled at the handsome, young man.

"I can't dance, you know. But I like to watch. My name is David. I used to be the captain of a football team in Dayton. One day I was just a normal teenager. Then wham, my world ended. I was at a football practice and took a hard hit to my head. When I came to I couldn't walk, and I was an epileptic. You know, I didn't even know what an epileptic was until I started having seizures," he said, looking into my eyes.

I stared at him. *Would this young man be spending the remainder of his life behind the wall?* That thought left me feeling very sad.

"Do you know when you are about to have a seizure?" I asked.

"Oh, yes. I can feel them coming on. I have what they call an aura. I see purple lights. I'm on the drug study and the seizures are coming less often now. There's no cure for epilepsy, as I'm sure you well know. But there is hope it can be controlled with drugs. How're you doing with yours?"

"Why do you think I have seizures?" I asked.

David stared at me for a moment. "Everyone in this hospital has seizures. You aren't in denial, are you?"

Good Lord! Did even the patients think I was in denial? I didn't try to tell him I was not an epileptic; that I'd had a brain injury; that I may or may not have had a few convulsions. And the injury was now healed and I was being kept prisoner here by an evil sister and someone inside Gatewood. Instead I said, "I'm getting better." By now a pretty, young patient came to ask David to dance. David took her hand, and the girl danced around the wheelchair.

There were dancing contests. And I wasn't surprised to see the most treasured prizes were jars of instant coffee. Lee Ann won a large jar for doing the Hula.

When the dance was over and I was walking beside Lee Ann back to the ward, I stopped on the sidewalk and closed my eyes. It was so nice out there in the summer night air. I longed to have the freedom to just sit on one of the benches that were outside each cottage. I yearned to sit in the grass, to take my shoes off and run at will over the grassy hill. These things all, I could have done just a few short months ago, now I had to ask permission to do just the simplest things.

"Come on, Jordan, and get on up here with the rest," Miss Jones's voice broke into my thoughts, reminding me of just how true my thoughts were. I sighed and ran to catch up to the others.

By the time we got back to the ward, it was time for bed. "Jordan," Miss Abner called, as I headed towards the lavatory. "You have an appointment with Dr. Kelso for 10 A.M. tomorrow."

"OK," I said.

"And another thing," Miss Abner added, "your sister will be there."

I felt my heart sank and suddenly felt sick. Would Julia be holding the letter I'd sent to Paul? Would I be getting a trip to C3? I went into the lavatory and was brushing my teeth when Lee Ann came to stand beside me. "I have an appointment with Dr. Kelso for tomorrow, and Julia will be there."

"I heard old Abner telling you," Lee Ann whispered. "Don't worry about the letter. I don't think your young man would give it to your sister."

Just then Miss Abner appeared in the doorway and barked, "You two, cut the whispering and get along to bed." We quickly put our toothbrushes in the cabinet and went our separate ways to bed.

Later, when all the lights were out, except for the one dim one in the hallway letting enough light into the dormitory for the attendants to see if everyone were in bed, I lay in my bed studying the shadows on the wall, feeling hollowness in my stomach. I saw in my mind how Julia would be acting for Dr. Kelso tomorrow. I figured Julia would have a long talk with Dr. Kelso before I even got to the meeting. *Why was Julia coming to Gatewood? Had Paul showed her my letter?* I hugged my pillow, as a feeling of dread swept over me.

It would do no good, and maybe even make my situation worse-if that was possible-, to accuse Julia of keeping me locked up in Gatewood, to Dr. Kelso. After all Julia was the one on the outside, while I was a patient and as Lee Ann had said, *"No one ever believes a patient over an attendant, doctor, or anyone on the outside. That's one of the rules."*

I hoped Lee Ann was right about Paul not giving the letter to Julia. I thought about what I would do when I saw Julia. I knew I would want to verbally, and maybe even physically, attack the woman who had done so much to destroy my life. But wait, Jordan, I asked myself, what would be the wise thing to do? What would great-great grandmother Jordan have done? How would Lee Ann handle it? The worst thing I could do would be to attack Julia. That would give them more reason to keep me locked up. I could almost hear Julia saying, "*See, doctor, I told you. She's dangerous and must be locked up for all eternity, for all our safety.*"

The next morning, I awoke to a beautiful, sun-filled day. I prayed I could get through the meeting with Dr. Kelso and Julia without making myself look like I was definitely in need of being locked up forever. As I dressed, I said a silent prayer God would grant me strength to bear the day without coming apart, and that Julia would not be holding the letter I'd written to Paul.

When I was let out the door to catch the bus for my appointment with Dr. Kelso, Lee Ann also went, to go to her job. As we were walking down the sidewalk, Lee Ann said, "Don't worry. Things will work out. You have a good head on your shoulders. Just watch what you say, weigh each word before it leaves your mouth. Remember, sometimes words you believe are going to hurt your enemy, sometimes end up hurting you more."

I thanked Lee Ann for her advice.

When the bus pulled in at the building where Dr. Kelso's office was located, a new, cream colored Cadillac was parked in one of the parking spaces. I had no doubt whose Cadillac it was. Taking a deep breath, I headed up the walk, wondering what the next few minutes held.

By the time I got to the office door, my heart was pounding wildly. I stood before the door for a moment, breathing deeply. Please, please let me appear calm, I silently prayed as I opened the door.

The secretary looked up and smiled as I entered. "Well, good morning, Jordan. Dr. Kelso said to send you right in. Your sister is already here."

I smiled, thinking, yeah, I bet that devil has been here for some time, filling Dr. Kelso full of lies. I felt hot anger beginning to rise up within me, but Lee Ann's words seemed to be overcoming the anger. I could almost hear my friend saying, *"Remember it is not how your words will hurt your enemy, but how they are going to hurt you."* I went through the door into the office, praying for wisdom and a tight tongue.

Julia was standing by the window, elegantly dressed in a light blue knit dress. I had to admit she looked beautiful. Beautiful until you saw her eyes. I had always thought Julia had the coldest eyes I'd ever looked into. I had noticed that when I'd been a small child. Why couldn't Dr. Kelso see that?

Dr. Kelso greeted me. "Jordan, how are you doing this beautiful day?"

I managed to mumble I was fine. Julia smiled at me. I just looked at my sister, thinking what a fake smile she has. "Jordan dear, you do look a bit pale," Julia said. "Dr. Kelso and I were just discussing you."

I'll just bet you were, I thought, wanting to shake Julia and demand to know how in God's name she could do what she was doing to her sister, or any other human being. But I knew I could not act on my feelings. I just hoped Julia didn't have the letter I'd written to Paul.

Julia smiled sweetly, "Is there anything you need, dear?"

"Yes, Julia, I need to go home. Did you come to take me home today?"

"Now, Jordan, you know, I can't take you home until your seizures are under control. And this other problem you've been having. I know the doctors have told you these things must be resolved. What I meant was do you need a bit more money for personal items?" Without waiting for me to answer, Julia turned to again look out the window.

I wanted to scream: *You know full well I'm not having seizures! And I'm not insane either! You and someone inside Gatewood are keeping me here!* Instead, I took a deep breath and said, "Sure, I can use more money for the canteen."

"By the way, Paul was over to see me," Julia said, turning from the window and looking directly at me.

I froze, hardly breathing as a wave of terror like a giant hand twisted at my insides. *Oh, God, now Julia is going to bring out the letter and Dr. Kelso will know I smuggled it out! I'm headed for C3!* I felt I was going to start hyperventilating and I might even throw up right there in the doctor's office.

"Jordan, are you all right?" Dr. Kelso was saying. "You look so pale."

"I'm, I'm ok," I managed to say.

"One of the reasons I'm here today," Julia said, "I thought I had better come down here and have a talk with your psychiatrist. Paul somehow found out you were in Gatewood. --He's back from the Peace Corps--I told him the first time he came and asked about you that you were out of town working and didn't want anyone to contact you. I didn't tell anyone about you being in the state hospital," Julia added, throwing up her hands. "But somehow he found out. He's claiming there's a new law allowing people like you to have an advocate. He's planning on becoming yours. I think his being away in the Peace Corps turned him into some sort of social nut. Now, of course, you don't need an advocate. I will always represent you. I'm going to ask Gatewood's superintendent to put a stop to all this nonsense. You don't want an advocate. I told that to Dr. Kelso. But he insisted the law is you have to make the decision yourself," Julia said, looking a bit perturbed towards Dr. Kelso. "Now, Jordan just tell the kind doctor you don't want this advocate. You won't have to be bothered with ever seeing Paul again. You can concentrate on getting your seizures and other problems under control. After all, Paul did lose that case with his brother. And the scandal is still the talk of the town. You don't want to get messed up with him again."

I looked at Dr. Kelso. My brain was spinning. *An advocate! Was this possible! And Paul had tried to find me when he'd returned from the Peace Corps.* My heart soared. "May I have an advocate, Dr. Kelso?" I asked, as Julia sucked in her breath.

"That's the new law. You will be allowed to meet with your advocate once per month." Dr. Kelso said. "We have to give it a try if you so request. Mind you, a trial run is what we have to give it. After an evaluation, if the staff in a state institution find the advocate is hindering the patient's progress, then we can terminate the advocacy."

I thought, the advocacy would certainly be terminated, Julia and the person or persons inside Gatewood would see to it. But maybe, just maybe, by that time, with Paul's help, I could expose Julia and whoever else was responsible for keeping me there.

"I think it's a stupid law!" Julia said.

"Well, now, maybe not" Dr. Kelso said. "I think it might help Jordan in her recovery to see an old boyfriend."

I was glad to see Dr. Kelso approved. I had for some time now thought he might be one of the people responsible for the false reports. I was seeing the little man in a different light now. Perhaps he did care about me in his own way.

"Would you like to stay and visit with Jordan and perhaps have lunch with her?" Dr. Kelso said, smiling at Julia.

"Oh, No," Julia said quickly, fluttering her hands. "I really would like to, but you see, I have a previous engagement: An appointment: A very important appointment. And I regret I have to get back to Harper City."

I left the doctor's office feeling hopeful that I might have a chance of getting out of Gatewood. Julia was still in Dr. Kelso's office, said she needed to talk with the doctor. I thought she was making one last desperate attempt to try and get my advocate taken away. But I knew if it was the law it would not be taken away without first giving it a chance. Because at Gatewood there was much respect for the law by *"the powers that be"*.

I could hardly wait until Lee Ann got in from her job. As soon as I saw her come up the walk, I went into the lavatory and waited for her to come in there. "Lee Ann!" I whispered, grabbing her arm. "We did it! The letter got through."

"I told you it would. Didn't I?" Lee Ann said smiling. "Girl, we'll get you out of here yet."

Just then Gladys passed the lavatory and looking in saw us whispering and said, "I'm a telling Mrs. Holt you two are in there whispering and plotting."

"Tattletale fool!" Lee Ann hissed.

"Lee Ann," I whispered, as Gladys ran towards the day room yelling for Mrs. Holt. "I have to find out who is conspiring with Julia. I have to know who inside Gatewood is helping her do such a terrible thing. I don't doubt the reason. I think she's paying them big bucks, and using my money to do it."

"We'll find out, honey. Remember I have a key. It unlocks the office door, too. The records are in there. We'll become detectives just like Dick Tracy or Miss Marple or Philip Marlowe."

Suddenly Mrs. Holt was in the doorway, "You two quit loitering in here."

For the next two days, I constantly thought about what I would do and say when Paul came. They hadn't told me what day he was coming, but on Thursday, Mrs. Holt called me to the desk. "You have been told about the new advocacy program. One will be visiting you on Monday."

I almost jumped for joy. "Now, there are rules you and the advocate must follow," Mrs. Holt said. "You may go to the canteen with the advocate or sit outside on one of the benches. The visit is to last not more than one hour. And by the way you have an appointment with Dr. Thorpe for tomorrow morning, just a routine exam.

The next morning I went to Dr. Thorpe office. He smiled kindly at me and I was relieved the anger, I'd witnessed coming from him that day he'd caught me in his files, was gone. Another patient now had my old job, an older woman. I remembered seeing her at the dance.

"I see your seizures have increased greatly this week," Dr. Thorpe said, reading from a folder in his hand. I wanted to scream that it was a terrible lie, but knew he would only say I was in denial. "Have you been under any unusual stress this week? How was your visit with your sister? I met briefly with her while she was here. How do you feel about having an advocate?"

"You know about that?"

"Of course. I was on the panel that approved it. It is only for a trial run. You do know that, don't you?"

"Yes, Dr. Kelso explained it to me."

"You do know your sister and Dr. Cole are against this, but it's the law so we have to give it a chance."

Dr. Cole? I thought. Why would he be against it? Of course, Julia had gone to him and told him all sorts of things to try to get him to use his influence on the rulers at Gatewood.

I left Dr. Thorpe's office knowing I was going to have to get into the attendants' office and have a look at my records. I desperately needed the names of the person or persons who were filing the false reports to give to Paul. The thought I could get caught sent shivers of fear all through me. If I were caught I'd be spending Monday in a smelly side room on C3, instead of an hour with the man I loved. But something deep inside me told me I could get in there, see my records and not get caught. Perhaps it was the spirit of old Jordan giving me strength; perhaps it was my believing Paul was coming back into my life; perhaps it was a belief in my own self.

On Saturday mornings some of the patients worked in the dormitory cleaning and changing linens on the beds. (This was a weekly routine at Gatewood). And Lee Ann always helped clean for those who couldn't do it for themselves. As I swiped the dust mop under my bed I whispered to Lee Ann, "I'm going to try and get into the attendant's office sometime today or tomorrow. Could I please have your key?"

Lee Ann didn't reply right away. She looked at me and then to the floor, and when she finally replied, the bottom dropped out of my heart. "I can't let my keys go into anyone else's hands," Lee Ann whispered, finally looking me in the eyes.

"But, I tell you what I will do. I'll unlock the office and you can get in there on your own."

"When will you do this?" I whispered, noticing Gladys was standing over in the corner, staring at us. And I thought Gladys would be heading for the day room to tell the attendant we weren't working, but gossiping instead.

"Tonight. I will unlock the door tonight," Lee Ann whispered even lower, and I noticed Gladys was creeping closer. Lee Ann continued, "I heard Miss Abner just last night telling Miss

Jones that Saturday night there will be a special on television and she intended to watch it. It's that singing fool, Elvis, everyone is so crazy over. Old Abner is planning on making a party of it. One is to bring the popcorn, the other the cokes. I'll wait until they're engrossed in the program then I'll unlock the door. Then, honey, you'll be on your own. I'm sorry, but I can't let my keys into your hands or anyone's. My keys are my only link to Sir Lancelot."

I looked at Lee Ann and nodded. "I understand."

Just then Gladys appeared at Lee Ann's elbow. "I'm a telling Mrs. Holt you and Jordan are up to something, Lee Ann. If you don't tell me what you're whispering about."

"Get out of here, you tattletale shitass," Lee Ann barked.

Anger flushed Gladys's red face making it even redder than was the norm. She ran towards the day room yelling, "Mrs. Holt! Mrs. Holt! Lee Ann and Jordan are back there whispering! They're up to something!"

By the time Mrs. Holt appeared in the dormitory doorway, Lee Ann was clear across the room turning a mattress on a bed in the corner. I viciously swept under a bed. Out of the corners of my eyes, I could see Mrs. Holt standing in the doorway with her hands on her hips staring at me. After a moment the attendant turned and went into the day room yelling for Gladys.

For the remainder of the day, I could hardly sit still. "What is wrong with you?" Mrs. Holt asked. "You sure are fidgety today"

"I'm just excited about my visitor coming on Monday." I had to believe Lee Ann actually had a key and would find a way to get to the office and unlock the door. What I was worried about was my own ability to get out of the dormitory and into the hallway to the office without being seen. All sorts of things flashed through my mind: What if the electricity went off and the attendants didn't get to watch their program? Stop it! Stop it! I scolded myself. Don't think about all the bad that could happen. Think about finding out who is behind the conspiracy to keep you here.

After Miss Abner had turned off the television and announced it was time to get to bed, I lingered in the lavatory hoping to be able to speak to Lee Ann

But Gladys was also lingering in the bathroom. Soon Miss Abner appeared in the doorway telling us to get on to bed.

I lay on my bed. It seemed all the other patients were taking an extra-long time to get to sleep. First it was Maylene. She discovered her pillowcase didn't have *"her name"* on it. I could have slapped myself. I had been the one that very morning who had changed Maylene's bed. I hadn't even looked or thought about the pillowcase having the state hospital stamp on it. Not all the linens were stamped, most were. Leave it to me to mess up, I thought. Maylene promptly got out of bed, pulled the pillowcase off the pillow and draped it over her walker. I quickly took my own pillowcase off my pillow. Seeing it had the stamp on it, I went across the room to Maylene. "Look, Maylene. Here's a pillowcase with your name on it"

Maylene looked at me and smiled. "No, honey, that ain't her name either. The attendant will get her one."

I was losing patience with the little, black-eyed woman, and almost shouted, "It's the same thing they will give you! The very same thing!"

“No, it ain’t, honey,” Maylene said and began inching her walker past me.

By now Gladys was out of bed and seeing an opportunity to have something to tell the attendants said, "I'm a gonna tell Miss Abner. I'm a gonna tell you are trying to make Maylene take your old pillowcase."

"Oh, shut up, you old turdhead!" I shouted, hardly believing the words coming out of my mouth. In defeat I went back to my own bed, taking my pillowcase with me, while Gladys went off to find the attendants and tell. And Maylene slowly scooted her walker, with the stampless pillowcase draped across it, down the aisle towards the day room calling, "Attendant, honey. She’s gotta have a pillowcase with her name on it."

I put my pillowcase back on my pillow and lay on my bed. Soon Miss Abner was in the doorway, followed closely by Gladys. Miss Abner flipped on the overhead lights. "What's going on in here?" she demanded.

Maylene was still shuffling down the aisle, "I say there, attendant honey. The answer to your problem would be to give her a pillowcase with her name on it."

"Damn it, Maylene," Miss Abner said, sighing in disgust. "Get on back to bed, and I'll get the stupid pillowcase."

Maylene said, "Ok, attendant honey." But she made no attempt to turn her walker around. I knew the little woman would not make a move toward the bed until an attendant laid a pillow case, with *"her"* name on it, over the walker.

Miss Abner turned to go get the pillowcase. "But Miss Abner, Jordan was---"Gladys protested.

"Oh, shut it up, Gladys!" Miss Abner said. "I've about put up with all I care to out of any of you!" With that she swiftly walked away towards the linen room.

After Maylene had been given a pillowcase with *"her name"* on it and had put it on the pillow, and the attendant had turned out the lights, I thought surely everyone but me would soon get to sleep. Not so. Mossie couldn't find her dog and was crawling on the floor, frantically looking, in the dim light, under all the beds, calling, "Koko! Koko!" Gladys was out of bed in a flash, on her way to *tell.*

In a matter of minutes, the overhead lights were on again. Miss Abner and Miss Jones stood in the doorway, looking very angry. "Now, what is the matter in here!?" Miss Abner demanded.

Gladys, looking smugly, returned to her bed and sat down, surveying everyone. Mossie came out from under one of the beds crying, "My Koko is lost! I gotta find my Koko!"

"Mossie, you get your tail in that bed, now!" Miss Abner yelled.

Instead of obeying, Mossie threw herself onto the floor and began kicking and screaming, "Koko! I have to find my Koko!"

Miss Abner looked at Miss Jones and said, "Oh, shit! Now, we'll have to throw her in the side room, and call the nurse to get a shot of Thorazine. Do you know how long that's gonna take?"

I was thinking the attendants were thinking they would be missing their Elvis show. And I would be missing a chance to get into the office. At that moment I hated Mossie.

Finally, Miss Jones said, "Why don't we just find the damn dog?"

Miss Abner was looking like she liked that idea, but said, "Jones, you know we can't encourage her hallucinations. We'd be in big trouble if anyone found out."

"Who's to know?" Miss Jones asked. "We'll just find the dog. The program starts in fifteen minutes. By the time we get security down here to help put her in the side room and Old Margo gets here, gives the shot, and lectures and leaves, it will be time for us to go home."

Miss Abner weighed that for a few seconds then said, "Ok, Mossie. We'll find Koko." Miss Abner squatted down on the floor by Mossie's bed and looked under it. "Here he is, Mossie. He's hiding under your bed. I got him. See," she said, holding her hand up in the air as if she was holding something.

Mossie must have seen what the attendant wanted her to see, for she quickly jumped up from the floor and ran to Miss Abner, and reached into the air above the attendant's hand. Mossie began stroking the air above her arm and said, "My, Koko. You don't run away and hide again." Soon Mossie was in her bed with the imaginary dog safely tucked under her arm. The attendants sighed and turned off the light and all was finally quiet in the dormitory on A2.

After what seemed like hours, I heard the low sounds of the television coming from the day room. I eased upon one elbow and looked around the shadowy dormitory. Everyone looked as if they were sleeping: Everyone except Gladys. Old Gladys was raised upon one elbow staring directly at me. Damn her, I thought, laying back down. If she ruins my chance to get into the office, I'll break her neck. I was surprised at some of the thoughts coming across my brain lately.

I lay very quietly for several minutes. I looked towards Gladys' bed. Gladys appeared to be sleeping. As quietly as I could, I slipped out of bed, and made my way towards the doorway, inching past Gladys's bed. Gladys was snoring softly. I breathed a sigh of relief. As I passed Matilda bed, she opened her eyes and I froze. Matilda smiled and whispered, "Her name is Tillie. Mom calls her Tillie."

"I know, Tillie," I whispered, reaching down to pull the sheet up to Tillie's chin. "You go to sleep now, Tillie." Matilda closed her eyes and happily returned to sleep. I thought if anything else happened I was going to have a heart attack before I even got out of the dormitory. I pressed against the wall and looked around the door into the dayroom. I was delighted to see the two attendants were captivated by the Elvis program, their backs to me, sitting in two of the cushioned chairs. I quickly covered the few feet across the dayroom to the hallway. Just then the phone rang and I darted into the lavatory knowing the attendant answering the phone could see into the hallway. I stood there in the darkened lavatory, feeling comforted by the shadows.

Miss Abner annoyingly said "Hello". The conversation only lasted a few yeses and nos. Then Miss Abner said, "Jones that was the dumb attendants over on Al wanting to know if we knew Elvis was on television."

I stood in the lavatory for just one more moment. If I was going to do this I had better not waste any more time and get on with it. I stuck my head out of the doorway, looking first towards the day room then towards the office. Lee Ann was strolling up the hallway, coming from the direction of the linen room and her private room, stopping in front of the office.

Lee Ann looked towards the day room and seeing me with my head stuck out of the lavatory doorway smiled. Reaching into a pocket of her robe, she produced a key and calmly unlocked the office door. She returned the key to her pocket, looked at me and gave the OK sign, then quickly turned and went back down the hallway, disappearing around the corner of the linen room.

My heart was beating faster than ever now, but I came out of the lavatory and went as fast and as quietly as I could to the office door. My palms were sweaty as I tried to turn the knob on the door. After wiping my hand on my robe, I tried again. The knob turned. The door made a small squeaky sound as I pulled it open far enough to get through. I hesitated for just an instant; the faint sounds of the television were still coming from the dayroom. I inched on into the room. My knees trembled as I sat down at the desk. The clock on the wall was at fifteen minutes till the hour. Elvis would be off the air in just fifteen minutes. I stared at the rows of metal charts in the chart rack. My hands shook as I pulled out one marked Jordan Walker.

I hugged the chart to my chest, thinking I was holding my whole life in my hands. With trembling fingers I opened the chart. The first thing I saw was a picture of me, looking like something out of a gangster movie. I remembered them taking that picture when I had gone for the first EEG. No time to be concerned about that, I thought and began to read.

It stated on page two that the history on this twenty-three-years-old female had been given by her well-educated sister. As I read on, I became more enraged with the lies Julia had told. She'd told I had been institutionalized as a child and my parents had used a fake name. I could hardly believe what was in the report. She'd told I had at the age of seven drowned my kitten. Dr. Kelso had asked me about that in my first session with him. God, what a wicked person my sister is, I thought as I read on. No wonder the staff at Gatewood thought I was a crazy person. The only truth about the kitten was I'd had one when I was seven years old. The kitten had disappeared. A horrible thought crossed my mind. Why would Julia have said it had drowned? Maybe Julia drowned it herself. That thought sent shivers through me. I read I had cut up all my mother's clothes. And that I had pulled a knife on my father and stabbed him in the leg. My God, I thought. How could someone make us such terrible things about their own sister? As I read on about the bizarre person I was supposed to have been, I began to realize my sister was not only a truly evil person but quite possibly very sick as well.

On the next page I found a document from the court. **Jordan Katelin Walker** was clearly printed at the top. And in bold lettering was the statement **Court Committed**. I almost went into a panic. How could that be? *I was admitted as a **Temporary!** Where was it stated about my ninety days! Dr. Cole had said ninety days!* I remembered going to a court, but Julia and Dr. Cole had told me in was just a formality to get me into the state hospital for the drug study. That day I could barely walk and had taken extra medication Dr. Cole had given me. He said I'd had a terrible seizure and the medication was to ward off another attack. I barely remember Julia and the doctor taking me into a court room. A judge and other people were there. Julia had put me in a chair and I passed out. When I came to, Julia was shaking me, telling me it was done.

In the document it was stated that a Psychiatrist: a Dr. Jacob Massingale was present at the hearing and had met with me on several occasions and that I was definitely mentally ill. Diagnoses: Paranoia. Schizophrenia. He recommended Gatewood State Hospital. Oh, *My God! Oh, My God!* How can this be? I had never heard of this person. My mind was racing, my heart pounding. And I still didn't know who was recording my false seizures and the other behaviors. I glanced at the clock, only seven more minutes before Elvis would be off the air. *"Please, Elvis hold the attendants' attention for just a few more minutes,"* I whispered, as I desperately searched through the chart. I finally found what I was looking for, written in my progress notes. I had believed most likely Miss Abner was the one who was charting the false seizures and behaviors.

The first entry about my seizures was the day after I'd had the first EEG. I stared in disbelief at the signature; the entry was signed by Mrs. Holt. I could hardly believe what I was seeing. I felt sick. Reading on, I found that only Mrs. Holt had recorded seizures on me. She'd also written that I often talked to myself, and sometimes conversed with an imaginary figure. And that I might even be planning to harm my sister. She wrote that I was a danger to others, and had attacked an attendant when I'd only been in Gatewood two days--(that was the only truth she'd written). I read on. She'd noted that C3 was where I most likely belonged. With my heart breaking, I wondered if she could get me sent to C3 for eternity. No one else had written anything about my seizures or bizarre behaviors. *Why wouldn't someone question the fact that this one employee was the only one who witnessed such things?*

There was also a report from Dr. Kelso. He wrote that I was in denial of all my problems. And all evidence pointed to my being mentally ill. And that I had a history of mental illness. He wrote that my sister had reported that our mother had episodes of mental illness, and he thought that most likely I had inherited it.

By now I was shaking and blinking back tears. *My God, how could someone do such horrible things?* I wanted to stay and read the entire chart, but knew I had to get out of there. Reluctantly, I returned the chart to the rack. The clock read two minute till eleven. I eased the office door open. I looked up the hall and seeing no one, went out the door, closing it as quietly as I could; it gave off a small squeak. I eased up the hallway until I got to the day room. The program had ended. The attendants were stretching. I darted across the corner of the day room to the dormitory door. As I went through the door I heard an announcer saying Elvis had left the building. I pressed myself up against the wall inside the door near Matilda's bed; afraid to go on back to my bed else the attendants might see me.

"God, I sure do love Elvis," I heard Miss Abner say. The voices on the television were silent as the attendant turned it off.

"Abner, I'll go on back to the office and finish filling out the report before the night shift gets here, if you will straighten up here," Miss Jones said. I heard the rustle of her uniform as she walked by the dormitory door. Seconds later: "Abner!" Miss Jones yelled, "You left the damn office door unlocked."

Miss Abner raced across the dayroom and stood in the doorway to the hall. "I did not leave it unlocked!" she said hatefully. "I never leave a door unlocked since somebody stole my keys!"

"Well, its unlocked now. How do you explain that?" Miss Jones said. I saw my chance to make it to my bed and high-tailed it across the dormitory. I jumped into bed, pulling the covers up over my head. I could still faintly hear the attendants arguing. I lay there for a long time, as despair and grief surged through me. Such lies Julia had told, not only about me, but about our dear mother. How could she have done something so horrible? And Mrs. Holt. She was the last person I would have suspected of conspiring with Julia. I remembered the young woman who did my EEG saying she had family from Harper City and Mrs. Holt was her sister. And her aunt was Julia's friend.

The aunt lived in Cincinnati, and was still Julia's friend. I felt that it all had to be connected.

As I lay in my bed, I was able to stop the tears, but couldn't do anything about my broken heart.

After the night shift made their rounds, I got out of bed and stood looking out the window. The stars were shining so brightly they looked like millions of diamonds. Could one of those diamonds really be my ancestor? For an instant I thought I saw a dark cloud roll across the stars, but it was going faster and didn't seem as big as it usually did. I had never mentioned the cloud to Dr. Thorpe or to Dr. Kelso for fear they would say I was insane. Well, they thought I was insane anyway, dear old Julia and Mrs. Holt had seen to that.

Chapter Eleven

Monday dawned a beautiful day. Not a cloud sailed across the perfect blue skies over Saberville. And not one showed its face above the walled village just on the outskirts of the city on that Monday morning in late August. I felt happy and anxious knowing I would soon be seeing Paul.

I had been at Gatewood for more than ninety days now. By all rights I should have been gone, I thought as I stood at the day room window, looking out on the sunlit day. By rights, I should never have been sent here. But thinking of what was right and wrong would not set me free from these walls. Thinking about what I could do about it would set me free, must set me free.

Mrs. Holt sat at the desk doing paper work. I turned from the window and just stared at her for some time, trying to see the evil lurking behind that kind-looking face. What had Lee Ann said on that first day I was here*? 'Some of these people aren't at all what they seem.'* Had she been trying to warn me? Did Lee Ann know what Mrs. Holt really was? I had talked very little with Lee Ann since Saturday. Every time I tried, Gladys was right at our elbows, her ears poised to hear anything she could *"tell".* I had managed to mouth, "Thank you." Lee Ann had smiled and nodded.

I had hoped I would be allowed to pick out my own clothes for this special day. I was disappointed with what had been laid out for me to wear, (it was the worst dress I owned, a gray one). I had asked Mrs. Sullivan if I could choose my clothes, although I knew well what the answer would be. Mrs. Sullivan had looked at me like I'd asked for a piece of the moon. "Missy, you will wear what is laid out for you. We can't be running back to the clothing room every time someone doesn't like what has been chosen for them."

"But it is a special day for me," I said.

Mrs. Sullivan had retorted, "You're not special. You're no better than the others. And the others don't get to pick out their own clothes."

I had felt such burning hate for the woman at that moment. I thought Mrs. Sullivan was the most hateful person in the world, even more hateful than Julia and Mrs. Holt, they were evil, Mrs. Sullivan was pure hateful. So here I was standing in a day room in a state hospital waiting for the man I loved. *Oh, God what is he going to think of me?* Just then Lee Ann came into the day room and handed me a little white collar. "To dress up your dress a bit," she said.

"Thank you, Lee Ann," I said, taking the collar. Looking around, I saw there was no one within ten feet of us. "I got into the office," I whispered. "'I know who is conspiring with Julia. Mrs. Holt is reporting the seizures. And other weird lies."

Lee Ann didn't look at all surprised. "I told you, didn't I, some of them aren't what they seem," she stared at the attendant for a moment; then turned back to me. "Has to be a lot of money in it for her. I'd sure as hell like to know how they are pulling this off. Do you think they hold meetings and take notes? Surely there are more people in on it than just your sister and old Holt."

"I believe the EEG technician is involved. She is Mrs. Holt's sister, and their aunt is a friend of Julia's. "

"Wow!" Lee Ann said. "A family affair."

Suddenly Mrs. Holt yelled, "Lee Ann, get on out there and catch the bus." Lee Ann raced for the door. I watched her hurry down the walk and get on the green bus, wishing there was something I could do to help my friend. But I thought of how Lee Ann reacted every time I said anything about her getting out of Gatewood. I didn't like the thought that this was the world Lee Ann wanted.

I went into the lavatory and put on the collar. The collar did something for the drab gray dress. Staring at the pale faced young woman looking back at me from the mirror, I pinched my cheeks to bring color to them. Mama had always been proud of my clear skin. A deep sadness fell upon me as I thought of her. It would have grieved my mother terribly to have known one daughter was in a state hospital, and the other was behind it all. *Had Mama ever seen the evil side of Julia*?

Paul was to arrive at ten o'clock. In the meantime, Mrs. Holt laid down a few rules for me. "I know this advocate person is an old boyfriend of yours. I want you to know you are not to hang onto him. You are to behave like a lady. There is to be no hugging or kissing. I want you to set a good example for the other patients. I warn you, should you even bend these rules, your advocacy will be terminated."

I was surprised Mrs. Holt would warn me. Why wouldn't a person in Mrs. Holt position (in cahoots with Julia) want me to fail?

I got the answer when I heard the booming voice of Nurse Margo coming from the other side of the room. "Very good, Mrs. Holt. I think you explained the rules very well." And Jordan, I hope you do as well in keeping with the rules."

"Nurse Margo, I will go strictly by the rules," I said, thanking my lucky stars Margo had been there to see that Mrs. Holt explained the rules. For once old Margo didn't look so intimidating. I could almost have hugged her. I believed if it hadn't have been for Nurse Margo, Mrs. Holt would only have written in my report that the rules had been given to me. And anything I would have said to deny it would not have been believed; my link with Paul and the outside world would have been snatched away before I had a chance. For I knew I would have at least hugged Paul. Now thanks to Margo, I knew the smallest sign of affection would most likely end the advocacy.

It was five minutes till ten when Paul came up the walk, the pass he had gotten at the switchboard in his hand. I stood at the window in the day room and watched him. He looked taller and thinner and a bit older than I remembered. I felt a tug at my heart. *God, I love him so.*

I wondered: Had his being away in the Peace Corps affected his old love for me? Would my being a patient in a state hospital affect his love? Was he the same man I had said good-by to so many months ago? How could he be? I was certainly not the same.

Soon Paul was at the door. Mrs. Holt went to answer the door. I knew he would not be allowed to come on the ward and would have to wait in the small vestibule just outside the door. Mrs. Holt came back inside. "Jordan, your advocate is here."

My heart was beating hard as I went to the door. Paul, more handsome than I remembered, smiled his old smile, as I stepped into the vestibule. I wanted to throw myself into his arms, but held out my hand and shook Paul's hand. "It's so good to see you, Paul. How are you?"

Paul held my hand and looked into my eyes. "Jordan it's so good to see you. How are you doing?"

"Paul there is so much to say. So much I need to tell you," I said low so Mrs. Holt couldn't hear if she was standing, listening on the other side of the door. "We can sit outside on one of the benches if you like." As we walked out onto the lawn, I made sure I didn't walk too close to Paul.

We sat under the maple tree on a park bench. I turned to Paul. "Every move I make is being closely watched."

"Jordan," Paul began, "When I got your letter, I was so stunned I didn't know what to do or think. I had no idea you were in a hospital. When I first came back from the Peace Corp, and went to your house to see about you, Julia said you were away working and didn't want any contact from anyone. And then in your letter you said you were kept against your will. I read the letter several times.

I looked into his eyes and saw the concern. Dare I believe love was there also? I ached to throw myself into his arms and feel the comfort of having those arms holding me close. *Can't do that. Maybe he wouldn't want me to.* "I know it all sounds unbelievable Paul," I said. "I was so afraid you would think I was in here because I'm crazy. If anyone would read what is written about me, I know they would think me insane. I got a look at my record and Mrs. Holt is conspiring with Julia. Everyone will believe what is in the record! Such horrible things about me have been written, and I can't do anything about it!" I knew I was beginning to sound hysterical; my voice was shaking and I was about to burst into tears. "I feel that I'm in a horrible nightmare, and I can't find a way out!"

"Easy, Jordan," Paul said, starting to put an arm around my shoulders. I quickly pulled away. "We're being watched. Can't touch. I know all I'm telling you sound like I'm paranoid, and totally a nut case. But please remember what I was like, who I was before you went away. I'm still inside here," I said, putting a hand over my heart, as tears stung my eyes.

"I managed to get into the office and read my chart. I found a court order that said I was court committed. I found nothing about the ninety days that Dr. Cole told me I was coming here for. He said I was coming here for a drug study! And there was a report from a psychiatrist, a Jacob Massingale, who I'd never met. He had written he'd met with me several times and that I was insane! And he recommended I be placed in Gatewood!" I looked into Paul's eyes and saw anger and pain.

"My God! How could something like this happen?" Paul said his voice stressed. "I'll find out what can be done. There has to be a way to expose them! I feel so helpless. I want to take you out of here. But with Julia being your guardian, she has total say. I know a judge who might help. We'll have to go through the system. To charge someone with a crime as serious as your sister has committed has got to be backed up with proof. I'll begin working today on getting proof."

"You believe me, Paul?" I whispered.

"Of course I believe you." Paul said. "I've known who and what you are since forever. I went to see Julia again, being careful like you warned in your letter not to let her know you had contacted me. She told me such horrible lies. All that stuff about when you were a little girl and had such problems. She told me it had been kept a secret but you had been institutionalized when you were a child. I didn't believe any of that. She said your parents admitted you under a false name and you were in a private hospital, so she wasn't able to give Gatewood your record."

"Good God, Paul, she has gone to such extremes to put me here and to keep me here! I was never in an institution when I was a child!"

"I know," Paul said. "When we get her into court, we'll be able to prove all that."

"You don't know her, Paul. I'm so afraid she will find a way to prove me insane and to keep me locked up forever!"

"No honey. She cannot do that. We will expose her, and she'll be the one locked up. Now, it can't be done in a day, but we will find a way!" Paul said fiercely

"I think Dr. Cole may have something to do with all this. Dr. Thorpe told me he was against my having an advocate."

"At Julia's insistence, I went to see Dr. Cole and I also think he's in on it. There was something about him I didn't trust.

And then he started telling me about you. He said you had terrible seizures when you were in the clinic, and there were other things too. He said he believed the accident had damaged your brain and in addition to your epilepsy, you were having hallucinations. A real doctor would never have shared that information with a total stranger. I'm having him checked out. Even the certificate claiming he's a doctor looked like a fake to me."

"That hurts me so much that he would say such things about me. I thought he was my friend."

"I ran into Thomas one day," Paul said. "He gave me an ear full. He said he found out Julia and Dr. Cole had been having an affair for years."

"To get the goods on them, I must let them think I believe them." Paul was looking into my eyes. "You must trust me. We must never forget they are desperate people, and they have gone to great lengths to set up this plan. I believe they are capable of anything to see it all through. I can go through the system and try to expose them, but it will take time. You must be brave and believe it will all work out in the end. It breaks my heart to have to leave you here. But I know for today there's not a damn thing I can do about it," Paul said with so much distress in his voice I wanted to put my arms around him and tell him not to worry.

All too soon our time was up and it was time for Paul to leave. I didn't know how I was going to bear to let him go. There was so much I wanted to ask him. I didn't even know how things had gone while he had been away in South America. "How was your trip to South America," I asked as we walked back to the ward.

"I grew up a lot while I was there, Jordan. I found out what is really important in this life. I found out I can't always win. I thought I could save my brother, but it was my brother who would have had to save himself. I took all my brother's problems on myself. So sad, such a promising young life wasted. There is not a thing I can do about it, so I have to try to let it go," Paul said, shaking his head. "But most of all I found out just how much you mean to me, Jordan. I love you more than life. I want nothing more than to take you in my arms right this moment and take you away from this place. I want to kiss you and say be damn with the system that says if I do we will be barred from seeing each other because of a rule some people made up!" Paul said, his voice trembling. I saw the frustration in his eyes. “We will get them! I promise you that!"

"Paul, please be careful. I believe they will stop at nothing."

"Don't worry about me. You just hang strong until all this is over. I’m so sorry we can only meet once a month. Hopefully by the next time we meet you will be out of here."

I knocked on the door and Mrs. Holt came to let me in. I told Paul good-by not knowing how I was going to stand to walk back inside that door. But I knew I must. I stood at the day room window and watched as Paul got into his car and drove away. I had such a hopeless, sinking feeling in the pit of my stomach. Would I ever see him again? Would something happen to my only contact with the outside world?

Soon it was time to go to lunch. I had been excused from going to work until after lunch. Mrs. Holt let me in on Al on the way back from lunch. I had missed the feeding but would get in on the changing.

Gladys, who was already on the ward working, came up to me as soon as she realized I had arrived. "So, you seen your old boyfriend today?" Gladys said, leaning her head to one side, and squinting her left eye.

"What are you talking about, Gladys?" I asked, not really wanting to be bothered with the biggest tattletale I had ever known.

"Well, now, I heard old Nurse Margo down there in the attendants’ office this morning, just before I left to go to the canteen. She was a talking to Mrs. Holt. I heard her say your old boyfriend was a coming to see you and they had better keep a close watch out on you. I said I would watch you for em, but they said to mind my own business, and they asked me if I wanted to be looking from the other side of the side room door. I said I didn't want that, so I didn't say any more. But did he come?"

"Yes, Gladys," I sighed. "A very dear friend was here."

Gladys just looked at me for a long moment, and then finally said, "Good." And turned and walked away.

A sudden thunderstorm came up just before it was time for me to return to my ward. I was in the dormitory checking on a small resident whose bed was near the back window. I put the sides up on the crib and was drawn to the window. Great, black clouds were rolling in from the east, and the world outside was a dark greenish color. From the window I could see the evergreens, looking like tall, green toothpicks shaking in the wind. And I found myself wondering what in the world Lee Ann and Sir Lancelot were going to do if the gazebo was blown away. And I realizing I was thinking of Lee Ann's stories as real. Well, Jordan, I thought to myself, you don't know they aren't real. Do you? And I had to admit I didn't know that at all.

Suddenly Gladys was standing beside me. "Whee, look at that," Gladys said. "Boy that old wind just might blow Lee Ann's playhouse down."

"What?" I asked.

"There's a playhouse out there behind them little green Christmas trees, that the wind is blowing around," Gladys said, pointing towards the evergreens. It's Lee Ann's playhouse. I seen her out there one time at night." Gladys leaned closer and whispered, "And she had a man with her, too. I told too. But they didn't believe me. Said if I ever told such a lie again they was a gonna put me in the side room. I didn't want that so I never did tell again. I can only see the playhouse from the window beside your bed. I think it is a doll house cause it looks so little."

I just stood there, with the rain beating against the window and stared at the big, red haired woman. Could all this really be true?

Gladys took a step back from me, her eyes wide with fear. "You gonna tell I was talking about Lee Ann's playhouse! You do, and I'll say you lied!" Gladys' voice shook as she looked at me.

I smiled and gently touched Gladys' arm. "Don't you worry, I won't tell a soul."

Gladys looked relieved. "That's good, that's good," she said. "Cause I don't wanna be in the side room."

Somehow I was able to get through the next few days. Paul had said I would have to be patient. Waiting was the hard part. I had read somewhere the wheels of justice turned slow, and I wondered why. Lee Ann had whispered it would all work out, not to worry. But I did worry. Sometimes the fear I was to be trapped forever in a state hospital weighed so heavy on my heart I felt as if I was smothering. Mrs. Holt was on vacation, and I was thankful. Each time I had looked at the woman knowing what was behind that sweet looking face, I had felt such a burning anger I feared I might say or do something to give away the fact I knew what Mrs. Holt really was.

I had an appointment with Dr. Kelso one rainy September afternoon. I got on the shuttle bus and was glad to see Rosa was there. I sat beside her. "I haven't seen you for a while," I said.

"I've only been back from C3 for two days. I remember seeing you there when they brought me in. What had you done to get sent there?"

I didn't answer for a moment. I was wondering if I should tell the woman I had broken into Dr. Thorpe's files. Oh, well, I thought, what could it hurt? "I got into Dr. Thorpe's files: The patents' personal files," I whispered so only Rosa could hear.

The woman's blue eyes lit up with interest. "Oh, really. You know, I have always wanted to see what they have written on me over the years. I would give anything to see what my ex-husband had to say about me. You know they take anything someone on the outside says as fact?"

"I found that out," I said. "I hope that will change in the near future."

"You can't change a thing," Rosa said, shaking her head. "You try and it really makes them mad. That is one of the reasons I had to stay on C3 for so long. For all the years I've been here, I was a model patient. They said so at each yearly staffing on me. They always bragged on me and told me to continue the good job. Well, they aren't doing that anymore," Rosa said, her eyes widening and her voice lowering, "They say what a disappointment I've become. They say now I'm a trouble maker. But lately, I've been thinking about my children," Rosa said, a tremble in her voice. And I saw the pain in her eyes and wished with all my heart there was something I could say or do to help her. She continued, "I keep remembering them, seeing them as little children, although, I know they are now adults. I keep wondering what they think of me, if they remember me at all. One time when my husband was here to visit, he said I was dead to them and it was best that way. I was in such a depression back then I thought him right, but now I don't know. I just wish I could lay my eyes on them. They wouldn't have to see me, but I wish I could see them." Rosa's voice trailed off into a whisper as she turned her head, staring out the window.

I felt hopelessness. Because I knew there wasn't a single thing I could do or say to ease the woman's pain.

By the time I arrived at Dr. Kelso's office, I was more than sad for Rosa's plight, I was burning with anger. And when Dr. Kelso asked me what was on my mind. I told him. "Just why is it, Dr. Kelso a patient can be locked away in this state hospital for years, sometimes even a lifetime, and not be allowed to have any say in that decision!"

I could see Dr. Kelso was taken aback. I knew he would say I was in denial. Somehow he would get that in, I just knew it.

"Now, now Jordan," he said, leaning back in his chair and puffing on his pipe as he studied me. "We must not let ourselves get all upset."

"Ourselves! Ourselves! It has nothing to do with ourselves! Why do you keeping saying ourselves?" I knew I was shouting and it would only make me look bad on the doctor's report, but I couldn't help myself.

"Do you think you are going to be able to continue this session?" Dr. Kelso asked, peering over his glasses as he put a hand on the telephone. I was afraid he was going to call security and I might get sent to C3, so I fought back tears of frustration and managed to say, "I'm sorry, Dr. Kelso. I'm calming down."

Dr. Kelso sighed, "I understand." But I didn't believe him. How could he understand what I was feeling? Had he ever been held in a place like Gatewood, against his will? I thought not.

"Just how much does your being upset have to do with the visit from your friend and advocate?"

Oh, no! I thought, now, he's going to use this to stop me from seeing Paul. Thoughts raced through my mind. What could I say to convince Dr. Kelso my behavior had nothing to do with Paul? "Oh, Dr. Kelso, I said, taking a deep breath, hoping my voice sounded calm. "I'm so sorry for my outburst. I think my nerves are shot and I just took it out on you. I'm so sorry you had to see me act this way. Will you please forgive me?" I waited, hardly daring to breathe; I could see the doctor was showing interest. He relaxed and leaned back again in his chair.

"Now, tell me, Jordan just what is making your nerves shot."

"Do you think, Dr. Kelso, my feeling so nervous could be because of all the bickering I hear each day between some of the other patients on the ward?" I stole a glance at Dr. Kelso. His lips were puckered like he was really considering what I had said.

"Yes. Yes, I think that could get on one's nerves," Dr. Kelso finally said. "What are the other patients saying that bothers you so much?

"I don't think it is what they are saying; I think it's the noise they make when they say it."

"I see," Dr. Kelso said, fingering his chin. "How would you feel about being sent to a quieter ward?"

"Like where?" I asked, wondering where in Gatewood could be found a quieter ward? And a wave of fear swept over me as I thought perhaps I would regret my complaints about the other patients on A2. What if Dr. Kelso sent me to another ward? I didn't want to leave Lee Ann. She was the only person I could count on. My only friend in the hospital. But then Mrs. Holt wouldn't be able to falsify my record if I was on another ward. I was weighing this when Dr. Kelso said he was sorry but there just wasn't any opening on any of the other wards. But he would make a note of it and I would be considered when an opening became available on one of the cottages.

I thought it would be to my advantage to try to get a good report written about me from Dr. Kelso. Maybe he'd forget about my outburst if I came up with something better for him to write down. Suddenly something Lee Ann had once said flashed across my mind --- *Dr. Kelso believes every action us patients have has something to do with sex.* So I leaned forward and asked, "Dr. Kelso, when I saw Paul it brought back some old memories and I just wanted to be with him so bad. Do you think that might be the reason I'm so edgy?"

Dr. Kelso smiled and leaned forward. "Yes. Yes, I think that is most likely the reason for your frustration. You are having memories of what it was like to be with your lover, and realizing such activity is impossible while you are in treatment here, your anxiety got the better of you and you acted out by being irritable."

I looked the little doctor in the eye, thinking of how great-great- grandmother Jordan would have handled this and said, "Dr. Kelso will you please forgive me? Do you think everyone will forgive me?"

"Of course, I forgive you. I understand. And I'm sure everyone else will also. I must congratulate you on recognizing your problem. The first step in resolving your problems is admitting to them."

"Now, all this knowing what my problem is won't keep me from seeing my advocate, will it?" I asked, and held my breath until Dr. Kelso answered.

Dr. Kelso smiled even broader and waved his hands in front of his face, "Oh no. I think your admitting your problem will help you to deal with it. And I see no reason to pull you from the advocacy program. I will continue to work with you and help you to understand your frustrations."

"Thank you for being so understanding, Dr. Kelso."

"Just doing my job. Now, you go on back to your ward and think about what I have told you. I'm sure we can work through all this. I'll schedule an appointment for next week."

I left the doctor's office thanking my lucky stars I had gotten out of there without losing my one contact with the outside world.

When I got back to the ward, I was delighted to find I had mail from Paul. Seeing it had been opened, I felt steaming anger and bit my tongue to keep from lashing out at the attendant. I went to a chair in the corner of the room near the window, taking the card out of its envelope. I knew there wouldn't be anything in the message that would cause the staff to be suspicious of Paul. But yet, I felt I had been violated in having someone else see the card, reading the words that should have been for my eyes only. Paul had only scribbled a brief message on the inside of the card, 'Everything is going well. Hope you are well. Will be seeing you before long.' Those words gave me hope. *Everything is going well;* meant Paul was progressing in his plan to free me from Gatewood. And with those thoughts running through my mind, I felt the weight lift a bit. But I had no warning of what was to come.

Chapter Twelve

Because of one unguarded moment my hopes of getting out of Gatewood were shattered.

On a bright, sunny morning in September, I as usual, got into line to get my medication. I stuck the pills into my mouth; then slipped them under my tongue. I took a sip of the water Mrs. Holt handed to me. I then went as quickly as I could to the lavatory to brush my teeth. Perhaps I was being careless, with my mind on hopes of soon seeing freedom. All I knew was that I had just spit the pills into the sink, when out of nowhere appeared Mrs. Holt, Nurse Margo, and Gladys. I just stood there in shocked silence, staring at the faces, knowing I was in serious trouble. I hadn't even known Margo was on the ward, and I suddenly realized it was a setup.

"Grab her! Pin her to the floor!" Margo said. And in the blink of an eye I found myself lying on the cold marble of the lavatory floor with Gladys sitting on top of me, holding my arms and Mrs. Holt holding my shoulders. I could see Margo with a tissue in her hand swooping in the sink. She came up with the foamy toothpaste and the tell-tell pills.

"Young woman!" Margo said, her face flaming red with anger. "You know better than this! This drug study is very important! And what you have done is unforgivable!"

The other attendant appeared in the doorway, wanting to know if her help was needed. "You get yourself back out there in that dayroom! You know better than to leave the medicine cart unattended!" Margo yelled at the attendant. "And call security. This patient is on her way to C3." The attendant took one look at Margo and swiftly headed for the day room.

I just lay there with the weight of Gladys pressing me into the marble floor. I didn't try to say anything. I knew anything I could say would not help me in any way. *Damn! Damn! Damn!* How could I have been so careless? And I realized Mrs. Holt had been suspicious for some time.

"I told you she wasn't taking the medication. Didn't I?" Mrs. Holt said, pushing my shoulders harder to the floor.

"That was very observant of you, Holt. Good job." Margo said. "Ha. You just wait till Old, Doc. Kelso hears about this. He was so sure in the last meeting that this one was coming to terms with her problems. This ought to put a hole in his ego. He's always acting so superior at all the meetings. And if anyone disagrees with him he tries to make out they are sexually frustrated. I think he's the one with the problem."

"Yeah," Mrs. Holt said. "I think everyone thinks he has sex on the brain."

I lay there realizing these two didn't hold Dr. Kelso in high regard.

“Better put this one in a straitjacket,” Nurse Margo said. “No telling what she may try to pull on the way to C3.”

Moments later, security was there, cramming my arms into a straitjacket. Mrs. Holt left the lavatory and soon returned with more pills. "I'll take the pills," I mumbled, not wanting them poured down me.

"You‘d better believe, you will, " Mrs. Holt said, dumping the pills into my open mouth. I wondered if I was getting an extra-large dose of something. I hadn't kicked and screamed; Thorazine hadn't been mentioned. I was thankful for that.

In a short while I was on my way to C3. I, secure in the straitjacket, rode in the back seat of the security car with the attendant. I looked out the window to my right, a dark cloud rolled in from the west. I realized my world that had held a glint of hope was now looking very dark indeed.

When we got to C3, I was helped out of the car. Inside the building, the C3 attendants looked me up and down. "Well," Miss Voiles said. "Couldn't stay away, could you?" They led me to a side room door and quickly removed the straitjacket. Even quicker my clothes left my body. "Get on in there," Miss Voiles said, swinging wide the side room door.

I didn't cry this time. I just numbly walked into the room and sat on the sticky, green mattress.

Cordelia was still there, still had her face pressed against the tiny screened window in her side room door, still screeching profanities at anyone she could see. She screeched at me, "You there, I knowed you'd be coming back. Didn't I tell you the other time when you left I'd be seeing your ass right back in here?" I remembered Cordelia had said exactly that, but I hadn't believed her then.

The day crept into afternoon. A routine I knew from the other time I’d been in this lockup began. I was let out of the room to use the lavatory, took my medication and ate the food pushed on the metal tray into the room. After a while I slept. Coldness awakened me. My mouth was dry and I longed for just a sip of water. How long had I slept? On shaky legs I stumbled to the barred window at the back of the room.

The entire skies were heavy with dark, rolling clouds. In the distant horizon, lightening flashed, sending daggers of orange clear to the ground. Between the flashes the side room was in almost total darkness. Soon rain started to beat against the window. I shivered as the room became cooler. I crossed my arms and rubbed my shoulders to try to warm up. I'd really blown it this time. There was no way I would be allowed to have any contact with Paul while I was on C3, and I was certain Mrs. Holt and Margo would have me pulled from the advocacy program. They would say my being in the program had influenced my destroying the medication. Nothing I could say would make a difference, even if I got a chance to speak, which I doubted very much I would be allowed to do. I thought of Paul back in Harper City. It made me feel a little better for I believed he was trying his very best to find a way to get me out of Gatewood. But the doubts kept coming into my mind. Would he really be able to buck the system? Would he really be able to prove I was being kept here by my evil sister? But I had to hope, I told myself. Hope was all I had to hang onto, hope and a belief in Paul.

That night, after I had eaten the food the attendant slid across the floor on the metal tray and had taken the drug study medicine, (No chance of hiding the medicine under my tongue). The attendants were on to that and checked under my tongue. I had no choice but to swallow.) I lay shivering in the darkness of the side room and listened to the patter of the rain. The thunder and lightning had ceased and only a steady rain remained. I could hear the sounds of some of the other patients in the other side rooms. Someone was singing. Someone was crying. And Cordelia was screeching, "This is hell. But you shitasses are going to a bigger hell. You're all just a bunch of whores! God sees what you do! You bitches! Bitches! Bitches! Whores and Bitches is all you are. All you've been since the day you were born!!"

Swiftly one of the attendants was in front of Cordelia's door, shouting through the tiny screen in the window. "Cordelia, you shut up this instant! One more sound out of you and we'll have to give you a shot!" The threat worked. All was quiet from Cordelia's room.

Suddenly, I felt something run across my foot and yelled out. One of the attendants peered in the little window in the door. "What the matter in there?" My heart was in my throat. Most likely it had been a cockroach and that would have been bad enough, but what if it had been a rat? "There's something in here! It ran across my foot. Would you please turn on the light?" The attendant flipped on the light.

I blinked in the strong light from a large, single bulb, concealed in a wire frame on the ceiling of the room. A large cockroach darted across the room, disappearing under the door. I heard a crunch and the attendant say "Ah, ha, got him. I swear the roaches in this place are big enough to put saddles on."

I said, "thank you" to the attendant. The attendant turned off the light and the room was in darkness again. I suddenly thought of great-great-grandmother Jordan. Had she ever had to deal with cockroaches? I bet the Jordan of old could whip a cockroach. Well, if the Jordan of old could do that, then so could I.

Most of the other patients soon quieted down. After a while I slept, but not very sound. The cold kept waking me up. And I was glad when the first light of dawn crept in the window. Soon the night shift attendants came to the hallway and opened the doors one at a time to let the patients go to the bathroom. That took a good fifteen minutes. I was glad to get to the bathroom. My skin felt gritty already, and I knew it would be days before I got a bath. I washed my hands in the sink and splashed water on my face before the attendant told me to hurry along.

The days seemed endless. I did everything requested of me, which was: be quiet, go to and from the bathroom without causing any trouble, take my medication and not piss on the side room floor. The last was the hardest one for me to do. Sometimes I thought I was going to burst before the hours for bathroom privileges came. But somehow I managed to wait. I was now swallowing the drug study medicine. I had no choice. One attendant gave me the medication and another stood by. After I put the pills into my mouth and drank the water, the attendant would have me open my mouth and lift up my tongue. They had explained if I didn't swallow it, they would force it down me. I didn't want that. I remembered Lee Ann saying, *"Honey, you never want that."* I always took the medication for I knew in the end it would go down my throat anyway. I believed the medication wasn't doing anything for me and thought maybe it was harming me!

Sometimes a few minutes after taking the medication, I had a ringing in my ears lasting for hours. And at other times I saw wavy lines before my eyes. I told this to the attendants, once. They said they thought I was just saying that to get off the medication and it wouldn't work. I wondered why no one was concerned about the side effects of the drugs. Maybe all they wanted to know was if the medication controls seizures.

The attendants took me out of the side room and gave me a shower. I asked if I could dress and go to the dayroom. The attendant said that I would have to return to the side room, that destroying the drug study medicine was a serious offence and that they would have to get permission from the nurse to release me.

Since I was out of the reach of Mrs. Holt, my seizure report should show me as seizure free. I was wrong.

The next day, to my horror, Mrs. Holt was standing outside the side room looking in at me. I saw the face for an instant before it was gone and thought I was having hallucinations of the worst kind? For a moment I stood frozen in the middle of the room. With heart pounding I ran to the window in the door. No doubt about it, Mrs. Holt was walking towards the dayroom. An attendant from the day shift was coming into the hallway and I heard Mrs. Holt say: "I was just looking in on Jordan and she was in a very hard seizure. She's out of it now. I'll do the write-up on it."

The other attendant said, "That's too bad. We thought the drug study medication was working well with her. Holt, I'm so glad you decided to volunteer to be transferred up here to help us out while Arnet is off sick. We do need someone who knows how to handle the patients." Their voices faded off as they went out of sight, into the dayroom.

For a moment I had just stood there in stunned silence. My knees were like rubber and I sank to the floor and held my head in my hands.

"Dear God!" I thought, what is to become of me? My worst nightmare was there, just outside that door. What in God's name was I to do?" I sat there in the floor for what seemed like a long time; then numbly crawled across the floor, throwing myself onto the mattress. I felt as if all the will to fight had been stripped away in one instance in time when that evil face stared through the tiny window at me.

After a few minutes, I heard voices outside the door. I recognized one of the voices as Mrs. Holt's. The light was switched on and I kept my eyes shut.

"See, she's sleeping off the seizure," Mrs. Holt said. The light was switched off, then the sound of their footsteps as they walked away.

After a while I slept. I awoke sometime later to the jingle of keys. I rose upon one elbow. Mrs. Holt and another attendant stood at the door. They had come to let me out for bathroom privileges, and to give me more medication. When Mrs. Holt handed me the medication, I noticed there was more pills than I had been taking. "Why are you giving me more medication?" I asked.

Mrs. Holt looked at me and smiled. And I saw the ugly evil behind that smile. "Your seizures have become more severe," Mrs. Holt said. "The doctor has ordered an increase in the medication for you. Now, hurry up and take it. You do want to get better, don't you?"

I took the pills because I knew I had no choice. It would do no good to appeal to the other attendant in any way. To say anything against Mrs. Holt would not be believed by anyone in the state hospital.

I later realized I was being given a powerful drug, when my mind was clear enough to think at all. I noticed after Mrs. Holt had given me medication, for several hours I became barely able to function and could barely get up off the mattress. My brain was so cloudy that everything appeared as in a gray, far-away haze. When Mrs. Holt wasn't there to give the medication, I didn't have that reaction. I believed Mrs. Holt was giving me something other than what the doctor had ordered. In the time Mrs. Holt was off duty, I tried to get my mind to function enough to think of what I could do. I feared if this continued I would be a dead woman. Chills of terror swept across my body, as I thought that was exactly what Mrs. Holt wanted.

Sitting in the darkening side room, I tried to clear my mind enough to think of what I could do to survive until Paul could find a way to rescue me. He had probably gone to all the legal people he knew in an attempt to get me out. And I thought with such hopelessness, if he'd had any luck, why was I still here? In that desperate moment, I almost gave up with despair flooding my very being. Maybe I should just give up and let Mrs. Holt and Julia destroy me as I was sure they had planned. But something, perhaps a spark of who I really was, refused to surrender. A small flame of hope or defiance begin to slowly burn from somewhere deep within me, as I forced my mind to think, to try to find a way out of the nightmare. In my foggy state I tried to focus on what I could do to get out of taking the medication. Mrs. Holt always gave the medication in a hurry, telling me to, "Swallow, Now!" Perhaps so the other attendant wouldn't suspect anything, wouldn‘t see there were more pills than what the doctor's order called for. Then she would carefully look in my mouth to be sure the pills weren't under my tongue: That done, she always quickly shut the door and would hurriedly walk away. I thought the next time Mrs. Holt brought the medicine I would try to get the medicine to come back up, just as soon as the attendants were out of ear shot. Would the other patients hear and tell? I would have to think of something to mask the sound of my vomiting. How was I going to get the vomit out of the side room?

I gave the vomiting a try with the night medication. I got some help from Cordelia, who was throwing such a fit the attendants were threatening a strong dose of Thorazine. I had been given my medication and let out of the side room to use the bathroom. When the attendants' attention was momentarily averted to Cordelia's door, I quickly went to the toilet stall at the farthest corner of the bathroom. Flushing the toilet to muffle the sound, I ran my finger down my throat. The medication came up, along with my supper. If I could manage to stay alive for a little while longer, I might have a chance. Help came the next day.

Chapter Thirteen

I had managed to fake taking my medication that morning. I had spit the medication into the white, hard-plastic glass, hoping and praying the attendant wouldn't look in the glass. She didn't. I asked if I could have my bathroom privileges and use the glass to get another glass of water. After the attendant had looked into my mouth to be sure the medicine was gone, I went into the bathroom, poured the pills into the sink and washed them down the drain. I stumbled along a bit and tried to look stunned, which I didn't think was too hard to do. As I looked into the mirror I thought I looked a sight with my hair all matted, and my eyes dull. I thought surely I would be getting out of the side room sometime that afternoon.

Just before noon I heard someone yelling and cursing, "Let go of me, you God Damn sons of bitches! You rotten assed tubs of lard!"

"Hold her! Get the Thorazine!" Someone yelled.

I hurried to look out the window of the side room door. "Oh, no," I whispered. The source of the disturbance was Lee Ann. The attendants: Mrs. Holt and a short, dark-haired woman I had never seen before, along with two security guards, were dragging a fighting Lee Ann into the side room, directly across from me.

Soon another attendant appeared with a needle and ran into the side room. I watched them strip off Lee Ann's clothes. One of the security guards yelled, "Better hold her arms and legs tight, this one is a hellcat!"

The attendant jabbed the needle into Lee Ann's hip injecting the Thorazine. On the count of "Three", the attendants and security guards made a run for the door. They had barely cleared the doorway, when Mrs. Holt slammed the door and locked it. "That'll fix her for a few hours," Mrs. Holt said triumphantly. I watched as the attendants and security guards straightened their clothing. "Whew, that was a workout," the tall guard said, wiping his sweaty forehead.

"Come on into the office and I'll fix us all a cup of coffee," Mrs. Holt said.

I watched until they disappeared towards the dayroom. I tried to call to Lee Ann, but was unable to make myself heard. After a few minutes the cursing and screaming from Lee Ann ceased. And I thought the shot had kicked in. After all was quiet, Cordelia remark, "So much damn racket around this place. How do they expect a person to get any rest around here?" Many times, I had wondered the same thing when Cordelia was doing her screaming and cussing.

I managed to get my noon medication to come up. Mrs. Holt had given me the medication, checked under my tongue, and then let me out of the side room to go to the bathroom. Mrs. Holt stood just inches away as I sat on the commode, wondering how in the world I going to get the medicine up? All of a sudden Cordelia and another patient began screaming at each other. "You are a skinny, sorry excuse for a patient!" Cordelia screamed. "Your old man came to see you only one time in all the years you've been in this hellhole and he looked like shit too! I'm sick of hearing you talk about him! Don't you know the fool's out there sleeping with whores!?"

"Shut up! Shut up your lying mouth! You're nothing but a bushy headed lying fool!!" the other patient screamed back.

"I'm not putting up with that!" Mrs. Holt said, rushing out of the bathroom.

I quickly jumped off the commode, flushed the toilet and ran my fingers down my throat. The medicine came up. I flushed again. Mrs. Holt yelled out in the hallway, "Shut this racket up this instant. There will be no coffee for either of you this noon! And if I hear another word from either of you, there will be none this afternoon!" Silence.

I was washing my hands when Mrs. Holt came back into the bathroom. "Get on back into that side room," she said. I shook the water off my hands and returned to the side room.

I felt sad Lee Ann was on C3 and wondered what she had done. I got my chance to find out that evening. To my great relief, the afternoon shift let me out of the side room. "Guess what," an attendant with a name tag of Brown said. "You get to sleep in the dormitory, but there has been an added rule. When a patient is released from the side room, they have to clean and disinfect the room and mattress. You can do that after you have your shower. Do you think you are going to be up to it? You look awful dragged out. The attendant leaned closer to me and whispered, "I'll help you out if you don't think you can manage it."

"I can do it. I'm fine." I said. I was touched by her kindness. I didn't remember seeing this one before and guessed she was new. "Thanks," I said. "After the shower, I think I'm going to be feeling a lot better."

The attendant took me into the shower room and turned on the water. I thankfully stepped under the warm water, letting it wash away the dirt and grime, thankful I was able to feel my body was getting clean. And later when the attendant handed me the drab, gray dress that was the regular state supply, I caressed the stiff denim-like fabric. To me it felt wonderful.

I was given my evening dose of medication. (I managed to spit it into the sink when the attendant wasn't looking) A minute later, she apparently remembered she was supposed to check under my tongue. "Wait a moment," she said. She looked under my tongue and said, "That's good."

We went to the mop room and the attendant poured disinfectant and scrub soap into a mop bucket, filling it with hot water. She also fixed a small bucket with disinfectant, water and put rags into it. Telling me, "You be sure and wash the mattress and wall real good."

I was hoping I would be allowed to clean the side room unsupervised. I wanted to take a look through the tiny window of Lee Ann's side room. If I got caught, I would be in more trouble. But if the attendant went into the day room I wouldn't be seen. To my relief, the attendant said, "If you are ok, I'll go on and get my work done in the dayroom. You be sure and clean that room good."

"I'll do a real good job," I promised. I turned the mattress on its side and washed the top and bottom, thinking even the strong disinfectant wouldn't kill the horrible odor in the room. I guessed the odor had been accumulating for decades, and I wondered about the countless souls who had shivered within those walls. And I felt deep sadness at their plight as well as my own. Before starting to mop the floor, I went into the hallway, looking first towards the day room and then towards Lee Ann's door. All was quiet from Cordelia's room, and I guessed Cordelia was sleeping. I thought the attendants were taking a break and were probable watching television with the patients who were in the dayroom.

I went to Lee Ann's door, peeking in at the window. Lee Ann lay naked, on the bare mattress. "Lee Ann," I whispered.

Lee Ann opened her eyes, looking towards the door. She slowly sat up and crawled to the door, and managed to stand leaning against the door. Smiling, she said thickly "Good Lord, Jordan, you get caught talking to me, you know what'll happen to you."

"I just got released from the side room," I said, keeping a watchful eye towards the day room. "They're having me clean it. What did you do to get in here?"

Lee Ann sighed heavily and looked bleary eyed at me. "I decked that damned old Margo."

I could hardly believe my ears. "You hit Nurse Margo!"

"Knocked her flat on her fat ass," Lee Ann said. "And I'm not one bit sorry either."

"What on earth made you do that?"

"You know my black, sequined dress: The dress I had when I came in here. I've told you how much that dress means to me. I wore it when Joe and I used to go dancing."

I recalled Lee Ann had mentioned many times, the dress and this Joe character who had supposedly been her lover when she had been a young woman, before her illness. Lee Ann always got a special glint in her eye when she told tales of Joe and the beautiful dress. I guessed Lee Ann must have loved this Joe person just about as much as she now loved Sir Lancelot. I still didn't know if Sir Lancelot was real. But hoped he was.

"Well," Lee Ann continued. "That bitch Margo decided I was not to have my dress anymore." Lee Ann's voice broke a bit, and she staggered, bracing herself against the door. And I thought she was about to cry. I had never seen Lee Ann anything close to tears, and I didn't want to see it now.

Lee Ann didn't cry. She continued with the story. "Margo made the attendants clean all the old clothes out of the clothing room. And my dress was the first to hit the trash can. Old shitass Margo said, *'I've hated that ugly dress for years. Get rid of it.'* Just like that. Well, I made a run at the trash can, determined she was not going to throw my beautiful dress away. I know I've not had it on in years, but it holds the most precious memories for me." Again, Lee Ann's voice had the hint of tears in it. And I felt my own throat tightening.

"I grabbed the dress and Margo tried to stop me. Before I knew it I had popped her one up the side of the head, and that hateful bitch was on her ass, flat on the floor, in a wink of an eye. I'm not sorry either," Lee Ann added. "Well, the attendant grabbed me, and with the help of Gladys, pinned me to the floor. They pried the dress from my hands and threw it back into the trash can. They called security, and here I am. I fought all the way though. They were out of Thorazine, had to wait until they got me here to give me the shot. I sure gave them a rough time."

"I heard," I said. Hearing voices coming from the day room, I quickly ran across the hall and viciously began mopping the side room floor.

It saddened me deeply that Lee Ann was in the smelly side room, and she had lost her beloved dress. I thought about what a complex character Lee Ann was. On one hand she shunned, and even seemed to fear, the outside world. On the other she held onto bits of what the outside had once held for her. And what of this Sir Lancelot character? Was he of the outside world? And I found myself wondering as I had so many times since I'd first heard of him: did he really exist outside Lee Ann's imagination? The only thing I was sure of was that Lee Ann was truly my friend.

The attendant inspected the side room. Smiling she said, "Jordan, you have done a good job. Now, would you like to mop the hallway? This can be your job each evening, and we will even let you clean the lavatory too. I thought that job was supposed to be the afternoon shift's responsibility, but readily accepted it. Maybe I'd get a chance to talk to Lee Ann as I cleaned. "You can start this very evening, after all the other patients are in bed," the attendant said. "But don't mention it to the day or night shift."

"Not a word," I promised.

After the dormitory patients were in bed, the attendant fixed the mop water and I began mopping the hallway. I peeked in the window of the room where I'd spent the last few days; thankful I was looking in the window, instead of out of it. I knew it wouldn't be empty long and wondered who would fill it? Most of the patients in the side rooms had quieted down for the night. One little woman at the end of the hall was still softly talking to herself, "They're going to make me a pretty birthday cake. I'll eat it all up."

Cordelia had been cussing earlier, but the attendant's threat of a shot had silenced her.

I thought I had better appear to still be having the side effects of the medications when Mrs. Holt returned to work. I was dreading her return; afraid she would catch me when I tried to destroy the medication. And I didn't know how long I could endure taking the added medication, I was sure she was giving me. How long would my body, could my body hold up?

If only there was a way I could escape and get to Paul. Lee Ann had always said to make things happen, you had to have a plan. I had none.

I mopped to Lee Ann's room and found her face pressed against the window in the door.

"Hey, Jordan," Lee Ann whispered. "How's it going? Got you swinging a mop, have they?"

I looked towards the day room wanting to be sure an attendant couldn't see or hear me before I stopped to talk with Lee Ann. Seeing no one I edged closer to Lee Ann's door. I whispered, "I'm scared, Lee Ann. More scared than I've been since I got put in this place. Mrs. Holt is giving me medicine the others don't give me! I'm afraid she is trying to do me great harm! Maybe even kill me!" This was the first time I had allowed myself to voice these thoughts. And I found the words terrified me. I knew if I told anyone no one would believe me, no one except Lee Ann. And if Mrs. Holt found out I was saying these things, she might just finish me off sooner. Lee Ann was the only person I dared tell.

Lee Ann stared at me, not saying anything for a good moment. "I believe you," she said slowly. "We have to get you out of here."

"How in the world am I going to be able to get out those doors?"

"We'll find a way," Lee Ann said, biting her lip as if she was at that very moment making a plan. "You have to go over the wall."

"If I did make it over the wall, then what? Where would I go? I'd have to get to Paul. But, how?"

"You are getting out of here," Lee Ann said, looking me in the eyes. "You go over the wall and get to Sir Lancelot. He'll help you find your young man."

Just then I heard voices coming from the dayroom. Attendants were coming into the hallway. I began mopping as fast as I could. One of the attendants asked, "Is this all you have done?"

"I-I-I was just taking my time and trying to do the very best job I could for you," I said, hoping my voice wasn't shaking too much, and my speech was slurred enough so the attendant would think I was slow because of the side effects of the medication.

"Well, you're going to have to work faster than this," the attendant said. "Now hurry up. You have to get to bed." The attendant gave me a disapproving look, turned and walked back towards the dayroom, stopping in the dayroom doorway.

I knew I wouldn't have a chance to talk anymore to Lee Ann and hasty finished mopping the hallway. "I haven't done the lavatory yet," I said.

The attendant sighed and looked even more disapprovingly at me. "Well, if you are going to keep this job, you're going to have to learn to work faster. Go on, get on to bed. I'll do the lavatory myself."

I mumbled, "Sorry. I'll use the bathroom and get right to bed."

"Well, hurry up." the attendant said. You sleep in the third bed on the left. There's a gown on the bed."

I went into the dimly lit dormitory. Most of the other patients were already sleeping. An old, faded, flannel gown lay on the bed. I hugged the gown to my chest, thankful I had a gown to sleep in. I took off my clothes, then slipped on the ward-supply gown and slid between the sheets. The smoothness of the sheets felt so good. I had never imagined in my whole life how terrible the feel of a sticky plastic mattress was on bare skin.

I lay there for a long time, sleep eluding me. I ran my mind back over the unbelievable occurrences of the past four months. My ninety-day stay had turned into one hundred and twenty-one. A heavy fear gripped my heart, and I tried to erase the thoughts that kept returning to haunt me time after time. Even if I survived, what if these days that had turned into weeks and now months, turned into years? What if they turned into a lifetime? I shivered and pulled the covers tighter around me. I must not dwell on that possibility. I must think of getting out, of getting to Paul.

Lee Ann had said Sir Lancelot would help. I thought of what the odds were that this character existed and admitted to myself the odds were pitifully low. I had to believe in him. I had to believe this odd character was not just something out of Lee Ann's fantasy. Gladys had said she'd seen a man in Lee Ann's playhouse.

I thought of Paul. It seemed he was as far away as the stars. I tried to imagine what he must be up against trying to go through the legal system to try to get me out. He had no absolute proof Julia was a greedy, evil woman who wanted to keep her sister locked away forever in a state hospital. The hospital would simply produce their record on me, and I had to admit from a judge's point of view my record wouldn't look like a person who was a victim of the system. I could just see some old white-haired judge going over my record and saying, *"Well, this woman reads likes she is insane. Look here, she has been in the lock-up more than once. And there is report after report of her erratic behavior*." The truth would be enough to convince him I was a loonie, added to the false reports on me, no doubt signed by one Mrs. Holt. What chance, would I have? Mrs. Holt's reports, along with the false things Julia had reported, I was certain, would keep me locked behind the walls forever, in spite of what Paul might try to prove. And I knew now I would be forbidden to see Paul again: The advocacy program was closed to me. The "*powers that be*" had deemed the program wasn't for me.

I shivered and my knees knocked together and fear was a heavy weight on my chest. What would the ancient Jordan have done in a situation like this? The answer was clear. There was only one thing I could do. I had to go over the wall.

Chapter Fourteen

Just as dawn was breaking, I awoke. I lay in the soft gray light, surprised I had slept so well, and my sleep had been without the usual nightmares. Everything was so quiet, just the sounds of the other patients sleeping. Soon the glaring, overhead lights would be flicked on by the night shift attendants. On the foot of my bed was the familiar bath bundle. I quietly got out of bed and made my way through the doorway into the day room. Two night shift attendants sat at the desk, their heads down, resting on their arms. Soon they would be stirring and the dreadful day would begin. I had never known C3 to be so quiet. Ordinarily, Cordelia would have been cussing by now. I tiptoed across the day room floor and into the hallway, making my way to the lavatory. I stood looking out the small window at the fire in the morning sky: A beautiful, blazing red covered the eastern horizon. I marveled at the beauty before me, yet the sight left me feeling lonely sadness.

I stood there for just a few seconds then made my way down the hallway to Lee Ann's room. "Lee Ann," I whispered through the tiny window.

In an instant Lee Ann's face appeared in the window. "Girl, what are you doing here?" she whispered.

"I'm going over the wall," I whispered. "I have to go before Mrs. Holt gets back off pass. Last night, I heard one of the attendants saying that Holt would be off until tomorrow. I'll have to go today. I don't know how. But I know I have to!" My voice shook, my heart pounded crazily.

"Okay," Lee Ann said simply. "Listen, they'll take me out of here at one o'clock for my appointment with Dr. Kelso. That can't be missed, you know. He insists on it. One attendant should have all you patients who are out of the side rooms out in the fenced yard for the afternoon fresh air time. They will take me through the yard to the back parking lot. Now listen carefully," Lee Ann whispered so low I had to strain to hear. "When the attendant unlocks the gate, I will fake the worst seizure anyone has ever seen. The attendant and the security guard will be occupied with me. You run out the unlocked gate. Run like hell; scan the rock wall back there, then as fast as you can get into the woods. Run straight until you come to a creek, go up it. About two miles or so you'll find a cabin. Sir Lancelot should be there. You'll know him by the patch covering one eye. Just tell him your name. He knows all about you." Just then I heard voices coming from the day room and ran back to the lavatory. Soon the lavatory was filled with patients and I went to the dormitory to get dressed. I felt a heavy load had been lifted from my shoulders as excitement flooded through me. Yet a nagging fear played at the corners of my mind. What if I didn't make it? What if I got caught? What if Mrs. Holt had another opportunity at me? Trying to push the doubts out of my mind, I looked out the window as I dressed. The deep red of a few minutes ago had turned to gold and purple. I prayed that I would be watching my next sunrise from the other side of the wall.

I managed to get my morning medicine back up and flushed, and as the morning wore on, I ran over and over in my mind what I would do when Lee Ann faked the seizure. But what if they took Lee Ann out the front door? Stop it! I told myself. Stop thinking negative thoughts. Lee Ann had said they would take her out the back way. I was thankful I had on my sturdy oxfords, the black and white ones, and wished I had on jeans instead of the damned state supplied dress. I pictured in my mind Lee Ann faking a seizure. I'd seen some of the patients have horrible seizures and someone would always say, usually a patient, *"She's faking a seizure!"* I wondered how anyone could tell. They sure looked real to me. Just last week, Gladys had a horrible seizure and Miss Abner said to the other attendant, 'I know she's faking, but the new rule Old Margo put out says we gotta count them anyway. So we'll mark her up.'

I became more and more nervous as the morning turned towards afternoon, pacing back in forth in the day room.

Luck was with me again with the noon medication. The attendant passed out the medication and didn't ask to look under my tongue. I quickly went to the lavatory, took the pills from my mouth and flushed them down the toilet. When Mrs. Holt returned I would be watched much closer while taking my medication than the other attendants watched. I had to believe this plan of Lee Ann's would work. It had to work. My life depended on it.

When everyone was back from the dining room after the noon meal and all the trays had been passed into the side rooms, one of the attendants opened the back door. "Everyone get out there in the yard," she said. I, along with all the patients from the dayroom, scampered out the door, into the fenced yard. The attendant soon followed.

The fence was old, make of strong crisscross wiring. The top was about ten feet up and had a metal railing topped off with a strand of barbwire. I didn't think I would be able to scale the fence since ugly barbwire was there. Maybe I could hook my finger in between the wire and pull myself to the top, but the barbwire would tear my hands and legs to bits if I tried to go over it. Had anyone tried in all the years the fence must have been there? I bet a few had. A long rock wall, like the one in front of the building, sat several yards beyond the fence, and disappeared from sight down the hill. I felt lightheaded and my breathing was coming faster. I stayed as far away from the attendant as I could, afraid she might guess I was up to something.

There were eight other patients in the yard. Most were permanent patients on C3, who most times were kept highly medicated, but were considered too dangerous to be put out on other wards. One patient had all her teeth pulled. "Cause I bite everybody," she told me. "I eat um up." She smiled and moved along the fence. And I wondered how many patients had suffered bites before the teeth had come out. I remembered seeing a terrible scar on Gladys's arm and Gladys saying that years ago a mean patient on C3 had tried to eat her up. I shivered and wondered how one patient was to be protected from the other violent ones? Gladys was a very strong person, and most likely could protect herself, yet she had the horrible scar.

As it turned out, the toothless patient was an enormous help in my run for freedom. Not wanting to draw attention to myself, I stood several feet away from the gate when they brought Lee Ann out. An attendant and a security guard escorted her. Lee Ann's eyes met mine and she nodded. I held my breath and got set to run as the attendant unlocked the padlock on the gate, then swung open the gate. Then everything started happening at once:

Lee Ann let out a loud cry, flopped to the ground, and began thrashing about. I thought, now is the time. Go! In that instant, the toothless patient also made a run for the gate, running past the startled attendant. The other attendant in the yard began yelling at the security guard, "Get that patient! Stop her! She'd getting away!" The guard ran out the gate. By this time the runaway patient was now going out of sight towards the front of the building.

I ran as hard as I could out the gate. The attendant furled her arms, screaming, "Lock the damn gate! There goes another one! She's going for the wall! She's headed for the woods!"

I didn't look back to see what the security guard did. I hoped he was still running after the other patient. I ran as hard as I could towards the wall. Grabbing onto rocks at the top of the wall, I kicked and clawed until I made it up, jumping to the ground on the other side. Only then did I look back. One attendant was bending over Lee Ann. The other was looking through the fence yelling, "Jordan you get back here! You're in big trouble now!" Looking over to the right I saw the guard dragging the toothless patient, who was kicking and screaming, back towards the gate.

I didn't hesitate any longer, but began running as hard as I could toward the shelter of the woods. It would only be a matter of time before the search team would be called out. I ran on into the woods, the underbrush tearing at my clothes and legs. My heart pounded in my ears and my breath came in gasps. Still I ran as fast as I could, going as straight as I could.

Lee Ann had said to just go straight and I would run into the creek. Soon I came to a creek, sinking onto its bank to catch my breath, listening for the sound of the searchers coming after me. But the only sounds in the woods were a bird singing and my own heavy breathing. I stayed there for only a minute more before getting to my feet and running along the creek bank, going upstream as Lee Ann had said. Coming to a place in the creek which had a lot of large rocks, I climbed across to the other side and kept going upstream. I felt a bit safer with the creek between me and the hospital. A sharp pain in my side forced me to slow. Lee Ann had said to just follow the creek and it would take me to Sir Lancelot, to safety.

I didn't like the fear-filled thoughts swimming through my mind. What if there was no Sir Lancelot? What would I do? What could I do? Would I wait to be captured and thrown back into that smelly side room for Holt to have another chance at me? Don't think about that I told myself; just think that help and freedom are ahead. I went on up the creek, stopping from time to time, listening for voices and of someone running through the brush. I heard none of that. I had a good start on them and doubted they would know which way I had gone once I had gotten into the woods.

I ran on for what seemed like hours, stopping once to rest and to drink from the creek water. I splashed some of the water over my face and realized I was sweating profusely. I thought again of what my options were if there was no Sir Lancelot. I didn't believe Lee Ann would have told me he would help if she didn't believe it. But one thing worried me. What if Lee Ann believed it, but it was only in her mind?

So if there was no Sir Lancelot what would I do? If I could get to a phone without getting caught, I could call Paul and wait for him to come to me. Looking like I did I wouldn't dare show my face in town, even if the town's folk hadn't been warned about an escapee, and I figured they had by now. I had State Hospital Patient written all over me with my ragged appearance. Maybe if I could hide out till dark, I could find a house with no one home, break in and use the phone.

I began running again. After a while I came to a clearing with high, almost dead grass. A gravel road ran through the clearing and disappeared down a hill. At the far end of the clearing sat a large cabin. This had to be the cabin Lee Ann had talked about, the one she had found the time she had gone over the wall. But would I find Sir Lancelot there?

I stood staring at the cabin, wondering what I should do. I didn't think I had time to wait. What if the search party came this way, this far? Slowly I walked towards the cabin.

"Oh, God," I whispered as I approached the cabin, "please let there be a Sir Lancelot." A wide porch wrapped around the front of the cabin, running down the right side. I climbed the three steps to the porch and with pounding heart said aloud, "Sir Lancelot!"

"At your service ma'am," said a voice behind me.
I whirled around to face a tall man with salt and pepper hair protruding from a black cowboy hat. A black patch covered his left eye. Breathing a sigh of relief, I realized I was looking at Lee Ann's Sir Lancelot.

Chapter Fifteen

For a moment I stared at the man. His face was the saddest I'd ever seen. I heard myself saying, "My name is Jordan Walker! I know Lee Ann! Will you help me?!"

The man looked at me for a few seconds, and then said. "I will help you in any way I can. First let's get you inside." He climbed the steps, stepped around me and pushed the door open.

I stepped out of my mud caked shoes, walked across the threshold, and found myself in a large living room. It was well lit from the many long windows. Paintings of birds were everywhere. Some were framed and hung on the wall. One was of a giant eagle hanging over the stone fireplace. And still many were just lying around in various stages of completion. "You are an artist? I asked, realizing Lee Ann had not told me this about her Sir Lancelot.

"Yes. This is what I do. And I see for this day you are an escapee."

I looked at him, trying to read his face to see if there was a sign he was friend or enemy. "Yes," I said. "Lee Ann said to find you, that you would help me."

He shook his head and said, "Lee Ann. The most fascinating woman I've ever met. Committed to that place I think would be a living hell, yet she feels the world outside that wall is more of a hell. I have tried for a long, long time to change her mind. But even my love cannot unlock the fear she has of the outside world." His face looked so sad I wished I could wipe away the sadness. "Lee Ann told me about you," he continued. "She said you were falsely put into Gatewood and was being kept against your will."

"Yes," I said. "And I would still be there if Lee Ann hadn't helped me escape. She's in the lock-up. She thinks she'll be there for a couple of weeks."

"I wish I could do something," Sir Lancelot said, sadly, shaking his head. "I've dreamed for so long of rescuing her from that place. But the thing is she doesn't want to be rescued. So hard for me to understand, but I just have to let it be. But, seems like you are in need of a rescue?"

I felt here was the first person, besides Paul and Lee Ann, who was willing to listen to me and maybe believe what I had to say. I found myself telling this man everything, even about my suspicions Mrs. Holt was actually out to kill me.

He just sat there in the big, leather chair, and listened, as I sat across from him on the couch. "Well," he finally said, rubbing his hand across his chin, "First we'll have to get you cleaned up and those scratches taken care of. Then we'll see about a plan to get you to this Paul person. Hopefully, he'll be able to find a way to get you out of your predicament once we get you to him."

He got up and went into another room which I thought must be a bedroom. He came back with jeans and a blue denim shirt. "Here," he said. "The bathroom is just down the hall. These might be a bit large, but guess they'll have to do. You get yourself cleaned up and then we'll see about the scratches."

I took the clothes. "What if the search party comes here?" I asked fearfully.

A wry smile formed on his lips. "If they come, they won't stay long. I'm known as the crazy birdman. This is my sanctuary. They won't be thinking I would allow anyone in here, patient from Gatewood or otherwise."

I walked down the hallway and found the bathroom. Inside, I flipped on the light and closed and locked the door. I stared at my reflection in the mirror above the sink. I looked a fright. I picked a couple of twigs from my tangled hair. I picked up a comb and smoothed out my hair and then peeled of my filthy, torn, state hospital dress, dropping it on the floor. I soaped over the scratches on my legs. There were many but they didn't seem to be very deep. I also had a few scratches on my arms. I had run through some briars. Remembering Rosa and how she had looked after her encounter with the briar patch, I realized I was lucky. I thought about the man just down the hall in the living room. I had believed him when he said I was safe here. And I wondered how he came to be here and about the patch on his eye. I dried my legs and arms off with a giant, brown bath towel and then began to put on the clothes Sir Lancelot had given me. The jeans were way too big. I didn't see how I was going to be able to keep them up. Maybe a belt? I looked around the bathroom and found a tie belt around an old bathrobe. I took it, looping it through the jeans and found it worked ok. I tied the shirt tails in front, rolled up the sleeves. It would have to do.

I thought of Lee Ann and how she had helped me. And about what Sir Lancelot had said about his love not being able to wipe out Lee Ann's fear of the outside world. It was all beyond my understanding.

Suddenly it came to me. Lee Ann's dress! The dress that meant so much to my friend. The black sequined dress Lee Ann held so dear: The dress that held beautiful memories of her life before Gatewood. The trash truck hadn't come yet. It wouldn't come until tomorrow for the weekly pickup. That meant Lee Ann's dress was somewhere inside the trash house out behind A1. I sometimes helped the day shift's staff take the trash out. There were two small buildings several feet behind Al. One was for the wards' trash and the other was for the kitchen's trash. Both were padlocked. The trash houses were used by all four wards of the Wallace building. The attendant had explained the trash houses were locked to keep the patients out because some of them loved to go through the trash cans.

I figured if I could get back to Gatewood, I could break the lock with a rock and get inside. I would find the dress for Lee Ann. Sir Lancelot could take it to her on their next rendezvous. On second thought he couldn't give it to her. The dress had been put in the trash and couldn't ever go back inside the clothing room. Hopefully Sir Lancelot would keep it for Lee Ann.

I thought the gravel road down a ways from Sir Lancelot's cabin would lead into Gatewood's grounds, if I followed that I could find my way onto the grounds. Surely the search party would be called off after dark. And I could hide in the ditch by the roadside if a car came by.

Part of my brain was screaming *are you insane*. And maybe I was (my record at Gatewood sure said I was) but it was something I knew I had to do. One little thing I could try to do for my dear friend who had done so much for me.

I went into the living room to tell Sir Lancelot of my plan to go back to Gatewood to rescue the dress. He might think I had lost my mind, for real and maybe I had. But I didn't care. I had to go back. I shivered with fear at the thought of going back to Gatewood. I would have to go under the cover of darkness else I was certain to be captured. Perhaps Sir Lancelot would lend me a flashlight.

I found him on the front porch, sitting on the first step, scraping mud off my saddle oxfords with his pocketknife.

He turned as I approached. "You do look much better," he said, handing me the shoes. "Come on inside and I'll see if I can find some socks."

I took the shoes and followed him inside. I waited while he went into a bedroom. He soon came out with a pair of black socks and a jar of some kind of salve for my scratches I rubbed the salve over the scratches; then pulled on the socks. The heels went almost to my knees, but I didn't care, they felt warm.

"Sorry, I don't have a phone," Sir Lancelot said. "I know you need to call your friend. If I could I'd take you to a phone booth, but my truck is being repaired and my friend and mechanic won't have it back until late tonight. All I have is that old truck in the barn, it will run, but barely. No way would I take it out on the main highway. You'll have to stay here tonight. We'll head out first thing in the morning."

“Thank you.” I said.

I sat at the table in the kitchen while he fixed supper and told him about my plan to go back to rescue Lee Ann’s dress.

If he thought me a complete fool, he didn't let on. He fixed pancakes and sausages, and I realized I was starving as he set them before me. As we ate, he told me he would help me get the dress. "Can't have you stumbling around in the dark. And it wouldn’t be safe for you out on the road. We'll take the old truck --should be ok to drive it that far.”

"What if security sees your truck?"

"Oh, I'll not be on state property. The area across from the Wallace building is my property. I’ll park there. It’s a bird sanctuary, left to me by my grandmother Santon. Grandmother was a very special woman,” Sir Lancelot said and then added softly, “She believed in me.”

"I really appreciate your helping me. I don’t know if could make it without you," I said.

"Well, Miss," he said slowly. "Sometimes you gotta have friends. Lord knows I have few. But the few I got, I know I can count on if I need them. You say you are a friend to Lee Ann and I believe you."

He got up from the table, and went to light the fire in the fireplace. I watched as the wood caught fire and the flames began licking at the larger logs. "It's getting cold," he said turning to look at me. "Lee Ann never told me about a sequined dress," he said sadly. "I know she has a lot of secret thoughts I'll never be able to touch. It has to be enough just to be her Sir Lancelot for a few hours now and then." He turned sideways, looking into the fire.

Sadness lined his face. "You mean so much to Lee Ann. She has told me about dancing in the moonlight with you. She says she lives for those times. At first I didn't believe you were real. Even till today, I had my doubts. I thought you might be just a figment of her imagination. But I thank God you are real."

"Thank you, Miss. You are very kind," he said, looking at me.

"What happened to your eye?" I asked, hoping I wasn't prying too much.

"Korea. I got hit two days before I was to come home. I lost an eye. My best friend lost his life," he added softly.

"I'm so sorry," I said.

"We all have our demons, Miss," he said staring back into the fire. "Lee Ann has hers. They keep her behind that wall. What are your demons, Miss Walker?" he said, turning back to me.

"My sister, Julia is the biggest demon I have right now, and Mrs. Holt. But I think I can whip my demons with a little help from my friends."

"I'm betting on you, Miss Walker."

Darkness had fallen by the time we started for the dress. An almost full moon was just touching the treetops. I wondered if Sir Lancelot would have been planning on a few hours in the gazebo with Lee Ann on this moonlit night if he hadn't known she was locked in a side room on C3. I thought about asking, but didn't. Perhaps that would have been invading too much on his private world. I was feeling a bit fearful I would be captured, but I knew the tinge of fear was nothing to what I would have been feeling if I had gone alone. Yet, I knew without doubt I would have gone, and I felt good about myself knowing that. I thought about my namesake. Was I perhaps getting some of my courage from an ancient ancestor?

Sir Lancelot parked the old truck on the lane to the bird sanctuary. At times I had wondered if the truck was going to just stop, as it rattled over the pavement.

Lights were shining brightly from the Wallace building. From this distance, the lights had a soft glow, an almost welcoming look to them. I shivered. I knew the misery that lay behind those walls. I said a silent prayer that God would keep me from seeing the inside of those walls ever again.

Sir Lancelot pulled a flashlight from under the seat. "We might need this inside the shed." He pulled out a tire iron. "To break the lock."

It was just past eight o'clock and I knew this was one of the busiest times of the evening, as the attendants would be giving baths and getting the patients ready for bed.

At the bottom of the hill, we scaled the wall, avoiding the well-lit walkway. We silently made our way, lit by misty moonlight, though the trees to the top of the hill just behind Al. The trash houses stood a few yards behind the building.

My heart was beating so hard I thought Sir Lancelot could probably hear it. What if we got caught? I knew what would be in store for me. But what about my new-found friend? What would be his punishment? I tried to push those thoughts from my mind and get on with the business of getting Lee Ann's beloved dress out of the trash house.

We came closer to the trash house, first darting behind a large oak tree. We looked around the tree towards A1. All was quiet and still. We ran to the side of the trash house; then eased to the front side, beside the door. Sir Lancelot pried off the lock with the tire iron and opened the squeaky door. I looked around fearful someone might be outside, although I knew it was unlikely. Sir Lancelot shined the flashlight inside the small building, revealing several large trash cans. "I'll dump the trash cans, and you hold the light and keep a lookout towards the building," Sir Lancelot said, handing me the flashlight.

I held the light while Sir Lancelot dumped several cans and rummaged through them without finding anything resembling a sequined dress. I shined the light on a can in the far corner and saw something glittering. A piece of the dress was sticking over the side of the can. "There! Near the back! I think I see it!" I was so excited I hadn't been watching towards the building and was startled to hear a grinding, squeaking sound.

I flipped off the light. "Listen!" I whispered, looking towards A1's door. In the cool moonlight, I saw a white uniformed figure bringing a wheelchair down the steps onto the walk. I had heard that grinding sound before. When I had helped the day shift attendant take the trash out we always used an old wheelchair to carry the trash can in.

Sir Lancelot came to stand so close I could feel his breath on my hair. We watched as the attendant came closer. My knees shook, as I pressed against the wall, praying the attendant wouldn't see us when she shoved the trash çan into the shed. On no, I thought, she'll see that the lock has been pried off. When the attendant had pushed the squeaky chair to within about twenty feet of the trash house, Sir Lancelot sullenly bellowed, "Come to me my pretty one!"

I was startled and jumped, and for an instant, the attendant froze in her tracks, then she began screeching and gave the wheelchair a violent push forward, causing it to tip over, sending it and the trash can crashing onto the sidewalk, making a terrible banging sound. The squeaky wheel spun around and around, it spokes glistening in the moonlight. The attendant ran screaming towards Al. "Help! Help! Call Security! Call Security! Somebody's in the trash house!" she screamed at the top of her lungs. Beside me, Sir Lancelot chuckled softly.

"Oh, God!" I said, "Security will be here. We'll get caught!" I turned on the flashlight, ran to the trash can in the corner, grabbed at the sparkly piece of cloth hanging over the side. I tugged until the dress came free. Holding the dress to my chest, I flipped off the light, and I, quickly followed by Sir Lancelot, ran out the door and down the hill, just as flashing, red lights appeared around the side of Al.

I was out of breath by the time we got to the truck. We climbed into the truck and Sir Lancelot turned on the light in the cab. "Let's see what this venture was all about," he said, reaching for the dress. He gently touched the dress. "Some dress," he said shaking his head. "I bet Lee Ann was a beautiful sight in this."

We were on the gravel road nearing the cabin, when a siren blasted the night. "Quick! Get down on the floor!" Sir Lancelot said. I quickly slid to the floor, taking the sequined dress with me. Sir Lancelot brought the truck to a stop as flashing red lights came through the back window. "It's the police," he whispered.

I froze. If the police found me, I would lose my only chance at freedom. There was no way, even with Sir Lancelot's help, I could escape. If Sir Lancelot was scared his voice didn't show it as I heard him say, "What's the problem?"

"Oh, there's a runaway from Gatewood, Mr. McBride. Just wanted to warn you to be on the lookout. Better be sure all your doors are locked tonight. They say she's very dangerous, a wild one."

"I'll sure keep that in mind," Sir Lancelot said.

Soon, I heard the police car on the gravel, moving away and the flashing, red light dimmed. "Safe to get up now," Sir Lancelot said.

I climbed back onto the seat as Sir Lancelot put the truck into gear and pulled back onto the pavement.

Mr. McBride? I thought, stealing a glance at the man beside me. So that was his name. I'd seen that name at the hospital, on a brass plate on the wall next to the multipurpose room. Miss Jones had said it was the name of the richest man in Saberville who had donated the funds for the multipurpose building. I wondered if he was related to Sir Lancelot.

When we got back to the cabin, I hung Lee Ann's dress on a hanger and carefully inspected it for damage. There were a few sequins missing from the right sleeve, but otherwise it seemed in good shape. I looked at the dress, trying to picture a young Lee Ann in it.

"I'll get the dress cleaned and tell Lee Ann it is safe," Sir Lancelot said as he stood before the fireplace. "Of course she can't have it back at Gatewood, but maybe she'll be happy just knowing I have it here with me."

"I'm sure that will make her happy," I said. As I looked at the tall, rugged-looking man standing there, I wondered if he was related to the man whose name was on the brass plaque. "Are you related to a man who donated funds for the multipurpose building at the state hospital?" I asked.

"Yes," he said, turning to look at me. "Samuel McBride. He's my grandfather. He's about ninety now, but still very active. A very strong man. He doesn't understand, nor approve of, my seclusion. In town," Sir Lancelot said, a half smile on his mouth, "they refer to me as an eccentric. I know full well if I were from a poor family I would be called plain crazy."

"What's your full name?"

"Michael Samuel McBride," he said thoughtfully. "I guess everyone thought I would be a doctor or a politician. They said I showed such high potential when I was a young man growing up in Saberville. Korea changed all that." He stopped talking, turning to again stare into the flames. Finally he said, "When I came back from the war all I wanted was this cabin, and to paint my birds. I've always had a love for painting, and for birds. When I was a teenager I tried to tell this to my parents. They said, oh son, you can do better. But I learned in Korea life is sometimes very short. I've seen it snuffed in the blink of an eye. So when I came back, I just took to doing what I wanted. I suppose that might sound selfish to most people. But I find my peace here in my solitude. I found Lee Ann here," he said, looking at me again. "Or should I say she found me. You know she ran away just to feel freedom for a day. She had no intention of ever leaving Gatewood. She stayed with me one day and a night; then went back in spite of anything I could say." He looked back into the fire, and shaking his head sadly, said, "It's those damn demons, those fears that have hold of her that I can't touch."

I looked at him, wishing there was something I could say to wipe the sadness from his face. Standing there staring into the fire with his high-top boots, jeans, western shirt and hat, he looked like a cowboy from an old western movie I'd seen as a child. But I didn't think this cowboy was going to ride happily into the sunset. I thought both he and Lee Ann were two lost souls, and the thought gave me a deep, sad feeling.

"You must be very tired," he said, turning from the fire. You take the bedroom at the end of the hall. I'll be staying up for a while, going to work on my paintings."

"Good night," I said, rising from the chair. "I'll never be able to thank you for your help."

"Glad to help a friend of Lee Ann's. In the top drawer of the chest you'll find tee shirts. You can sleep in one if you want," he called as I went down the hall.

I called back thanks. Later as I lay in the big bed I looked out the window at the moonlit night, and thought of all that had transpired that day. I felt safe in the secluded cabin with Sir Lancelot in the room down the hall. And tomorrow I would, with his help, find Paul. I wished Sir Lancelot had a phone so I could call Paul. Instead I let a picture form in my mind of the man I loved. Surely my ordeal was almost over. God willing brighter tomorrows were ahead. I had to believe that.

Chapter Sixteen

The faint light of dawn was just coming in the window, when I was startled out of a sound sleep by wild pounding on the bedroom door. I jerked upright in bed. For a second I thought I was back at Gatewood, then reality came to me and I realized I was in Sir Lancelot's cabin. "Miss Walker!" The voice was urgent.

"What's the matter!?" I called as fear filled my body. Were they coming to take me back!? The bedroom door opened and I could make out the outline of Sir Lancelot. "Hurry up and get dressed," he said, worry in his voice. "We have to get you out of here fast!"

"What has happened?" But he had already gone. Quickly I jumped out of the warm bed and shivering pulled on the pants and shirt I had worn the night before. I ran into the living room to find Sir Lancelot waiting at the front door.

"I went down to the filling station on road 6, and good thing I did," he said, his face grim. "Your sister is raising hell about you escaping. I saw the police chief and he said your sister hired three private detectives to come down here and get you back in that hospital. The chief wasn't too happy about that. He doesn't want out-of-towners coming in here telling him how to run his business, vowed he'd catch you himself no matter what. A judge has granted warrants for every house for miles to be searched. We have to get you far away from here. We'll find your friend Paul and hope to God he can help. Hurry and put your shoes on," Sir Lancelot added, eyeing my bare feet.

I quickly put on my shoes; then ran with Sir Lancelot towards a truck parked in the drive. "They returned my truck late last night." Sir Lancelot said. "Lucky for us."

Lucky for me. I thought, climbing into the cab.

"Get down on the floor!" Sir Lancelot said, as we sped down the gravel road, the truck tires spewing loose gravel, and then the smooth sound of pavement as he turned onto road 6. I lay on the floorboard of the truck, hardly daring to breath, expecting any moment to hear a police siren blasting in behind us. What must have been about ten minutes later, Sir Lancelot spoke, “You can get up now."

I pulled myself up onto the seat. The sun was topping the horizon, like a giant, red ball in a purple haze. Above the sunrise, I saw a huge, black cloud rolling high in the sky. But it wasn't coming towards me as it had all the other times I'd seen it. I watched as it rolled away and then fully dissipated. A quiet peace filled my body. Was this an omen that my ordeal was coming to an end?

"I'll stop at Winnsboro and you can call your friend," Sir Lancelot said.

"I feel everything is going to turn out all right. Just get me to Paul. We'll find the legal help that will forever free me from Julia and Gatewood." I suddenly thought: *Would Sir Lancelot be arrested if they found out he had helped me.* "What happens to you if the law finds out you helped me escape?"

Sir Lancelot looked over at me and smiled a slow smile. "Don't worry about me. After all you aren't a dangerous criminal. It not like you escaped from a prison. Is it?"

Images of Gatewood flickered across my brain. "Yes, Sir Lancelot," I said slowly, "I think a prison is exactly what I escaped from."

Sir Lancelot covered my hand lying on the seat with his giant one. "It's all right," he said gently. "You're almost home free now."

With tears in my eyes I looked at him. "I owe you and Lee Ann so much."

Winnsboro is a small town. A green and white sign at the edge of town boasts: Population 800. Sir Lancelot pulled the truck into a filling station lot, parking off to the side, near an outside phone booth. He handed me a handful of change, "Go call your friend."

I realized I didn't even know Paul's number. If I called the old number I had called so many times in years past, I would most likely get his mother. He'd said he had his own place now since coming home from the Peace Corps.

I went into the phone booth thinking I would have to call information. Through the wide window of the filling station, I could see a large, round clock. 8:05. Would Paul be home, or would he have already left for work? With trembling fingers I dialed information, and asked for Harper City. I dialed the number the operator gave me and put in the money. I could hear the phone ringing. Oh, please Lord let him still be there, I prayed.

"Hello," came a strong voice, a voice belonging to the man I had loved since junior high.

"Paul!" I said into the receiver, knowing my voice was shaking.

"Jordan! Are you all right? Where are you!?" Paul shouted.

"I'm Ok," I said, my voice calmer now. "I'm with a friend. I broke out of Gatewood."

"I know," Paul said. "Your sister called here demanding to know if I'd seen you. I've been sick with worry all night. I wanted to come to Gatewood and help look for you but didn't dare leave the phone in case you tried to call me. Where are you? I'll come for you?"

"I'm at a phone booth in Winnsboro, about twenty miles from Gatewood. Can you meet us up the road somewhere? We're on route 6."

"Ok. Stockton is about fifty miles from here on route 6. That should make it about that far from where you are. If you can meet me there, I'll leave right away. There's a monument of a Revolutionary Soldier at the edge of town. We'll meet there. Just then the operator cut in saying time was up and to deposit sixty-five cents. I started to grab more coins, but dropped them onto the floor of the phone booth. Frantically I tried to pick them up, but they rolled through a crack in the floor. I looked towards the truck to see Sir Lancelot waving frantically at me and to my horror saw a state police car drive up. I could hear Paul's desperate cry, "Jordan! Jordan!" Then the click as the operator cut us off.

I stood frozen. I didn't dare leave the phone booth and try to get to the truck. So many things were going through my mind. What must Paul be thinking? What were the policemen going to do? What would the policemen do to Sir Lancelot? What was going to happen to me? Was my short flight to freedom coming to an end? To my relief, the policemen went inside the station. I hunkered down, crept to the truck, and crawling into the cab beside Sir Lancelot.

"Stay down," Sir Lancelot said, putting the truck in gear and slowly driving away from the station. "Whew," he said when we were safely on the road. "For a moment there I thought they were after us."

"Yeah," I sighed, leaning my head back against the seat. “Paul and I got cut off. I dropped the money; it rolled through cracks in the floor. So I couldn’t call him back. But he said he’d meet us in Stockton at a soldier's monument at the edge of town. I don't know what he's thinking right now."

"Stockton is about an hour's drive from here," Sir Lancelot said. "When we get to Henryville, about ten miles up the road; I'll get us something to eat. Hungry?"

"Yes. I really am," I said, surprised I wasn't too scared or excited to think about food.

Sir Lancelot pulled into a parking lot at a doughnut shop. "Good coffee here," he said. "I'll get doughnuts and coffee and we'll eat in the truck." Sir Lancelot handed me several dines. “Go to the phone booth and try to call your friend.”

Inside the phone booth, I gave the operator Paul’s number. The phone rang several times. No answer. I could only hope Paul was on his way to meet me. I returned to the truck.

Sir Lancelot returned to the truck with warm doughnuts and cups of streaming hot coffee.

Almost an hour later, we arrived in Stockton. I could see the statue of the soldier in the distance, and a red, Thunderbird parked nearby. Please, God, let it be Paul, I prayed.

By the time Sir Lancelot pulled the truck alongside the car, Paul was out of the Thunderbird. With a sob I jumped out of the truck and fell into his waiting arms. Paul crushed me to him. I felt him tremble. "Jordan, Jordan," he whispered, his breath warm against my ear. "Thank God, you're out of there. I was so worried, so afraid I wouldn't ever hold you again."

I looked up at him, gently running my fingertips over his handsome face. Tears wet my face, and I could see tears in his eyes. My voice trembled as I said, "I've been to hell, Paul. If it hadn't been for a friend inside Gatewood, and Sir Lancelot, I would still be there." I turned my head towards the truck: Sir Lancelot had gotten out of the truck and was standing near the rear fender looking at us. "Paul I want you to meet a true hero," I said, leading Paul towards Sir Lancelot. "This is Sir Lancelot. Formally he's Michael McBride."

Paul extended his hand to the older man. "I cannot thank you enough for what you have done for Jordan, for us."

Sir Lancelot shook Paul's hand warmly. "Glad to help. Now you two had better get going, and get on with the business of getting this mess cleaned up."

I looked at the tall, rugged man and threw my arms around his neck. "Thanks, Sir Lancelot. Thanks for giving me back my life. You are a true knight in shining armor," I whispered, kissing his leathery cheek.

He hugged me to him for an instant, then gently pushed me away, "Get on with you," he said.

As Paul held the car door I climbed inside. Paul got into the car, put it in gear, backed up and we began driving away. I looked back at Sir Lancelot standing beside his truck and thought surely there was not another like him in the entire world. I looked back at him until we drove around a bend in the road.

"Jordan," Paul said, reaching over to cover my hand with his. Most people in the legal system didn't want to believe what happened to you was possible, but I found one judge who was willing to consider it. Finally Marsha Rayburn, a reporter for channel 9 said if everything works out, she'd do a story on you. She got in touch with a psychiatrist who used to work at Gatewood and is in a bitter feud with the administration of the hospital. The psychiatrist is now head psychiatrist at Meadowbrook, a private hospital over in Clayton. He said he'd be glad to do a work up on you and if everything turns out like I told him, he knows a lawyer who would be happy to take your case." He drew me over against him and I laid my head on his shoulder. "It will all be over soon, darling.

"You couldn't be my lawyer?"

"The judge thinks I'm too close to the case."

"Is Meadowbrook a mental hospital?"

"It is that, Jordan. But it isn't a thing like Gatewood. You will get a full examination, and you shouldn't have to stay more than a few days. But we have to get you cleared by a psychiatrist. That was the only way I knew to go. And I know the people at Meadowbrook. I trust them. Trust me Jordan." Paul said, pulling the car to the side of the road and taking my face in his hands and looking deep into my eyes.

I looked into his eyes and knew wherever he took me would be a safe place. "I trust you," I said. He kissed me; then I rested my head on his shoulder, feeling the roughness of his tweed jacket, feeling I was truly safe now.

Harper City was on the way to Meadowbrook. As we neared by hometown, Paul had me lie down in the seat in case someone spotted me. I longed to drive by my home, but knew it was too risky. We stopped at Paul's place. Paul drove into the garage and let the door down. Inside he handed me a bundle of clothes his sister had left. I took the clothes thinking *bath bundle.* I quickly put on the clothes and soon we were on our way to Meadowbrook, a good two hour drive. Paul explained that I would be admitted under an assumed name: Lillian Webb.

We had lunch at a drive-through and arrived at Meadowbrook in the early afternoon. Meadowbrook was a large, three-story, sprawling building. It, too, had beautiful grounds. There was no wall around it. We were met by the superintendent, a Dr. Sampson. Paul introduced me to the doctor, and explained that he knew him through the doctor's son, who had been a roommate when Paul had been in Law School.

Dr. Samson had snow white hair and looked like someone's grandfather. "You will be safe here. Paul has told us about you and we are looking forward to hearing your story. You will meet the administrator in a short while," he said, taking us to a large room that looked much like a lounge room. "Tomorrow, you will meet with Dr. Greeley, the psychiatrist." Dr. Sampson said. Morgan Jones the administrator will be with you shortly." He then excused himself and left the room. A few minutes later, a young man, who looked to be not much older than myself, came into the room, introducing himself as the administrator, Morgan Jones.

"Paul has told me a great deal about you, Miss Webb. And we want very much to help you. We will admit you for an evaluation. There are no guarantees our findings will be what you want them to be, but I can promise, you will get a full psychological as well as an intense physical workup."

I sat there with my hand held tightly in Paul's. *What kind of risk was this man taking to offer to help me? He must trust Paul a lot.* I wanted to scream to him that I had been in hell; that someone had tried to kill me at Gatewood; that my sister Julia had tried to put me away for a lifetime. That Dr. Cole, who I thought was my friend, was a fake, and part of the conspiracy. But I held back, fearing he would think I was a raving lunatic. I said simply, "I was held against my will at Gatewood. Records were falsified to make it look like I am an epileptic and mentally ill and a danger to myself and others. My sister is my guardian and wanted me kept there. It is all about money and greed."

"If all this is true, we will make it public," the administrator said, leaning towards me. "We find this very disturbing that something like this could happen in our state, but greed can cause people to do unbelievable things. Marsha Rayburn, a reporter from channel 9, will also be meeting with you. We have alerted law enforcement that you have been found, and are in protective custody. Law enforcement also contacted your sister."

"Julia knows where to find me!"

"No. No, she doesn't know your location. Paul and Meadowbrook have assumed total responsibility for you. A judge grated us temporary custody. Please know this: you are safe at Meadowbrook."

I thanked him, but I was more than a little uneasy that Julia knew I had been found, even though she didn't know exactly where I was.

I was taken to a sunny, tastefully decorated room on the second floor. The room had a large window overlooking the well-kept lawn. But what I liked best was the adjoining bathroom.

Paul stood in the middle of the room looking at me. "Jordan," he said, pulling me into his arms, "so much has happened. I should never have gone away. But I know I'm stronger for the journey that took me to the Peace Corps. I appreciate more what we have here in America. And at the same time, I'm appalled that what has happened to you could happen in our country."

"Paul," I said, "Why didn't you answer my letter I sent when I was in the clinic?" I searched his face as he answered.

"I never got a letter. I'll bet if Julia or Dr. Cole seen it, it never made it out of the clinic. But it will all be over with soon, my darling." He kissed my hair, gently running his fingers through it.

I thought, as I stood there in the shelter of his arms, *Yes, my darling, hopefully the nightmare will soon be over.*

"I have an appointment with the psychiatrist tomorrow. I pray he finds me sane."

"Don't worry," Paul said. "Everything will be ok."

After Paul left, a soft knock came at the door. "Miss Webb," a voice said as a woman stuck her head in at the door. "I'm Stella Cory, the day nurse. Is there anything I can get you?"

I told her thanks, but I had everything I needed. I watched the nurse leave, thinking this place was, in many ways, more like a hotel than a hospital. But as I looked out the window, at the well-kept lawn below, I thought although this place didn't look or feel like Gatewood, I still couldn't get out if I wanted to. I couldn't walk out the front door, right now if I choose to. Maybe no one would tell me to hurry up, or make me go to the dining room if I didn't want to, or tell me to stay off the bed if I wanted to take a nap, but this was still a mental hospital. This place must cost a fortune, but I was still locked up, and knowing that caused a wave of sadness to come over me. But soon, surely soon, my ordeal would be over.

I thought of the others back at Gatewood: Lee Ann: she wouldn't come to this place if she could. Gladys: I didn't know if she would be better off in a place like this. Matilda: She wouldn't know the difference. And Maylene: I smiled as I thought of the little beady-eyed woman. I didn't know where Maylene belonged. But what about the patients like Rosa who were trapped, forever wards of the state? Most, if not all, could never afford such a place as this. And I vowed to help those inside Gatewood who could be helped. Surely justice would come to people like: Mrs. Holt and Julia. And the so called *Dr.* Cole.

I went into the bathroom, ran water into the tub; and then gratefully sank into the hot water, realizing no one was going to pour buckets of water over my head. And there wasn't a time limit on how long I had to take my bath, and most of all no one was watching. Fear was still a knot in my stomach. Could Julia somehow find a way to take me from this place? Suppose she went to another judge, got them to override the order of the one Paul had been to? Would she be able to come and take me back to Gatewood? I tried to push such thoughts out of my mind.

I was to get my physical that afternoon. And tomorrow an EEG, then I would be meeting with the psychiatrist. I was sure the results of the EEG would show I was not an epileptic. But what would the psychiatrist think of me? I felt a bit dizzy. Everything was happening so fast. I was looking forward to seeing this news reporter Paul seemed so impressed with. He'd said by going public with my story, public outcry would force an investigation into my allegations. And the state would deal with Mrs. Holt and Julia. If anybody had their dues coming, it was Julia. "Please, God", I prayed. "Please let this be over soon, and let me return to my own home."

The rest of the afternoon went quickly. I was given an intense physical by a Dr. Frank Cross and his assistant, Dr. Ruby True. Afterwards I took a quick nap.

Later, I dressed, and then ran a comb through my hair. A nurse knocked on the door and introduced herself as the evening nurse, Lynda Mack. She told me dinner was being served, and if I chose, she would be delighted if I joined her. I followed her down the hallway to a candlelit dining room. The room was filled with small tables with linen tablecloths. Several patients were going through a cafeteria line.

Three nurses and a couple of men in suits, who I thought were doctors, were also in line. Everyone, me included, took china from a stack at the beginning of the line. After getting my tray, I had a choice of roast beef or baked chicken. "The chicken is absolutely delicious," Nurse Mack said. I thought I would give it a try. I followed the nurse to a small table near a window. As the nurse chatted on about what a fine place Meadowbrook was, I observed the other patients. No one was dressed in drab clothing. But the faces: the expressions I saw on many of those patients' faces, were much the same as what I'd observed on the faces of the patients back at Gatewood. Some had a look of bewilderment like they didn't know what had happened to their world; others looked listless as if they didn't know or cared where they were. Still others looked happy like they were out to dinner with friends. I realized after all, this was a mental hospital. And I was going to have to prove I didn't belong at Gatewood or here.

The next morning I had the EEG: I hated that flashing light. Meadowbrook's wasn't any easier to take than Gatewood's. Next it was on to a session with Dr. Greeley the psychiatrist. He told me to just talk. I told him about losing my parents, and about being sent to Gatewood and of my belief of the conspiracy between Julia, Dr. Cole and Mrs. Holt to keep me there. Even about my suspicions Mrs. Holt had tried to kill me. But I didn't tell him about the black cloud. I was afraid that was too far-fetched. I didn't want to give him any reason to think I had visions or anything like that. Not once did he suggest I was in denial.

Late that afternoon Paul came to visit, bringing a large shopping bag filled with new clothes, and a friend. "This is Marsha Rayburn," Paul said. "The reporter I was telling you about. She wants to hear your story.

Marsha Rayburn barely topped five feet. She had short blonde hair, sharp brown eyes, and a voice that would have made Howard Cosell envious. I liked her instantly.

"Now let's hear your story," she said, setting a tape recorder on the table and taking a small notepad and pen from her jacket pocket."

I told her everything that had happened to me. I studied her face and couldn't tell if she believed me or not. But guessed with her being a reporter she would be proceeding with the possibility I could be making it all up "I tell you what," Marsha said, "When we get the clear from the doctor's reports, I'll know more about how to proceed with this. I hope to do about a three session part for the evening news. Would you be willing to go on camera if it works out?"

"I'll do whatever it takes."

“Of course we have been covering about your escape on our regular news, as have the other stations.”

“I’m on the news!?”

Marsha grinned. “Oh, yes. You are the top story on all the stations.”

After Marsha left, Paul said. “She has to know your story is the truth. I know she believes you, but she would have to have proof before making an accusation against Gatewood. The judge issued an order to get your records out of Gatewood," Paul said. "That way there won't be a chance of someone altering them."

After Paul left, I was exhausted and fell across the bed to rest for a little while. I wanted to be sure I went down to the living room and watched the eleven o'clock news and saw what was being said about me. As I lay there I thought of Julia in my house. I bet she was a bit worried by now. Worried her little scheme was about to unravel.

At five till eleven I went into the living room. I was relieved very few patients were there and the television was turned to channel 9. One of the main newscasters was speaking, "Investigator newswoman, Marsha Rayburn, is beginning a series of reports on Gatewood State Hospital, starting tomorrow at 6 o'clock. The report will include a segment about Jordan Walker, the woman who escaped from there. As has been reported earlier she has been found and is in protective custody, in an undisclosed place. Marsha is in the newsroom now and we will speak to her on this."

The cameras focused on Marsha. "Thank you Tad," Marsha said. "This report is very disturbing indeed. This young woman said false reports were filed by a staff person. And that a conspiracy with the staff person and someone or persons on the outside was carried out against her. I understand that her records are in the hands of the governor.”

The cameras turned back to the other newsman, a dark haired man in his early forties. "Marsha does the governor know the exact whereabouts of Miss Walker?"

"Yes," Marsha said, as the cameras turned back on her. "She's in a safe place."

"Very disturbing situation," he said. "We'll have more on Gatewood tomorrow. Thank you, Marsha."

I sat there for a long time; one thought going through my head-- Someone was going to do something about Julia and Mrs. Holt and Dr. Cole. They were actually going to be held accountable for the evil they'd done.

The next-evening I watched the 6 o'clock news with Paul. The lead story was about Gatewood. The segment started with a picture of the beautiful landscape, and the old wall. Marsh's powerful voice narrated. My throat tightened when I saw the outside of A2 and then the cameras swung around to view C3. It looked so beautiful, so peaceful from the outside.

Paul put a protecting arm around my shoulders. "It's all over, Babe," he whispered. "That place will never touch you again."

Marsha appeared on the screen saying, "We have an interview with a Dr. Kelso who treated Jordan Walker. Also we have with us the superintendent, Dr. Woodrow Grayson. As you will recall in last night's episode," Marsha continued. Miss Walker had escaped from the institution and was in protective custody in a private hospital. This is Dr. Woodrow Grayson, superintendent at Gatewood State Hospital." Marsha turned to Dr. Grayson. "Just what kind of patients would one expect to find in Gatewood, Dr. Grayson?"

The superintendent looked directly into the camera. "Well, Miss Rayburn, anyone admitted to Gatewood must have a diagnosis of epilepsy. Of course many have other issues: such as retardation, and some are also mentally ill. We are trying to find a drug that will allow an epileptic to be totally seizure free. We have a drug study going on as we speak and have found the drug to be very promising.

"Dr. Grayson, did you ever meet Jordan Walker?" Marsha asked.

"Yes. Yes, I met the young woman on the day she was admitted to Gatewood." Dr. Grayson said, looking a bit uncomfortable. “With an institution the size of Gatewood, it would be impossible for the superintendent to get to know all the patients on a personal level. I would like for all the viewers out there to realize Gatewood is a top of the line hospital. And I am very disturbed by the allegations printed in the newspapers and coming from your station."

"Are you then saying, Dr. Grayson, that all Jordan Walkers charges are false?"

"I am saying," Dr. Grayson replied, his voice showing irritability, "Jordan Walker has a history of very bizarre behavior."

"Where did you get that history?" Marsha asked.

"Well, it came from her family of course, and from our staff's’ observation of the patient. And the court record." the superintendent said, showing further annoyance with Marsha's line of questioning. "Dr. Kelso treated her. Perhaps he can shed some light on what state of mind Miss Walker may be in."

The camera turned to Dr. Kelso. He looked directly into the camera and smiled.

"Did Jordan Walker ever tell you false reports were being filed on her?" Marsha asked.

"It's against my policy to reveal what is said between doctor and patient, but I can give you a general idea of how someone like Miss Walker might behave."

"You do that for us, Dr. Kelso," Marsha said.

"Often, patients have thoughts of persecution by family members. This is not uncommon at all. You must understand," Dr. Kelso said, leaning towards Marsha, “mental illness is something not to be taken lightly. These people need professional care.”

“Are you saying Miss Walker is mentally ill, along with having a diagnosis of epilepsy?

I stared at the little man knowing soon he was going to give Marsha his analysis on denial. And sure enough the next words out of his mouth were: "You must understand, Miss Rayburn many of these patients don't want to admit they have seizures or other problems and go into denial."

"In your opinion could someone who wasn't an epileptic be a patient at Gatewood?"

"No. Epilepsy is the criteria for admittance."

"So, could someone fake epilepsy?"

"Well, they could, but they couldn't fake the results of the EEG."

"Marsha," the male reporter cut in, "if Miss Walker is able to prove any of these bizarre allegations, will there be any charges filed against anyone?"

"I certainly hope so." Marsha said.

"We welcome an investigation," the superintendent said."

"Look for Marsha's special report on this case," the male reporter said.

I sat there in the shelter of Paul's arms as the television station went on to more news. "It's almost over," Paul whispered. "You'll soon be able to put this nightmare behind you."

Chapter Seventeen

The next few weeks flew by for me. All tests done at Meadowbrook showed I wasn't an epileptic, nor was I mentally ill. The governor was outraged by the conduct of the staff at Gatewood and ordered a full investigation. Marsha was on the news every night with an update as new allegations became public. I learned my EEGs had been substituted with a read-out from a patient who had severe seizures. That was why Dr. Thorpe had kept repeating my seizures were getting worse. I was happy to learn Dr. Thorpe was in no way a part of the conspiracy.

Nell, the EEG technician had been part of the conspiracy, and when questioned by the police panicked and told everything. She said she had switched the EEG reports on the orders of her sister, Mrs. Holt. The technician told the police she was sorry she had taken part and had done it for a large pay-off from Julia, and had only done it because she was in desperate need of money. And the technician's aunt, an old friend of Julia's, along with Julia and Dr. Cole, and the aunt's husband had come up with the plan from the beginning. As I had suspected: It was all about money.

The so called psychiatrist, Jacob Massingale, one of the main players in getting me committed to Gatewood, didn't exist. Dr. Cole had gotten fake credentials for a friend. The doctor's friend turned out to be the husband of Julia friend, Marge Slater. His name was Simon and he worked as a handyman. The friend was arrested and confessed all. Marge was also arrested.

A warrant was issued for Julia's arrest. Not for anything related to my allegations, but she was found to have stolen hundreds of thousands of dollars from the political fund she was in charge of. She had been under investigation for months. For two days she eluded authorities before finally being captured in Miami. My charges against her would have to wait.

I watched on television as Julia was brought back to Harper City to face charges. My sister was taken out of a police car and taken into the police station. Her hands were in handcuffs, her head bowed. I had longed for so long to see her get what was coming to her and thought I would be jubilant when I saw Julia in that condition, but all I could think of was the pain my mother would have been in if she could have seen her oldest daughter in handcuffs.

After Nell, the EEG technician had confessed all. Mrs. Holt had also been arrested. When faced with the evidence she had confessed, but only to taking money from Julia and falsifying my records. She denied she had tried to harm me physically. Mrs. Holt, too, had done it all for money. I thought it was ironic my own money had been used to cause me so much pain. Julia had taken huge sums of my money out of my special fund my father left me. She had written large checks to her friend, the friend's husband, Mrs. Holt, and the EEG technician.

And Dr. Cole fled the country before he could be arrested for impersonating a doctor and his role in the conspiracy. With fake credentials he had been running his special clinic for years. When he is found Dr. Cole will also face justice.

Chapter Eighteen

I left Meadowbrook on a beautiful Indian Summer Day. As Paul and I drove to my home, I marveled at what this year had brought me. Despite the horrors, I wouldn't have missed what I went through for anything. I'd had to dip to the core of my very soul to see who I was, what I was made of. And I found I liked the person I found there very much. And I knew I emerged from the ordeal strong, very strong, maybe even as strong as my namesake. God, I'd survived Gatewood State Hospital! I knew I could survive anything that came my way.

As Paul turned the car into the drive to my beautiful, old house, tears filled my eyes as I looked at the home that held so many happy memories of Mama and Daddy. I was a bit apprehensive about going inside as we walked up the walk, afraid of what Julia might have done to the house. We entered through the kitchen. I was relieved to find only minor changes had been done. There was new wallpaper in the hallway and new carpeting in the kitchen. I would replace the carpet soon with marble tile. I ran to the foyer and, to my relief, found the ancient portrait of great, great-grandmother Jordan hanging where it had hung all the years of my memory. I gently touched the painting.

Paul and I set January 1st as our wedding day. "A new year, a new beginning," Paul whispered as he held me close.

I will ask Sir Lancelot to give me away. And just maybe Lee Ann will break the binds of Gatewood and come to the wedding. A reason for everything: I believe that absolutely.

The End